用英文介紹臺灣

實用觀光導遊英語

Third Edition

Paul O'Hagan, Peg Tinsley,
and Owain Mckimm

著

CONTENTS

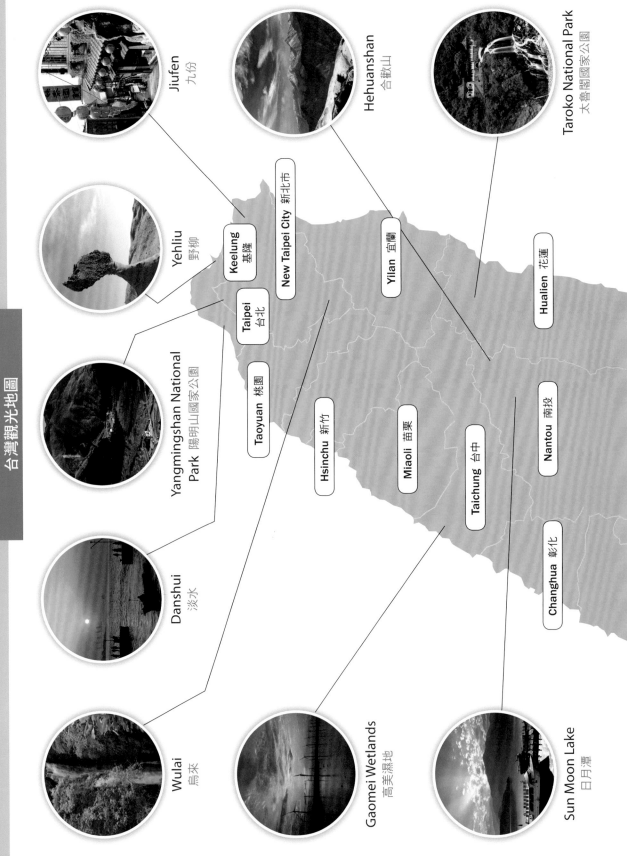

台灣觀光地圖

Jiufen 九份

Hehuanshan 合歡山

Taroko National Park 太魯閣國家公園

Yehliu 野柳

Yangmingshan National Park 陽明山國家公園

Danshui 淡水

Wulai 烏來

Gaomei Wetlands 高美濕地

Sun Moon Lake 日月潭

Keelung 基隆

Taipei 台北

New Taipei City 新北市

Taoyuan 桃園

Yilan 宜蘭

Hsinchu 新竹

Miaoli 苗栗

Taichung 台中

Changhua 彰化

Nantou 南投

Hualien 花蓮

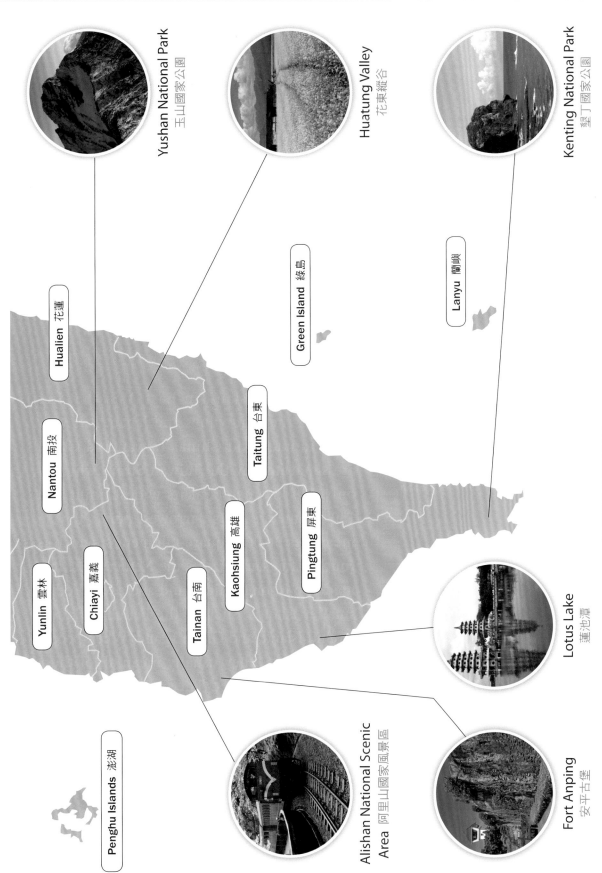

Yushan National Park 玉山國家公園

Huatung Valley 花東縱谷

Kenting National Park 墾丁國家公園

Green Island 綠島

Lanyu 蘭嶼

Hualien 花蓮

Nantou 南投

Taitung 台東

Yunlin 雲林

Chiayi 嘉義

Tainan 台南

Kaohsiung 高雄

Pingtung 屏東

Lotus Lake 蓮池潭

Penghu Islands 澎湖

Alishan National Scenic Area 阿里山國家風景區

Fort Anping 安平古堡

台灣觀光地圖

Geography 地理

🎧 Reading Passage

Taiwan's Yushan (Mount Jade) is the highest mountain in Northeast Asia.
台灣的玉山是東北亞第一高峰。

Taiwan is an island in East Asia that lies between the Philippines and Japan. It is very close to mainland China. Taiwan and China are **separated** by the Taiwan Strait, which is only 220 kilometers at its widest point and 130 kilometers at its narrowest point. Taiwan **measures** 36,000 square kilometers, which is **roughly** the same size as the Netherlands. It is **made up of** one main island and several other smaller islands, such as the Penghu Islands, Orchid Island, and Green Island. When people say "Taiwan," they usually mean all of these islands put together. The main island is also known as Formosa. When Portuguese sailors first discovered the island nearly five hundred years ago, they called it "Ilha Formosa," which means "beautiful island."

The island is very mountainous. Yushan (Mount Jade) is 3,952 meters tall, making it the highest

1   **Beautiful Sun Moon Lake**
    美麗的日月潭

2   **Taiwan is home to many bird species.**
    台灣有很多本土特有鳥類。

3   **Mt. Qixing** 七星山 **in Yangmingshan National Park is an extinct volcano.**
    陽明山國家公園的七星山是一座死火山。

mountain in Northeast Asia. The middle part of the island is covered by the Central Mountain **Range**. This massive range of mountains is 340 kilometers **in length**. Taiwan's mountain roads have lots of beautiful scenery. However, drivers must be careful on these roads as there are sometimes **landslides**.

Many of Taiwan's mountains are covered in thick forests. These forests are home to many interesting plants and animals. There are several different kinds of snakes. Some of them are very **poisonous**. But, visitors are unlikely to see them. It is also very hard to catch a **glimpse** of Taiwan's black bears. Visitors may have a better chance of seeing birds. There are many bird species which are only found in Taiwan. The **Taiwan Blue Magpie**, for example, can now be seen in some scenic spots. It has a very long tail, about 40 centimeters in length. Because they aren't afraid of people, visitors may have a chance to **encounter** these beautiful birds.

Many millions of years ago, Taiwan was home to **active** volcanoes. Today, they are either **extinct** or **dormant**. But, that doesn't mean that they can't provide hot water for Taiwan's hot springs! Most of Taiwan's hot springs are found in the mountains. Taiwanese people like to **soak** in hot springs waters because they are good for your health.

Quiz

1. Where is Taiwan?
2. How big is it?
3. Name the highest mountain in Taiwan.
4. What animals are very poisonous? Are people likely to see them?
5. Why do Taiwanese people go to hot springs?

♪2 **Conversation**

Taiwan was once called Formosa, which means "beautiful" in Portuguese. 台灣曾被稱為福爾摩沙，在葡萄牙文裡是「美麗的」的意思。

Ethan	So, tell me about Taiwan.
Laura	It's an island in East Asia that is off the coast of mainland China.
Ethan	How big is it?
Laura	It measures 36,000 square kilometers. It's roughly the same size as the Netherlands.
Ethan	Why's it called Formosa?
Laura	Portuguese sailors called it that when they discovered it nearly 500 years ago. It means beautiful in Portuguese.
Ethan	Is it still beautiful? I heard there are lots of **factories** there now.
Laura	The mountains are still beautiful, and there are still **plenty of** nice places on the plains as well. Most of the factories are **concentrated** in **certain** areas. Have you been to Yangmingshan National Park?
Ethan	I've been trying to find the time. I heard it's beautiful.
Laura	It is. We're lucky that it's so close to Taipei.
Ethan	Tell me a little about what it's like.

A beautiful chrysanthemum field in Taiwan 台灣的美麗菊花田

Laura	Well, it's a place where you can be close to nature, so it's great for walking around. There are lots of paths and several tourist centers.
Ethan	I hear you can also visit some hot springs where the water is always warm.
Laura	Yes, millions of years ago this area was full of volcanoes. They are not so active now, but they can still give us hot water. Just remember to try and go during the week.
Ethan	And I imagine it's best to go early. Those springs get pretty crowded, eh?
Laura	Yes. The hot springs in Yangmingshan attract a lot of visitors.

Pointed-Scaled Pit Viper
龜殼花

cc by vegafish

Formosan Sika Deer
台灣梅花鹿

by Yuyu

Formosan Black Bear
台灣黑熊

Formosan Rock Macaque
台灣獼猴

Birdwing Butterfly
珠光黃裳鳳蝶

Vivid Niltava
棕腹藍仙鶲

Animals
Endemic to Taiwan

Taiwan Blue Magpie
台灣藍鵲

Swinhoe's Pheasant
台灣藍腹鷴

Mikado Pheasant
帝雉

cc by Colinwen

Formosan Landlocked Salmon
櫻花鉤吻鮭

01 | Listening

Listen to the sentences describing something in Taiwan. Check the thing that you think is being referred to each time.

1. ◯ Central Mountain Range   ◯ Taiwan Blue Magpie
2. ◯ Hot springs   ◯ Volcanoes
3. ◯ Snakes   ◯ Black bears
4. ◯ The Penghu Islands   ◯ Yangmingshan National Park

02 | Reading

Choose the correct answer.

_____ 1. What does the Portuguese phrase "Ilha Formosa" mean?
     (a) Beautiful island.   (b) Lonely mountain.   (c) Dangerous animal.   (d) Blue sea.

_____ 2. Which countries is roughly the same size as Taiwan?
     (a) China.   (b) India.   (c) England.   (d) The Netherlands.

_____ 3. Which of the following is NOT true about Taiwan?
     (a) Taiwan is made up of one big island and several other small islands.
     (b) Taiwan is very mountainous.
     (c) Taiwan has many volcanoes which are still active.
     (d) Many interesting plants and animals can be seen in Taiwan.

_____ 4. What separates Taiwan from China?
     (a) The Central Mountain Range.   (b) The Taiwan Strait.
     (c) The Philippines.   (d) Green Island.

03 | Writing

Unscramble the sentences.

1. the / Taiwan / China / Taiwan Strait / and / are / separated/ by
   Taiwan and China are separated by the Taiwan Strait.

2. Yushan / the / mountain / Northeast Asia / is / in / highest

   _____

3. is / afraid / people / The / Blue / Taiwan / of / not / Magpie

   _____

4. to / springs / love / Visitors / in / Yangmingshan's / soak / hot

   _____

The sunrise and famous Sea of Clouds at Alishan
阿里山日出雲海

The summit of Yushan
玉山主峰

Alishan National Scenic Area
阿里山國家風景區

Hehuanshan (Mount Hehuan)
合歡山

Sun Moon Lake 日月潭

Gueishan Island 龜山島

↑
Yangmingshan
National Park
陽明山國家公園

Meihua Lake (Plum
Blossom Lake), Yilan
宜蘭梅花湖

→
Heping
Island
和平島

Climate 氣候

Word Bank

Tropic of Cancer 北回歸線	**humidity n.** 濕度	**crowded a.** 擁擠的	**value v.** 珍惜
tropical a. 熱帶的	**a variety of** 各種	**spectacular a.** 壯麗的；壯觀的	**escape v.** 逃避
subtropical a. 亞熱帶的	**fierce a.** 強烈的	**eye-catching a.** 吸睛的	**accompany v.** 伴隨
seldom adv. 很少地	**offshore a.** 離岸的；近海的	**delicate a.** 雅緻的	**destructive a.** 破壞力強的
	mild a. 溫和的	**chilly a.** 寒冷的	
	blossom n. 花朵		

🎧 4 Reading Passage

Yangmingshan National Park in summer time
夏季的陽明山國家公園

Taiwan's climate is hot and rainy, making it easy for plants to grow. Around 2,500 mm of rain falls on Taiwan every year. The **Tropic of Cancer** crosses central Taiwan, which makes Taiwan's climate half **tropical** and half **subtropical**.

It can be extremely hot in summer. The temperature **seldom** drops below 30 degrees Celsius and the **humidity** is high. It's a great time to enjoy the cool mountains and **a variety of** water activities. Visitors are suggested to wear hats and sunglasses and put on sunscreen as well.

From July to October is the typhoon season. Several typhoons pass by or hit Taiwan during this time of year. These storms can be **fierce** and cause great damage. Visitors must avoid coastal areas and **offshore** islands during a typhoon.

In spring, the weather tends to be **mild** and pleasant. It's the perfect time to visit scenic spots outside the cities and enjoy a wide variety of flower **blossoms**.

Typhoons may 颱風可能會

Typhoons may bring about mudflows.
颱風可能會引發土石流。

Typhoons may flood cities.
颱風可能會釀成都市水災。

Typhoons may blow down trees and destroy houses.
颱風可能會吹倒樹木、摧毀房屋。

The Plum Rain Season comes in mid May and lasts until June. During this time, it is quite likely that you will be caught in a shower. An umbrella is a must for tourists during the rainy season.

In autumn, it is cool and the humidity starts to drop. It is as pleasant in autumn as in spring.

Although Taiwan is very hot, the north can get quite cold during the winter. It can get even colder at the summits of Taiwan's high mountains. Up there, the temperature can drop to as low as -10 degrees Celsius. There is even snow on the ground. People travel to the mountains, such as Mount Hehuan 合歡山, just to see the snow. So, don't forget to pack some warm clothes if you're visiting Taiwan at this time of year.

Taiwan has lots of things to see. There are beautiful temples and **crowded** night markets in almost every city. Just outside the cities is the countryside, which is often **spectacular**, with beautiful mountains, rivers, and forests. There are also several flower seasons in Taiwan. Each of them has its own unique features and is very **eye-catching**. Every year, during the cherry blossom season, families go to places like Alishan 阿里山, Yangmingshan 陽明山, and Wulai 烏來 to see these **delicate** pink blossoms.

Cherry blossoms on Yangmingshan
陽明山的櫻花

Quiz

1. What kind of climate does Taiwan have?
2. What disasters can typhoons bring about?
3. When is the Plum Rain Season?

↑ **Flip-flops** 人字拖

Down jacket 羽絨外套 ↘

5 Conversation

Ethan	What about the weather? It's pretty hot, right?
Laura	Most of the time, but not always. In the north, winters are often **chilly** and occasionally very cold.
Ethan	Really? What do people do to heat their homes?
Laura	There isn't much central heating in Taiwan because it's not cold for very long. People usually use small electric heaters and put on more layers of clothing.
Ethan	What about in the mountains? How cold is the winter up there?
Laura	It can be surprisingly cold in the mountains during winter. A friend of mine who went camping there one year said it dropped to -10 degrees Celsius.

Cap 帽子 ↘

↙ **Sunglasses** 太陽眼鏡

↖ **Umbrella** 雨傘

Rain boots 雨鞋 ↗

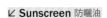

↙ **Sunscreen** 防曬油

Ethan	I suppose Taiwanese people **value** the mountains. They give them a great chance to go out and enjoy nature.
Laura	Yes, mountain areas are becoming more and more important. People go there to **escape** the heat of summer and view the beautiful flowers and plants.
Ethan	So, in summer, it's really hot!
Laura	Definitely. There are also typhoons during the summer.
Ethan	Is it very stormy during a typhoon?
Laura	Yes, a typhoon is usually **accompanied** by strong winds and heavy rain, which can be very **destructive**.

Seasonal Festivals

Alishan Cherry Blossom Festival
阿里山櫻花季

Miaoli Tung Flower Season
苗栗桐花季

Yangmingshan Flower Festival
陽明山櫻花季

Wulai Cherry Blossom Festival
烏來櫻花季

Baihe Lotus Festival
白河蓮花季

Practice

01 | Listening

Listen to the statements and mark the information you get from each one.

1. ○ Taiwan lies in the Pacific Ocean.
   ○ The Tropic of Cancer runs through Taiwan.
2. ○ The summers in Taiwan are hot and humid.
   ○ There can be snow on Mount Hehuan during winter.
3. ○ Typhoon season runs from July to October.
   ○ It rains a lot during the Plum Rain Season.
4. ○ If you visit Taiwan in winter, pack warm clothes.
   ○ Don't visit the outlying islands during a typhoon.

02 | Reading

Match the two halves of the sentences.

1. During the winter, people _____
2. In summer, people _____
3. Typhoons often bring _____
4. The north of Taiwan _____
5. It's likely you'll get caught in a shower _____

(a) strong winds and heavy rain.
(b) can be surprisingly cold in winter.
(c) heat their homes with small electric heaters.
(d) during the Plum Rain Season.
(e) go to the mountains to escape the heat.

03 | Writing

Use the following words to fill the blanks.

destructive   offshore   blossoms   crowded   mild

1. Each spring, thousands of people flock to the mountains to see the beautiful pink cherry _____.
2. Taiwan's _____ islands are a great place to do a variety of water sports such as diving and surfing.
3. The best time to visit Taiwan is during the spring or autumn when the weather is pleasant and _____.
4. The _____ winds of a typhoon can completely destroy houses and cause major problems like landslides.
5. Night markets attract visitors with freshly cooked food and a fun atmosphere; however, they can get very _____ on weekends.

More About the Climate of Taiwan

Taiwan is located in both the Tropical and Subtropical zones. It generally has a subtropical climate with high humidity. The northern part of Taiwan has a subtropical climate with an average temperature of around 22°C. The southern part of Taiwan has a tropical climate with an average temperature of 24°C.

The summer season is from June to August. The temperature can reach as high as 38°C during this time. The winter is relatively mild. However, in the high mountain areas, it is possible to see frost or snow. During the rainy season, especially in May and June, there are often heavy showers in the afternoon but they do not usually last very long.

	Jan	Feb	Mar	Apr	May	Jun	Jul	Aug	Sep	Oct	Nov	Dec
Average Temperature	17	18	21	24	26	27	28	27	27	26	23	19
Lowest Temperature	12	12	14	17	21	23	24	24	23	19	17	14
Highest Temperature	19	18	21	25	28	32	33	33	31	27	24	21

Unit 3

Population 人口

🎧 Reading Passage

There are over 23 million people in Taiwan. Because Taiwan is very mountainous, most of its population lives on the western plains. There are over 640 people per square kilometer in Taiwan. Taipei, undoubtedly, has the highest population **density** in Taiwan, with over 6.8 million people **inhabiting** this city.

The **indigenous** peoples were the first people to live on the island. Today, there are officially 14 tribes, and indigenous people make up about two percent of Taiwan's population. The largest tribe is the Amis. The Amis live mostly in Hualien and Taitung. The indigenous peoples depend on farming and fishing for a living.

Taiwan's indigenous people were no longer able to live in peace once other peoples began arriving seeking to **claim** power. In 1623, the Dutch **took over** Taiwan. They **ruled over** most of the island until the first large Chinese army arrived in 1661. This army was led by a Chinese **general** named Koxinga 國姓爺 (Zheng Chenggong 鄭成功). He was fighting the **Manchu** Emperor in China and

The 14 officially recognized indigenous tribes

Amis 阿美族
Paiwan 排灣族
Atayal/Tayal 泰雅族
Bunun 布農族
Rukai 魯凱族
Puyuma 卑南族
Tsou 鄒族
Saisiyat 賽夏族
Tao/Yami 達悟族
Thao 邵族
Kavalan 噶瑪蘭族
Truku 太魯閣族
Sakizaya 撒奇萊雅族
Seediq 賽德克族

Quiz

1. What is the population of Taiwan?
2. Where does most of the population have to live?
3. Who were the first people to live in Taiwan?
4. Who took over Taiwan and when?

had to escape to Taiwan. He died soon after he got to Taiwan. Following that, many Chinese people came to live on the island. Most of the indigenous people escaped to the mountains, but some stayed on the plains. The ones who stayed behind married the Chinese **settlers**. This is why most Taiwanese people are actually a **mixture** of different races.

Nowadays, the population of Taiwan consists of Taiwanese, also called Hoklo or Holo, mainlanders, and indigenous people. There is also a group of Chinese called **Hakka**. Hakka people have **managed to** keep their own language and customs. Most of the mainlanders came to Taiwan in 1949 because of political problems in China. Today, the population of Taiwan is 70% Hoklo or Holo, 14% Hakka, 14% mainlander, and 2% indigenous. Many foreigners also live in Taiwan.

Koxinga (Zheng Chenggong)
國姓爺（鄭成功）

Koxinga's Shrine, Tainan, Taiwan
台南延平郡王祠

🎧 8 Conversation

Ethan	There sure are a lot of people here.
Laura	Yes, the cities are pretty **lively**.
Ethan	Even when I go to the countryside or the mountains, I sometimes still have a hard time finding a place that is completely quiet.
Laura	I know what you mean. Sometimes when you climb a mountain to watch the sunset there's a crowd of people waiting for you at the top!
Ethan	How many people are there in Taiwan?
Laura	Over 23 million, and they mostly live on the western plains.
Ethan	I guess the indigenous people were the first people to live here?
Laura	Yeah, which is the same as in the US.
Ethan	Does anyone know where they came from?
Laura	No one knows for sure, but some people think they came from southern China.
Ethan	So, when did the Chinese come to Taiwan?
Laura	Around 400 years ago, but they had to **get rid of** the Dutch rulers first.
Ethan	Was there much of a fight?
Laura	Yes, the **battle** lasted for several months. A Chinese general called Koxinga wanted to use Taiwan as a base to fight the Qing Dynasty so he **drove out** the Dutch.
Ethan	What does Hakka mean?
Laura	The Hakka are a Chinese people who live all over China.
Ethan	Are there many of them?
Laura	They make up about 14% of the population. They have a **reputation** for working hard and they also have unique customs and food.
Ethan	What about the Holo people?
Laura	They make up about 70% of the population.

Indigenous Culture

cc by takunawan

The largest indigenous tribe in Taiwan, the Amis, is a matrilineal society, which means that family affairs were traditionally decided by the women. The Harvest Festival is the most important event of the year.

台灣最大的原住民種族阿美族屬於母系社會，一般來說，家中事務是由女性作主。阿美族每年最大的盛事便是「收穫祭」。

Photo provided by the Formosan Aboriginal Cultural Village

Paiwan artisans excel at wood carving. They are the second largest tribe in Taiwan and are known for their intricately decorated clothing.

排灣族工匠擅於木雕，他們是台灣第二大的原住民族，以華麗的服裝著稱。

The Bunun tribe lives mostly in the Central Mountain Range and is a representative high mountain tribe. The Bunun observe many traditional rites and ceremonies, such as the Ear Shooting Festival.

布農族多分佈於中央山脈，是典型的高山族群。他們的儀式在所有族群之中最是繁瑣，例如「射耳祭」。

The Atayal is the third largest tribal group in Taiwan. "Atayal" means "brave warrior" in the tribe's language.

泰雅族是台灣第三大原住民族，他們的族名「Atayal」在該族的語言中指的是「勇士」。

The Tao live on Lanyu 蘭嶼 (Orchid Island). They are the only indigenous tribe to live on this outlying island, and also the only one to make traditional fishing boats. The Boat Launching Ceremony is a major event for the Tao.

達悟族居住在蘭嶼，是唯一一個住在外島的原住民族，也是唯一以會建造傳統漁船的族群。「船祭」是達悟族的重要慶典。

01 | Listening

Listen to the dialogue and mark the information that you hear.

1. ○ Koxinga fought the Dutch in 1661.
2. ○ There are more Hoklo people than indigenous people in Taiwan.
3. ○ The Amis mostly live on the east coast of Taiwan.
4. ○ Hakka people have their own language and customs.

02 | Reading

Choose the correct answer.

_____ 1. Which of the following statements is TRUE?
    (a) Taiwan has the highest population in the world.
    (b) There are 8 million people living in Taipei.
    (c) Taipei is the most crowded city in Taiwan.
    (d) Most of Taiwan's population lives on the east coast.

_____ 2. Most mainlanders come to Taiwan in 1949 because (of)
    (a) a natural disaster in China.   (b) the population of China was too high.
    (c) business opportunities in Taiwan.   (d) political problems in China.

_____ 3. Which of the following is NOT true about Hakka people?
    (a) They have their own language.
    (b) They were the first people to live in Taiwan.
    (c) They have a reputation for working hard.
    (d) They are a Chinese people who live all over China.

03 | Writing

Use the prompts to write a sentence. You'll need to add necessary words or change the verb tenses to make correct sentences.

1. population / Taiwan / 23 million
    The population of Taiwan is over 23 million.

2. largest / tribe / Taiwan / Amis tribe
    _____

3. over / 640 / people / square kilometer / Taiwan
    _____

4. the Dutch / rule over / Taiwan / until / Koxinga / drive out
    _____

Indigenous Culture

Indigenous culture is an important part of Taiwan's cultural diversity. In the 1990s, there was a revival of indigenous culture even though the government had tried to repress it for many years. Now, indigenous singers, such as A-Mei, have become quite famous. However, it is difficult to see traditional indigenous culture up close. Also, indigenous culture itself is very diverse. There are 14 different indigenous tribes on the island. Each of these tribes has its own unique customs and way of life.

Fortunately, Taiwan has several museums and numerous villages where you can learn about indigenous culture. Indigenous communities can be found all over Taiwan, with many of them concentrated in Hualien, Taitung and Nantou counties. There is also a diversity of indigenous arts such as music, dance, wood carving, weaving and basket weaving. There is even an indigenous TV station.

Indigenous clothing, food and dance
原住民服裝、食物與舞蹈

The Pacuntapana Bridge 排灣族觀流橋 **in the Taiwan Indigenous Peoples Culture Park, Pingtung**
位於屏東台灣原住民族文化園區內的排灣族觀流橋

Unit 4

Language 語言

Word Bank

recognition **n.** 承認；認可
decline **v.** 減少
launch **v.** 推出；推動
tonal **a.** 聲調的

pronounce **v.** 發音
dialect **n.** 方言
communicate **v.** 溝通
character **n.** 字；字體
govern **v.** 統治

defeat **v.** 擊敗
flood **v.** （如洪水般）湧入
apart from 除了……之外
relate **v.** 和……相關
frequently **adv.** 經常

🎧 Reading Passage

Because Taiwan has so many different people, there are also a lot of different languages spoken. However, Mandarin Chinese is the only official language. The government uses Mandarin in its publications and other activities. Children are also taught in school using Mandarin. In the last few years, there has been some **recognition** of other languages. Taiwanese (also known as Hokkien or Minnanhua) is spoken by 80% of the people and it can be heard on TV and the radio. Taiwanese originally came from a language spoken by people in Fujian 福建 Province. Most people in Taiwan can speak both Mandarin and Taiwanese. Some people can also speak Hakka, but their numbers have been **declining**. Steps have been taken to save the Hakka language. For example, a Hakka TV station was **launched** in 2003.

Chinese languages are very different from European ones. They are **tonal**, making it difficult for non-

Chinese people to **pronounce** them. One word can have several different meanings depending on the tone. The word "ma," for example, has at least four different meanings depending on which tone is used. Therefore, Westerners have to study hard to learn Chinese. Because Chinese **dialects** are so different, a person who can only speak Hakka cannot understand someone who is speaking Taiwanese. Fortunately, nearly everyone speaks Mandarin. However, even if they cannot, writing can be used to **communicate**. Chinese **characters** are taught to everyone. If people cannot understand each other, they can just write something down. Even people who speak different dialects use the same characters for writing.

Japan **governed** Taiwan for fifty years, so there are some elderly people who can speak Japanese. There are many young people who study Japanese at university as well. It is the second most popular foreign language in Taiwan after English.

Most Taiwanese people can understand a little English. The ones who can't understand spoken English can usually understand it in writing. While most of the older Taiwanese people never had a chance to study English, young people begin to study English in elementary school. The government has also tried to create an English environment, such as putting up lots of English street signs all over Taiwan. Now, it is much easier to find your way around cities and towns.

English street signs are put up all over Taiwan.

台灣各地都設有英文路標。

Quiz

1. Why are several languages spoken in Taiwan?
2. What is the official language in Taiwan?
3. Can individuals who speak only one Chinese dialect understand another Chinese dialect?
4. Why do some of the older people speak Japanese?

Conversation

Ethan	Following the **defeat** of the Dutch by Koxinga, the Chinese started **flooding** into Taiwan. Is this why Mandarin is the official language here?
Laura	Not really, Mandarin caught on much later. But you know, Mandarin isn't the only language that is spoken in Taiwan.
Ethan	There are other ones? I mean, **apart from** the indigenous languages?
Laura	Yes, there are Taiwanese and Hakka.
Ethan	Are they like Mandarin Chinese?
Laura	They are **related** to Mandarin, but are still very different.
Ethan	But, the official language of Taiwan is Mandarin Chinese, right?
Laura	Yes. Most people speak Mandarin, although Taiwanese is much more **frequently** spoken in the south.
Ethan	Where did the Taiwanese language come from?
Laura	It is similar to what people speak in Fujian, a province in southern China.
Ethan	Are there TV and radio programs in these languages?
Laura	Yes. There are more and more programs in Taiwanese. A Hakka TV station has also been launched. More and more people are becoming interested in these languages.
Ethan	Are there any other languages?
Laura	Well, it's not an official one, but quite a few people can still speak Japanese.
Ethan	I hear it's mostly old people who speak it, right?
Laura	True. But quite a few young people also choose to learn it in university. Some even go to Japan to study.
Ethan	Of course, English is the most popular foreign language. Am I right?
Laura	I don't know if it's "popular," but many people here know they need to learn it.

Hakka Culture

Around 4.5 million Hakka people live in Taiwan. They first came from China. The Hakka have a distinctive language, customs and food. Some of them live in small villages, such as Meinong in southern Taiwan, and have preserved their culture.

The Hakka people have a reputation for being hardworking and frugal. The Hakka cuisine differs from other types of Chinese cuisine. Some famous Hakka dishes are Fried Pig Intestines with Shredded Ginger, Hakka Stir-fry, and Preserved Mustard and Pork Soup 福菜湯.

Oil paper umbrellas are one type of traditional Hakka craft. The frame of the oil paper umbrellas produced in Meinong is made from bamboo, mainly moso bamboo. Persimmon oil and hand painted images are added to complete the umbrella.

Fried Pig Intestines With Shredded Ginger
薑絲炒大腸

Hakka Stir-Fry
客家小炒

Simmered Bamboo Shoots
滷竹筍

Lei Cha
擂茶

Practice

01 | Listening

Listen to the statements and fill in the blanks.

1. There are many different Chinese _____, such as _____, Hokkien, and Mandarin.

2. A Hakka TV station was _____ in 2003 in order to save the Hakka language.

3. Mandarin Chinese is a _____ language, which makes it difficult for foreigners to _____ the words correctly.

4. Taiwanese, which is _____ to Mandarin, is spoken a lot more _____ in the south.

5. Because Taiwan was _____ by Japan for fifty years, many of the older people can speak Japanese.

02 | Reading

Put the dialogues in the correct order.

1. (a) Yes, they're both Chinese dialects.
   (b) Can you speak Hakka?
   (c) No, but I can speak Taiwanese.
   (d) Are they related?   → _____

2. (a) What about the older people?
   (b) Yeah. So most young people can speak pretty good English.
   (c) Taiwanese people start to learn English in elementary school, right?
   (d) Not so much. Some of them might be able to read a little though.
                                            → _____

3. (a) Yeah. No one understands me when I talk!
   (b) You just need to practice your pronunciation, that's all.
   (c) I'm trying to learn Chinese, but it's so hard.
   (d) Are you having problems with the tones?   → _____

4. (a) Will people in the south understand me if I don't speak Taiwanese?
   (b) Everyone gets taught Chinese characters, even if they don't speak Mandarin very well.
   (c) You should be OK. But if you get into trouble, just write the sentence down.
   (d) What do you mean?   → _____

03 | Writing

Fill the blanks using the words given.

1. *Hakka, declining, number*

   The _____ of people who can speak _____ has been _____.

2. *communicate, speak, dialect*

   People who don't _____ the same Chinese _____ can use writing to _____.

3. *English, around, foreigners*

   Putting up _____ street signs all over Taiwan has made it much easier for _____ to find their way _____.

4. *characters, tones, tricky*

   _____ make learning Chinese _____ for foreigners, and learning to write Chinese _____ is also a big challenge.

5. *Mandarin, recognition, official*

   Though the _____ language of Taiwan is _____, in recent years there has been some _____ of the island's other languages.

Lots of people in Taiwan speak Taiwanese (Minnanhua). The pronunciation of Taiwanese is very close to that of ancient Chinese. While many sounds in ancient Chinese have disappeared over time, they still exist in Taiwanese. It's interesting to note that if the Chinese poems of the Tang or Song dynasty are read in Taiwanese, the pronunciation will be more accurate than if read in modern Chinese.

Religions 宗教

🎧13 Reading Passage

Matsu, folk goddess of the sea
媽祖／天上聖母（海神）

She is said to be the protector of fishermen and sailors.
媽祖被認為是漁夫和水手的守護者。

Buddhism and **Taoism** are the two major religions on the island. There is also an important **philosophy** called **Confucianism**, and **folk** beliefs are widely practiced. Most Taiwanese follow a mix of religions and folk beliefs.

Traditional folk religion is a mixture of several beliefs concerning gods, goddesses, ghosts, ancestors, and luck. It is not unheard of for some Taiwanese people to go and see a **fortune teller** before making a big decision. There are different customs and beliefs throughout Taiwan. For example, people in fishing villages prefer to **worship** Matsu, the folk goddess of the sea. People from other areas may worship Guanyin, the goddess of **mercy**, or Guan Yu, a famous soldier from China. Farmers, on the other hand, prefer to worship the land god because he better understands the importance of a good harvest. Taiwan's folk beliefs are colorful and **diverse**.

Lots of local festivals in Taiwan are actually religious activities. One of the largest religious festivals is the International Matsu Cultural Festival, which takes place during the third month on the lunar calendar. The **pilgrimage procession** sets out from Zhenlan Temple 鎮瀾宮 in Dajia 大甲, Taichung. It stops

at several places in central and southern Taiwan before returning to the Zhenlan Temple after nine days. The statue of Matsu, puppets of gods, dancing lions and dragons, performing groups, and exploding firecrackers together form a loud and lively **parade** watched by crowds of people. Worshippers from all over the country walk along with the procession, hoping to receive a blessing from Matsu.

Shun Feng Er 順風耳 ("With the Wind Ear"), one of two guardians of Matsu
順風耳，媽祖的兩名護衛之一

Another important local festival concerns the city gods 城隍. For example, the city god of Taipei's birthday is celebrated every year in the fifth month on the lunar calendar. Other gods' birthdays are celebrated in front of temples and include performances that attract large groups of people.

Quiz

1. What are Taiwan's main religions?
2. Which god or goddess do people in fishing villages worship the most?
3. What kinds of festivals are held in her honor?
4. Which god do farmers tend to worship? Why?

Performers celebrate the birthday of Baosheng Dadi 保生大帝 (Emperor Baosheng) in front of the Baoan Temple 保安宮, Taipei.
表演者於台北保安宮前慶祝保生大帝壽誕。

Worshipers bow down at Fengtian Temple 奉天宮, Chiayi.
嘉義奉天宮前伏跪之信徒

🎧14 Conversation

Ethan	Tell me about the religions in Taiwan.
Laura	Buddhism and Taoism are the most important religions in Taiwan. However, most Taiwanese believe in a mix of these two, as well as Confucianism and other folk beliefs.
Ethan	It's a good thing that people with different religions can live together in **harmony**.
Laura	No doubt. Ancestor worship is also very important to the Taiwanese.
Ethan	You really worship a lot of gods and goddesses! Can you tell me something about the folk beliefs here?
Laura	For example, Matsu, the goddess of the sea, is widely worshipped in Taiwan. There are many **legends** about her, and she is said to be the protector of fishermen and sailors. People usually worship Matsu for good luck and safety.
Ethan	The folk beliefs here are quite **vivid** and interesting!
Laura	Yes. You may have heard of the Eight **Infernal** Generals 八家將.
Ethan	Who are they?
Laura	They are eight messengers from the underworld. They're in charge of **capturing** or **expelling** evil spirits and monsters. They are also the defenders of the chief **deity**. That's why you can often see them lead religious processions.

Eight Infernal Generals
八家將

Local Religious Festivals

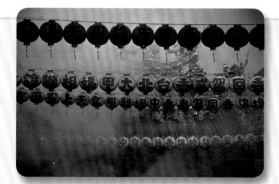

Matsu Cultural Festival/Matsu Touring Procession
媽祖觀光文化節／媽祖遶境

Donggang Burning the King Boat
東港燒王船

Danshui Chingshui Yan Cultural Festival
淡水清水巖文化節

Taipei Dadaocheng Welcoming of the City God
台北大稻埕迎城隍

Common Battle Array Performance

Song Jiang Battle Array
宋江陣

God General Battle Array
神將陣

White Crane Battle Array
白鶴陣

(15)

01 | Listening

Listen to the descriptions and check the thing that you think is being referred to each time.

1. ◯ Traditional folk religion   ◯ The lunar calendar

2. ◯ Confucianism   ◯ Fortune telling

3. ◯ Matsu   ◯ The land god

4. ◯ The Eight Infernal Generals   ◯ Performing groups

5. ◯ Buddhism and Taoism   ◯ Guanyin and Guan Yu

02 | Reading

Match the sentences to the pictures you think they best describe.

 **a**   **b**    **c**   **d**

_____ 1. Dancing lions and dragons, performing groups, and exploding firecrackers all form a big part of religious parades in Taiwan.

_____ 2. Guanyin, the goddess of mercy, is widely worshipped in Taiwan.

_____ 3. Before making a major decision in their lives, some Taiwanese people will go to see a fortune teller.

_____ 4. Matsu is the goddess of the sea, and as a result she is worshipped by people in fishing villages.

03 | Writing

Some of the information in the following sentences is incorrect. Write the sentences out again with the correct information.

1. People usually pray to Matsu for good harvests and money.

   _____

2. The Eight Infernal Generals are eight dragons from Heaven.

   _____

3. The International Matsu Cultural Festival takes place during the seventh month on the solar calendar.

   _____

   _____

Common Puppets

in Taiwanese Religious Parades

"Thousand Miles Eye
千里眼" (left) and "With
the Wind Ear 順風耳"
(right)—the two
guardians of Matsu
千里眼（左）與順風耳（右）
——媽祖的兩名護衛

Eight Infernal
Generals
八家將

Ox Head 牛頭 &
Horse Face 馬面 —
two guardians of
the underworld
牛頭與馬面——
兩名陰間的差使

Electric-Techno
Third Princes
電音三太子

General Hsieh/
Seventh Lord
謝將軍／七爺

General Fan/
Eighth Lord
范將軍／八爺

SAKYAMUNI BUDDHA
釋迦牟尼佛

Founder of Buddhism
佛教創始者

FUDE ZHENGSHEN
福德正神／
土地公

**God of Earth/
Land God**
土地之神

GUANYIN
觀世音菩薩

Goddess of Mercy (Guanyin means "listening to the cries of people.")
慈悲之神（觀音指「傾聽人們的痛苦心聲」）

GUAN YU/GUAN GONG
關聖帝君

Famous Chinese warrior who represents loyalty and righteousness
著名的中國戰士，代表了忠誠與正義

YAOCHI JINMU/ XI WANGMU
瑤池金母／
西王母

Goddess of Prosperity and Longevity
主掌繁榮興盛與長壽

ZHUSHENG NIANGNIANG
註生娘娘

Goddess of Fertility
生育之神

People worship Zhusheng Niangniang in the hope of having a child.
人們拜註生娘娘以求子。

WENCHANG DIJUN

文昌帝君

God of Culture and Literature 文化與文學之神

Students worship Wenchang Dijun in the hope of performing well on their exams. 學生拜文昌帝君以求考試順利。

EMPEROR BAOSHENG

保生大帝

God of Health
健康之神

YUE LAO

月老

God of Marriage and Love
婚姻與愛之神

XUAN WU/ DARK HEAVENLY UPPER EMPEROR

玄天上帝

SHENNONG EMPEROR

神農大帝

God of Medicine and Agriculture
醫藥與農業之神

TSAISHEN

財神

God of Prosperity/ Wealth
興旺與財富之神

MAITREYA BUDDHA/ MILEFO

彌勒佛

The Future Buddha
未來佛

Unit 6

Temples 寺廟

16 Reading Passage

Lungshan Temple and the performance of "bai bai" rituals
龍山寺與「拜拜」儀式

One of the first things that a first-time visitor to Taiwan notices is the temples. They are very different from churches in the West. Temples can be found all over the island, from **enormous** ones to small **shrines**. Many of them are decorated in a very colorful and eye-catching manner.

You may find that the various types of temples are a little confusing. This is because they are all built according to special rules, such as feng shui 風水 (wind and water). Of course, temples might also be built a little differently because of their own unique story and the history of their gods or goddesses.

Some temples are always crowded, like the Lungshan Temple 龍山寺 in Taipei. No matter what time you visit, you will always find people lighting **incense** and doing "bai bai" **rituals**. This is what it's called when someone puts their

Shengde Temple,
Hsichih, Taipei
by Yuyu 台北汐止聖德宮

hands together, often with an incense stick between them, and bows to an **altar**. This ritual can be used to **venerate** both gods and ancestors.

Taoist temples are usually managed by local people and they tend to be more decorative than Buddhist temples. Taoist temples aren't just places to **practice** religion. They serve as community centers where local people can get together. You might even find elderly people playing chess or card games around the temple grounds.

Many of Taiwan's folk arts are connected to temples, such as music, dance, **puppet shows** and Taiwanese opera. The architecture and decoration of the temples add a feeling of **vibrancy** to cultural performances. What's more, the carved decorations of gods, dragons, spirits, other **legendary** creatures, and educational stories are a traditional art form in themselves. During important holidays like Chinese New Year, people often go to temples to watch performances. Some temples even offer different performances every day for two weeks straight.

Puppet
show
布袋戲

Quiz

1. How are many Chinese temples decorated?
2. How are Taoist temples managed?
3. In addition to places of worship, what functions do temples serve in people's daily life?

⟨17⟩ Conversation

Ethan	There are so many temples in Taiwan.
Laura	Yes, it is a **distinguishing** feature here.
Ethan	So, which one are we going to today?
Laura	I'm going to take you to Lungshan Temple. It is one of the busiest temples in Taipei.
Ethan	I can hardly tell a Buddhist temple from a Taoist one.
Laura	Generally, Taiwan's temples are a mix. They are often **devoted** to the worship of a combination of Buddhist, Taoist, and folk gods and goddesses. Lungshan Temple is no **exception**.

Ethan and Laura arrive at Lungshan Temple.

Ethan	When was it built?
Laura	Lungshan Temple was built over 200 years ago. It is officially a second-grade historic **monument**. It has typical temple **architecture**.
Ethan	Wow, just look at the **antique** carvings all over the building!
Laura	Lungshan Temple was damaged and rebuilt several times. It has the only **bronze** dragon **pillars** in Taiwan. Here, let me show you.
Ethan	They're amazing! May I take a picture of them?
Laura	Sure.
Ethan	What kinds of deities are worshipped here?
Laura	The goddess of mercy, the goddess of the sea, the god of literature, and many other deities. You might be interested in the god of marriage, who is said to help people find their Mr. or Miss Right!
Ethan	No wonder it is crowded with worshippers every day! I'd like to make my wish to the god of marriage. Maybe I'll meet my true love here!

Practice

18

01 | Listening

Listen to the first part of each short dialogue. Match each one with the correct reply.

1. _____
2. _____
3. _____
4. _____
5. _____

(a) It was first built over 200 years ago.
(b) I think they're playing chess.
(c) Sometimes there are performances of Taiwanese opera.
(d) Let's take a picture of them. I think it's allowed.
(e) You should pray to the god of marriage, then.

02 | Reading

Complete the following short paragraph by choosing which of the given sentences should go in each blank space.

Taoist temples tend to be more decorative than Buddhist temples. **1)** _____ Sometimes, you'll even see elderly people playing chess or card games in the temple grounds. **2)** _____ This is when someone lights incense and stands in front of an alter with their hands together. **3)** _____ Some temples are incredibly busy and vibrant. **4)** _____ During Chinese New Year and other important holidays, you may even be able to see special performances.

(a) Lungshan temple in Taipei is a good example of how popular some temples can be.
(b) They are also managed by local people and serve as community centers.
(c) When you enter a temple, you're sure to see people doing a "bai bai" ritual.
(d) They then bow several times in order to venerate the god.

03 | Writing

Unscramble the sentences.

1. Temple / has / the / bronze / Taiwan / Lungshan / only / dragon / in / pillars

   _____

   _____

2. temples / are / according / shui / Taiwanese / built / to / rules / special / called / feng

   _____

   _____

3. used / "bai bai" / ritual / The / can / both / gods / be / venerate / ancestors / to / and

   _____

   _____

Features of Temples

Incense (stick) 香

Incense burner/censer 香爐

Hanging cylinder 吊筒

Ornate roofs The temple's roof is often decorated with deities and mythological animals to expel evil spirits and bring good luck.

華麗的屋頂 寺廟的屋頂通常都以神明或神獸作為裝飾，取其驅趕邪靈、招來好運之意。

Colorful paintings Temples are often decorated with colorful paintings of educational stories or legends.

彩繪 寺廟內之彩繪經常以富含教育意義的故事或傳說為主題。

Mythological animals

Lucky lions are commonly seen outside Taiwanese temples. The one on the left of the temple is male and the one on the right is female, and is accompanied by a cub.

神獸 台灣寺廟外經常可見代表幸運的獅子，位於左方的是公獅，右方的是母獅，母獅腳下有小獅子相伴。

Delicately carved pillars and walls

Dragons, phoenixes, other lucky animals and plants are popular subjects for temple carvings.

雕工精細的柱子與牆 寺廟內常見的雕刻主題有龍、鳳，和一些代表好運的動植物。

Lighting incense sticks 點香

Bracket 斗拱

Beam 樑；桁

Pillar/pole/column 柱

Door Gods

A door god is painted on each side of the door to keep the evil spirits away.

門神

每一扇門各繪製一位門神，以阻擋惡靈進入。

Candles

Candles are lit to show respect for the deities. They are also used to pray for good luck and safety.

蠟燭

點蠟燭表示敬神，也有祈求好運和平安的作用。

Famous Temples in Taiwan

台北
行天宮

Hsintien Temple, Taipei

台北艋舺
龍山寺

cc by Ellery

Lungshan Temple, Mengjia, Taipei

台北木柵
指南宮

cc by KasugaHuang

Zhinan Temple, Muzha, Taipei

台北大龍峒
保安宮

Baoan Temple, Dalongdong, Taipei

新北市汐止
聖德宮

by Yuyu

Shengde Temple, Hsichih, Taipei

新北市汐止
拱北殿

by Yuyu

Gongbei Temple, Hsichih, New Taipei City

台北松山
慈祐宮

Ciyou Temple, Songshan, Taipei

新北市
武聖廟

Wusheng Temple, New Taipei City

台北淡水
清水巖
祖師廟

Chingshui Temple, Danshui, Taipei

台北大稻埕
霞海城隍廟

Xiahai Chenghuang Temple/ Hsiahai City-God Temple, Dadaocheng, Taipei

新北市三峽
清水巖
祖師廟

cc by Winertai

Chingshui Temple, Sanxia, New Taipei City

台中大甲
鎮瀾宮

by Jingguo

Zhenlan Temple, Dajia, Taichung

台中鹿港
龍山寺

台中鹿港
天后宮

cc by a-giâu

Lungshan Temple, Lugang, Taichung

Lugang Matsu Temple, Lugang, Taichung

南投
中台禪寺

Buddhist temple

Chung Tai Chan Monastery, Nantou

台南
大天后宮

Great Matsu Temple, Tainan

cc by Winertai

台南
南鯤鯓
代天府

Nankunshen Temple, Tainan City

雲林北港
朝天宮

Chaotien Temple, Beigang, Yunlin

嘉義新港
奉天宮

Fengtien Temple, Xingang, Chiayi

cc by Peellden

高雄
佛光山

Buddhist temple

Fokuangshan, Kaohsiung

Confucianism
儒家思想

Word Bank

influence n. 影響	**discrimination n.** 歧視	**ornate a.** 華麗的
goal n. 目標	**in honor of** 向……致敬	**prevent v.** 預防
position n. 位置	**mentor n.** 導師	**adjust v.** 調節
fulfill v. 實踐	**possess v.** 擁有	
	solemn a. 莊嚴的	

🎧 19 Reading Passage

Confucianism, as well as Buddhism and Taoism, has had a great **influence** on Taiwanese society. People live and think according to Confucian thought even today. Confucius was a great philosopher. Since he lived in a time of war, it was his **goal** that one day people would live in peace. He wanted to change the way that people relate to each other in order to create a peaceful society.

He held the idea that everyone has his or her own **position** in society. It is important for all parts of society to work together in harmony. Each person must **fulfill** his or her duty. For example, a father should take care of his family and a son should love and respect his parents and look after them when they are older.

Confucius was also a great teacher. He believed that if people are educated, they will naturally do the right thing. "Education without **discrimination** 有教無類" is a strong Confucian belief.

Taipei Confucius Temple 台北孔廟

Today, Confucian temples are built in many cities **in honor of** this great **mentor** of China. The Taipei Confucius Temple was first built in 1879 and rebuilt in 1925. It is the largest Confucian temple in northern Taiwan. Every year on the 28th of September, a memorial ceremony is held to celebrate Confucius' birthday. Traditional dancing and rituals are arranged according to ancient practices.

by Yuyu

Pan Pond at the Taipei Confucius Temple
台北孔廟的泮池

The Taipei Confucius Temple **possesses** typical traditional Chinese architecture, with **solemn** entrances, grand red columns, **ornate** roofs, colorful paintings and decorations. The half-moon shaped pond, called Pan Pond 泮池, in front of the main gate, is designed according to the principles of feng shui 風水. It also has the function of **preventing** fire and **adjusting** the temperature.

Quiz

1. Other than folk religions, what philosophy greatly affects Taiwanese society?
2. Who established this philosophy?
3. What are some ideas of this philosophy?
4. What kind of architecture is seen in a Confucian temple?
5. What kind of ceremony is held every year? When?

🎧20 Conversation

Ethan   I visited a Taiwanese family last week. They really look after their grandparents well.

Laura   That's because Confucianism still has an influence on Taiwanese society.

Ethan   But, I suppose life is changing in Taiwan.

Laura   Yes. Elderly people in Taiwan used to stay with the eldest son. But that's been changing over the past few years.

Ethan   In what way has it been changing?

Laura   Well, sometimes there isn't an eldest son. So, a daughter might look after them instead. What's more is that sometimes it's the daughters who get the best jobs these days.

Ethan   So, Confucius thought family was important, eh?

Laura   He did. But don't forget that he also had a plan for society as a whole.

Ethan   What kind of plan?

Laura   Well, he thought that everyone in society should act a certain way. There was a proper position for everyone.

Ethan   He must be a great mentor for the Chinese.

Laura   That's right. He is considered the greatest teacher in Chinese history. You may see Confucian temples in many Chinese and Taiwanese cities.

Ethan   Will I have a chance to visit one in Taipei?

Laura   Yes. The Taipei Confucius Temple is quite large. The architecture and decoration all follow the traditional manner and the principles of feng shui. It will really impress you!

Scenes from the Tainan Confucius Temple
台南孔廟數景

Features of the Taipei Confucius Temple

Hong Gate 黌門
(meaning "school"
in ancient time)

Lingxing Gate 欞星門
(The 108 studs on the door
symbolize 108 gods in heaven.)

Double eaves roofs
重簷歇山式屋頂

Octagonal plafond
八角藻井

Water dragon
水龍

Tungtien cylinder
通天筒

Hornless dragons
encycling a censer
螭龍圍爐

Dragon stone pillars
蟠龍石柱

Ji Qing 吉慶
(auspiciousness
and happiness)

Stone drums
抱鼓石

Photos by Yuyu

01 | Listening

Listen to the dialogue and mark the things that are mentioned in the conversation.

1. _____

2. _____

3. _____

4. _____

5. _____

02 | Reading

Circle the correct option in each sentence.

1. Confucius' goal was to create a **peaceful/violent** society.

2. One strong Confucian belief is "education without **wealth/discrimination**."

3. Confucius' birthday is celebrated every year with a memorial **party/ceremony**.

4. Confucius is considered a great **mentor/warrior** by the Chinese people.

5. The architecture of Taipei's Confucius Temple follows the **temperature/principles** of feng shui.

03 | Writing

Use the following words to fill the blanks.

influence   in honor of   ornate   fulfill

1. All around Taiwan, temples are built _____ the great teacher Confucius.

2. Visitors to the Taipei Confucius Temple will be able to see grand red columns, colorful paintings and decorations, and _____ roofs.

3. Confucius believed that everyone has to _____ their duty for society to work peacefully.

4. Along with Buddhism and Taoism, Confucianism has a great _____ on Taiwanese thought.

Western Culture

Industrialization first happened in the West. Therefore, Western countries were the first to have their customs changed by industry. The West used to be made up of farming countries. These countries had their own traditional values, much like any other farming community around the world. Family, country, and religion were all important concepts. People would obey higher authorities like the Church (Christianity), as well as the state. However, as science progressed, people became more skeptical and religion became less of an important part of their lives.

Now, there is more emphasis on freedom of choice. Some children leave home as early as eighteen years old. They choose their own job, religion, spouse, and so forth. This is not the way it was done 200 years ago.

Some people argue that these changes are bad. They say that the family has broken up and that people do not respect the law anymore. They also think that modern life is lonelier and more stressful than it was before. Some even believe that we have forgotten how to respect one another.

Others say that freedom makes a better society. Freedom allows people to make their own decisions, and they will lead happier lives when they do so. Perhaps the solution is to find a comfortable balance between modern and traditional ways of thinking.

Traditional Arts
傳統藝術

divide v. 分成
craft n. 工藝
weaving n. 編織
ceramics n. 製陶業

acrobatics n.
  雜技表演
puppetry n. 偶戲
associate v.
  和……聯想在一起

paper cutting 紙雕
disappear v. 消失
promote v. 提倡
boost v. 振興
innovation n. 創新

dazzling a. 燦爛的
emerge v. 新興
exhibition n. 展覽
adopt v. 採用
appearance n. 外觀

🎧 Reading Passage

Taiwan has plenty of traditional arts, which can be **divided** into two categories: traditional **crafts** and performing arts. Traditional crafts include painting, carving, **weaving**, and **ceramics**. Performing arts include folk music, folk dance, folk opera, **acrobatics**, and **puppetry**.

Taiwanese folk arts 台灣民俗藝術

Although no longer living a traditional life, Taiwanese people are still interested in traditional crafts. You might discover traditional paintings or wood carvings when you visit a Taiwanese person's house. You might also see some traditional ceramics, such as cups, saucers, and teapots, which are both useful and decorative.

Taiwan is home to lots of different kinds of operas. The island's own "Taiwanese opera" is actually a mix of different styles of Chinese opera. It has also been influenced by indigenous music and Taiwanese folk songs. Taiwanese opera is often performed outside temples, and sometimes the whole community comes out to see a performance. In recent years, new forms of opera have been created. It is very much a living art.

This kind of performing art tends to tell the stories of human life and folk legends. Much of the time, it's **associated** with folk religions and is performed on many religious occasions.

Other folk arts, such as **paper cutting**, also still survive in modern-day Taiwan. Arts that require more skill, such as puppetry,

Lion dancing 舞獅

lion dances, folk opera, and acrobatics are slowly **disappearing**. The government and various community groups are trying to keep these folk arts alive. Much like other countries, the Taiwanese government has **promoted** festivals to help **boost** cultural activities. Some of these festivals have been very successful.

Meanwhile, the **innovation** of traditional arts has played an important role in their survival. For example, Taiwanese puppetry makes use of new lighting technology to create **dazzling** visual effects. The puppet costumes are colorful and designed to attract the young.

Taiwanese opera 歌仔戲

Quiz

1. Which folk arts do Taiwanese still take an interest in?
2. Who is supporting traditional folk arts?
3. Where is Taiwanese opera usually performed?
4. Which traditional folk arts are undergoing innovation in the modern world?

23 **Conversation**

Ethan	I noticed that there are many traditional folk arts in Taiwan.
Laura	There sure are. They include painting, carving, dancing, and so on.
Ethan	But with TV, the Internet, and other new attractions, have some traditional art forms declined in popularity?
Laura	Some of the arts such as puppetry and lion dances are having a bit of trouble. However, during the last few years, cultural life in the cities has improved a lot.
Ethan	Are we talking about modern culture, like theater, music, and so on?
Laura	I mean all kinds of culture, Chinese and Western, modern and traditional.
Ethan	Are there any steps being taken to save the disappearing arts?
Laura	The government is trying to promote the arts throughout Taiwan. This includes building a lot of cultural centers, supporting **emerging** art groups and holding lots of festivals and **exhibitions**.
Ethan	I heard that traditional arts have also **adopted** modern ideas to present a new **appearance**.
Laura	Yes, the performing arts use modern technologies and even Western materials in order to attract young people. Some of them are very successful.
Ethan	I have also heard about many interesting festivals related to traditional arts.
Laura	Yes, for example, there is the International Children's Folklore & Folkgame Festival in Yilan on the east coast.

Drum performance during the Culture and Art Festival in Danshui
淡水文化藝術節的擊鼓表演

Taiwanese Traditional Arts

Taiwanese puppetry 布袋戲

Ceramics 製陶

Paper cutting 紙雕

Wood carving 木雕

Taiwanese opera 歌仔戲

Stone carving 石雕

Taiwanese tops 台灣陀螺

Traditional music (erhu 二胡)
傳統音樂

Dragon dancing
舞龍

Taiwanese lanterns
台灣燈籠

01 | Listening

Listen to the short dialogues and fill in the blanks.

1. **A:** Could you tell me something about Taiwanese _____ arts?

    B: Well, Taiwanese performing arts include acrobatics, _____, and Taiwanese opera.

2. **A:** Is Taiwanese opera the same as Chinese opera?

    B: Not quite. Taiwanese opera has been influenced by _____ music and Taiwanese _____ songs. So it's a little different from Chinese opera.

3. **A:** What does the government do to _____ traditional arts in Taiwan?

    B: It holds _____ and sets up cultural centers which support _____ art groups.

4. **A:** How are _____ art groups attracting younger people to come and study traditional skills?

    B: They're combining traditional art with modern _____ and holding festivals specifically for kids.

02 | Reading

Choose the correct caption for each picture.

_____ 1.

    (a) Taiwanese opera is being performed.

    (b) Innovation is important for traditional arts.

    (c) Paper cutting still survives in modern-day Taiwan.

    (d) Indigenous music is being played.

_____ 2.

    (a) Learning how to make a traditional teapot

    (b) A cultural center built by the government

    (c) Attracting young people to traditional arts

    (d) The slowly disappearing traditional arts

_____ 3.

    (a) Taiwan's traditional arts can be divided into two categories.

    (b) New forms of Taiwanese opera have been created in recent years.

    (c) Traditional ceramics are both decorative and useful.

    (d) Traditional performances are often performed outside temples.

03 | Writing

Use the prompts to write a sentence. You'll need to add necessary words or change the verb tenses to make correct sentences.

1. Taiwanese / people / still / interested / traditional / crafts

   _____

   _____

2. carving / weaving / ceramics / examples / traditional / crafts

   _____

   _____

3. government / try / keep / folk / arts / alive / hold / lots of / festivals

   _____

   _____

4. folk / songs / indigenous / music / influence / Taiwanese / opera

   _____

   _____

5. performing arts / use / modern / technologies / attract / young / people

   _____

   _____

Acrobatic performances and kung fu demonstrations are quite common during local Taiwanese festivals.
台灣地方節慶中經常可見雜技表演與功夫展示。

Unit 9

Traditional and Modern Architecture
傳統與現代建築

🎧25 Reading Passage

Buildings have changed quite a bit in Taiwan over the past few **decades**. Fifty years ago, many buildings in Taiwan had **distinctive** Chinese-style roofs. Nowadays, most Taiwanese people live in Western-style apartment **blocks**. The population of Taiwan is too big for everyone to keep living in Chinese-style buildings. However, there are several public buildings that have been built in the old Chinese style. One such building is Taipei Railway Station.

Traditional buildings follow the **principles** of feng shui (wind and water). Feng shui is an ancient Chinese belief that tells us how buildings should be **positioned**. If they are not positioned correctly **in relation to** water, mountains

Taipei Railway Station 台北車站

Lin Antai Historical Residence 林安泰古厝，
a typical traditional Chinese-style house
林安泰古厝是典型的傳統中國式房屋。

Sun Yat-sen Historical Events Memorial Hall 國父史蹟紀念館 is a famous Japanese-style building in Taipei.

國父史蹟紀念館是台北著名的日式建築。

and other types of **terrain**, bad luck can result. Feng shui is sometimes used when **constructing** homes, temples, and even public or **commercial** buildings.

Japan controlled Taiwan for fifty years, so it is not surprising that there are still some Japanese influences on the island. For example, the Taiwanese language still uses many Japanese words. Japanese food is quite popular and many people study Japanese. You might occasionally see an old Japanese-style building. If you're interested in this style of building,

Sun Yat-sen Historical Events **Memorial** Hall, A Drop of Water Memorial Hall, and Huguo Chan Buddhist Temple of Linji School 臨濟護國禪寺 are good places to visit.

The Dutch and Spanish came even earlier than the Japanese. They **invaded** Taiwan in the early 1600's, and have left some historic structures. The main feature of Dutch-style architecture is the use of **bricks**. Sections of brick wall outside the Anping Fort 安平古堡 in Tainan are an example. There are also a few British-style buildings, for example, the former British **Consulate** at Takao 打狗英國領事館, located in Kaohsiung, which was built in 1865.

The original Anping Fort 安平古堡 was built by the Dutch in **1624**.

安平古堡原先是由荷蘭人建於 1624 年。

Quiz

1. Describe some of the changes in Taiwanese architecture.
2. What is feng shui?
3. Name some examples of buildings with Japanese-style architecture.

🎧 Conversation

Huguo Chan Buddhist Temple of Linji School 臨濟護國禪寺

Ethan   How is **Westernization** affecting Taiwanese society?

Laura   You can see lots of hamburger joints, Western movies, TV shows, and so on. But that's happening in other places, too. It's not just in Taiwan.

Ethan   I saw some Japanese-style buildings in Taipei. Is it because the Japanese ruled over Taiwan for a long time?

Laura   Taiwan was governed by the Japanese for fifty years. A lot of buildings were constructed at that time. Some **contemporary** architecture is built in the Japanese style.

Ethan   I have heard of "A Drop of Water Memorial Hall" in New Taipei City, I know it is Japanese-style.

Laura   Yes. After being moved to Danshui from Japan and **reassembled** in 2009, it was opened to the public in 2011.

Ethan   What are other examples of Japanese-style architecture that are worth seeing?

Laura   The Martyrs' Shrine in Taoyuan, the Huguo Chan Buddhist Temple of Linji School in Taipei, and the Memorial Hall of Founding of Yilan Administration are all typical Japanese-style structures.

Ethan   I also know that there are some Dutch, Spanish, and British historic **monuments**.

Laura   Yes. Taiwan's **colonial** background has resulted in a **diversity** of architectural styles and features.

The Memorial Hall of Founding of Yilan Administration 宜蘭設治紀念館

by Yuyu

WESTERN-STYLE
Architecture

Julius Mannich & Co.
安平東興洋行
cc by Pbdragonwang

Oxford College
牛津理學堂
cc by Kamakura

Former British Consulate at Takao
打狗英國領事館

Former British Consulate at Danshui
淡水英國領事館

Danshui Church
淡水教會

Office of the President
總統府

(27)

01 | Listening

Listen to the statements and fill in the blanks.

1. Taiwan's population has increased so much in the past few _____ that it's impossible for everyone to live in traditional, _____ houses.

2. Dutch-style _____ from the 1600s can be seen in southern Taiwan and can be recognized by the Dutch's use of _____ .

3. The Japanese-style building A Drop of Water Memorial Hall was moved to Danshui and _____ there in 2009.

4. To see a British-style building, go visit the former British _____ at Takao in Kaohsiung, which was built almost a hundred and fifty years ago.

02 | Reading

Match the two halves of the sentences.

1. Feng shui tells you how to _____

2. The Japanese ruled _____

3. Taiwan had a diversity of architectural styles _____

4. Some historic structures were built by _____

(a) over Taiwan for fifty years.
(b) because of its colonial background.
(c) position a building in relation to the terrain.
(d) the Dutch and Spanish in the 1600s.

03 | Writing

Complete the sentences using the words and fragments given.

principles   construct   old Chinese style   apartment   architecture

1. Feng shui is used to _____ modern commercial buildings as well as homes and temples.

2. Most Taiwanese people now live in tall _____ blocks, and the remaining traditional houses are no longer lived in.

3. The Japanese influence on Taiwan can be seen not only in the island's _____ but also in the Taiwanese language.

4. If the _____ of feng shui are not followed correctly, it can result in bad luck.

5. Though many visitors may not have noticed, Taipei Railway Station is one public building that was built in the _____ .

Taipei Guest House
台北賓館 [cc by 玄史生]

More
WESTERN-STYLE
Architecture

Anping Former Tait & Co.
安平德記洋行

Eluanbi Lighthouse
鵝鑾鼻燈塔

Unit 10 Traditional Etiquette
傳統禮儀

28 Reading Passage

Like any other country, Taiwan has its own traditional **customs** and **etiquette**. Many foreigners are not familiar with these customs and etiquette, so they sometimes **embarrass** Taiwanese people without even knowing that they're doing anything wrong. This can make foreigners very confused sometimes. In Taiwanese society, it's always a good idea to make people feel good. This is why Taiwanese people will often **compliment** their guests. At the same time, they tend to be **modest** about themselves and the food that they're serving. This mixture of compliments and modesty can be quite confusing to foreigners. For example, Taiwanese people might tell a foreigner that his or her Chinese is very good. But, if asked, they will say that their own English is very

Taiwanese people will usually ask their guests if they would like something to drink. Tea is a beverage they often serve to their guests.
台灣人通常會詢問客人是否需要喝點什麼。他們往往都會倒茶給客人喝。

People like to line up in Taiwan.
台灣人喜歡排隊。

Taiwanese people are very hospitable and ready to share.
台灣人十分好客，樂於分享。

poor. They will say this even if they speak English better than their foreign guest speaks Mandarin!

Taiwanese people **rely** on strong relationships with people to deal with both business and day-to-day problems. For example, if someone is looking for a job, one of his or her friends may know someone who is looking to **hire** a new employee. Thus, he or she may have a better chance of getting a job. This is because Taiwanese people value family and friends very much. "Helping each other" is a **virtue** in Taiwanese society. However, Taiwanese people are often willing to give **assistance** even if they don't know you. So, if you get lost in Taiwan, feel free to ask a Taiwanese for help. You'll find them to be very friendly.

Finally, under no **circumstances** should death ever be discussed with a Taiwanese person. Talking about death can bring bad luck. This is why Taiwanese tourists often skip "Death **Valley**" when they visit America.

Quiz →

1. What can confuse foreigners?
2. Do Taiwanese people often compliment guests?

Conversation

Ethan	It seems like it would be easy to make a mistake here and hurt people's feelings without meaning to.
Laura	You just need to get familiar with the etiquette here. Taiwanese people tend to **treat** people politely. That's why you shouldn't be too direct when talking to someone.
Ethan	So, I should be careful not to embarrass people in front of others.
Laura	That's right.
Ethan	Oh, and why does everyone think my Chinese is so good even though I can only say "ni hao"?
Laura	Generally speaking, making people feel good is important here, so compliments are common in Taiwanese society.
Ethan	So, they just want to make me feel good?
Laura	They're just trying to be polite. But, who knows, maybe your "ni hao" is the best they've ever heard.
Ethan	I doubt it, but it's nice of them to say so!
Laura	You may also want to think about complimenting others. Even though Taiwanese people are very **humble**, everyone enjoys some compliments every once in a while.
Ethan	Sure thing. That will give me an opportunity to practice my Chinese!
Laura	You may like to make some Taiwanese friends, too. It is the belief that relationships are very important, and that people should support one another whenever they're in need.
Ethan	I'm learning to build relationships here. It is really great that many Taiwanese are very friendly and **willing** to help me, even if they don't know me!

Western Customs

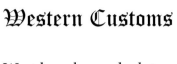

Life in the West has changed a lot over the past 200 years. Even compared to just 50 years ago, modern day societies are completely different. In the 1950s, people wanted to be thought of as polite so they would be careful about their manners. For example, whenever a man spoke to a stranger he would raise his hat. Men acted like "gentlemen," meaning they would open doors for women and let them go through first. Also, if a woman or a disabled person needed a seat on the bus, a man would offer theirs.

Just like in Taiwan, if you were invited into someone's home in the West, you would be expected to bring a small gift, such as flowers, chocolates, or a bottle of wine. Although people no longer expect this, it is still a nice gesture.

Why did things change? One reason may be the women's movement. Women wanted equal treatment, so they stood up and started opening their own doors. Another reason was the hippie movement of the 1960s. Back then, people started demanding more freedom and stopped believing in a stiff system of manners. As a result, people became less formal. Nevertheless, it is still quite important to say "please" and "thank you" in the West.

01 | Listening

Listen to the statements and match each one with the picture that best illustrates it.

1. _____
2. _____
3. _____

a

b

c

02 | Reading

Complete the following short paragraph by choosing which of the given sentences should go in each blank space.

1) _____ The Taiwanese are always very polite to their guests. **2)** _____
However, when the Taiwanese talk about themselves, they usually do so very modestly.
3) _____ And if they speak fluent English, they will insist that they only speak "a little." **4)** _____ If something goes wrong on your trip to Taiwan, don't worry. **5)** _____

(a) They will say that the banquet they serve you is nothing special.
(b) A Taiwanese person will always help a stranger as best they can.
(c) In addition to their politeness, Taiwanese people are also very helpful and friendly.
(d) Taiwanese etiquette can sometimes be confusing for foreigners in Taiwan.
(e) If you try to speak some Chinese, no matter how basic, you will almost always get complimented.

03 | Writing

Use the following words to complete the sentences.

valley   embarrass   virtue   assistance

1. Being ready and willing to help people is a major _____ in Taiwanese society.

2. It's always best to be familiar with Taiwanese customs before you arrive, otherwise you might _____ your host.

3. If you ever need any _____ in Taiwan, don't be afraid to ask a passer-by for help.

4. Taiwanese tourists often avoid visiting Death _____ when they visit the United States.

The Drinking
Culture in Taiwan

Drinking is an important part of Taiwanese culture. When getting together with friends, many Taiwanese people love to have a little beer or wine to relax.

When drinking wine or beer, the Taiwanese toast each other for any good things that have happened to them recently. They will usually drink all of the wine or beer from their glass at one time. This is considered to show support to one another.

Taiwanese people often say "gan bei" and then finish their drink. "Gan bei" means "cheers" in English. There is even a saying that goes, "Do not keep a goldfish at the bottom of your wine glass," which implies that one should never leave any liquid unfinished.

Today, the "gan bei" culture has gradually disappeared. The government has made great effort to raise awareness of the dangers of drinking and driving. So, now it is more common for people to take a sip when giving a toast. They do not ask their friends to "gan bei" very often.

Taiwan beer ↗

Unit 11
The Gifting Culture
送禮文化

🎧31 Reading Passage

In Taiwan, giving gifts is quite popular. Gifts can be given on many different **occasions**. When people get married, move into a house, give birth to a baby, start a business, and so on, they usually **receive** gifts from friends.

During Chinese New Year, children and the elderly receive money as a gift. Money is also given to the happy couple on their wedding day. Even when going to a **funeral**, you must give money to **the bereaved**. When money is given as a gift in Taiwan, it is always put in a red **envelope**, unless the occasion is a funeral, in which a white envelope is used instead. The color red **represents** good fortune while white is associated with death in Taiwanese culture. When giving a gift, foreigners should be careful not to give money in any **denomination** that has a four, as this number represents death. In Mandarin, the words for death and four sound almost the same. Therefore, Taiwanese people tend to avoid this number.

Money is often given in a red envelope at Chinese wedding receptions.
中式婚宴中，大家習慣致贈以紅包裝好的禮金。

Even today, hospitals in Taiwan don't have a fourth floor. If they did, nobody would want to stay on it.

When visiting a person's home in Taiwan, it is important to bring a gift. The gift can be fruit, chocolates, cake, wine or something similar. When you give your gift, you should offer it using both hands. Be modest about what it is and say that it's just something small. Don't be surprised when the person receiving the gift puts it down to open it later. Taiwanese people don't usually open a gift in  front of the person who gave it to them. If you are given a gift, it's best to act the same way. If giving an expensive present, it is a good idea to **wrap** it up nicely. Taiwanese people **regard** gift giving as an expression of **sincerity**. However, clocks and knives should never be given to a Taiwanese person as a gift. Clocks represent death because the word for "clock (zhong)" sounds the same as "the end of life (zhong)" in Mandarin. Knives represent the cutting of personal **ties**.

Taiwanese people always take off their shoes when they enter other people's homes. They may tell a visitor that it's not necessary, but you should take them off anyway. After someone removes their shoes, they are often given a pair of slippers to wear inside the house.

Another useful tip to remember is that it is considered **respectful** to greet the eldest person first whenever you enter somebody's home.

Quiz ➝

1. When are children given money as a gift?
2. What are two gifts you should never give people in Taiwan?
3. Why shouldn't you give these gifts?
4. What should you do if you want to give an expensive gift?

32

Conversation

> Ethan and Laura are buying pineapple cakes at a bakery.

Pineapple cakes
鳳梨酥

Ethan	Why are you buying so many pineapple cakes?
Laura	I'm visiting my aunt tomorrow. I'd like to bring some gifts along. Pineapple cakes are perfect to give as gifts.
Ethan	Is giving gifts part of the Taiwanese culture?
Laura	Yes. Gifting is very important in Taiwanese society. The gift can be cakes, fruit, wine, and tea. Even money is given on some occasions.
Ethan	On what kinds of occasions is money given?
Laura	Mostly at wedding **receptions** and funerals. Money is given either as a blessing or comfort.
Ethan	I have heard of the custom of giving red envelopes with money in them to children and the elderly during Chinese New Year.
Laura	Exactly.

Common Gifts

Wine 酒

Tea 茶

Fruit 水果

by Yuyu

Ethan	So, what's the occasion you're attending tomorrow?
Laura	Ha, Nothing! It has been a long time since I visited my aunt. I guess bringing gifts when visiting relatives or friends is simply a **behavior** or form of politeness and sincerity in Taiwanese society. Especially when going to an elder person's house, it is considered **rude** not to bring a gift.
Ethan	I see. So, you can give anything you want as a gift?
Laura	No, no. Clocks, knives, shoes, and umbrellas are not **appropriate** gifts. Clocks **imply** death, and knives are taken as a symbol of cutting relationships.
Ethan	But what **negative** meanings do shoes and umbrellas have?
Laura	Shoes imply asking a person to leave. Umbrellas represent separation because they sound alike in Mandarin.
Ethan	Wow! Thanks for letting me know. I should be extremely careful when choosing gifts.

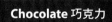

Chocolate 巧克力

Flowers 花

Egg rolls 蛋捲

33

01 | Listening

Listen to the first part of each dialogue. Match each one with the correct reply.

1. _____
2. _____
3. _____
4. _____
5. _____

(a) Yes. You should always offer the gift with both hands.
(b) Yes, definitely. It's considered impolite if you don't bring a gift.
(c) Yes. And make sure you put it in a white envelope.
(d) Because red represents good fortune in Taiwan.
(e) No don't! In Taiwanese culture it represents death.

02 | Reading

Choose the caption that best describes each picture.

_____ 1.

(a) Remember to wrap your gift nicely.
(b) Never give a clock as a gift.
(c) Taiwanese hospitals don't have a fourth floor.
(d) Be modest about your gift.

_____ 2.

(a) Pineapple cakes make good gifts.
(b) Always greet the eldest person first when visiting someone's house.
(c) The color red represents good fortune.
(d) An umbrella is not an appropriate gift.

_____ 3.

(a) Shoes and knives are both bad ideas for gifts.
(b) Gift giving is seen as an expression of sincerity.
(c) Don't give money in any denomination which has a four.
(d) Knives represent the cutting of personal ties.

_____ 4.

(a) You should give a gift when someone has a new baby.
(b) A gift of shoes represents asking someone to leave.
(c) People are often given slippers to wear inside the house.
(d) Elderly people receive money during Chinese New Year.

03 | Writing

Some of the information in the following sentences is incorrect. Write the sentences out again with the correct information.

1. Food is usually put in a yellow envelope when it's given as a gift.

   _____

   _____

2. Hospitals in Taiwan don't have a fifth floor because the words for five and death sound almost the same in English.

   _____

   _____

3. Umbrellas represent happiness in Taiwanese culture.

   _____

   _____

4. When you give a gift you should offer it with only one hand.

   _____

   _____

5. Remember to take off your socks when you enter someone's car.

   _____

   _____

Taiwanese people receive gifts when they give birth to a baby. However, to celebrate the completion of the baby's first month after birth, parents will send gifts to their relatives and friends. Usually, these gifts are cakes, red eggs and sticky rice with chicken drumstick, which are symbols of auspiciousness, propagation and promotion.

by Yuyu

12 Food Culture
飲食文化

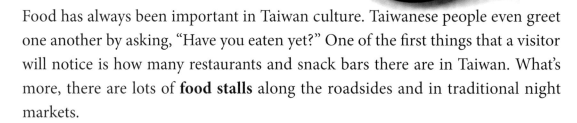

34 Reading Passage

Food has always been important in Taiwan culture. Taiwanese people even greet one another by asking, "Have you eaten yet?" One of the first things that a visitor will notice is how many restaurants and snack bars there are in Taiwan. What's more, there are lots of **food stalls** along the roadsides and in traditional night markets.

You may find different styles of Chinese food in Taiwan. Taiwan also has its own style of cooking that has developed over hundreds of years. You may even **come across** traditional indigenous food. Modern Taiwanese cities are also home to lots of restaurants serving different kinds of **cuisine** from all around the world. You can find Indian, Thai, Korean, French, and Mexican restaurants among others. In Taipei, you can even try Greek, Iranian, and Russian cuisine. Of course, American fast food is widely available. Taiwan also has its own fast food restaurants. Foreigners may find them strange, yet **oddly** familiar.

The two basic foods of Taiwan are rice and noodles. Since rice is so important, it should be no surprise that there are lots of tasty rice dishes in Taiwan. For breakfast, Taiwanese people sometimes eat watery rice **porridge** with **pickled** vegetables. This dish is called "**congee**" in English. For dinner, Taiwanese

Taiwanese Breakfast 台式早餐

1. **Watery rice porridge** 稀飯
2. **Salty duck egg** 鹹鴨蛋
3. **Pickled vegetables** 醬菜

families eat steamed white rice together with vegetable, fish, and meat dishes. Sometimes, a Taiwanese dinner can end up looking like a **banquet**!

Noodles are the other basic food in Taiwan. They became popular in China long ago because they are so easy to carry and store. Two popular noodle dishes in Taiwan are "soup noodles" and "beef noodles." Beef noodles have become more and more popular. In the past, people would not eat beef because

Beef noodles 牛肉麵

cows were seen as important **agricultural** animals. However, most Taiwanese people no longer have any problem eating beef.

Some noodles are made from rice flour. Delicious fried rice noodles and rice noodle soup are available in night markets and from roadside food stalls.

← Mung bean noodles 冬粉
↓ Rice noodles 米粉

Quiz →

1. When do Taiwanese people generally eat rice porridge?
2. What are a few types of international cuisine that can be found in Taiwan?

Chopsticks 筷子

35 Conversation

Ethan	You know, it's a little strange. If people aren't asking if I've already eaten, they're inquiring about whether I'm full or not. What gives?
Laura	I think they're being polite. As you know, Taiwanese people love their food. There's even an old Chinese saying that goes "for people, food is **paramount**."
Ethan	With all the delicious Chinese restaurants around the world, this isn't too surprising. Why are they so interested in food?
Laura	Some people say it's because Chinese people feared not getting enough food to feed their families in ancient times.
Ethan	I suppose there were lots of **famines** back then, eh?
Laura	Famines, **droughts**, and wars. Any of these **disasters** could leave people hungry. This made rice very important.
Ethan	Sounds like the way the Irish feel about potatoes. Potatoes were their main food. As long as you had potatoes, you could survive.
Laura	That's right. Chinese people also **associated** rice and food with prosperity. Rich people could eat as much as they wanted.
Ethan	So, even in modern Taiwan where everyone has enough to eat, people still think this way about food.
Laura	That's right.
Ethan	Do Taiwanese people have rice with every single meal?
Laura	They do, more or less. Whether they're at home or attending a fancy banquet, rice goes with pretty much everything.
Ethan	So, all of the main Chinese styles are available in Taiwan?
Laura	Yes, that's why it's a great place for food lovers! You can also find various kinds of foreign food in the big cities, such as Thai, Vietnamese, French, and Indonesian cuisine.

Soup spoon 湯匙   Bowl 碗   Sauce dish 醬料碟

Common Breakfast
& Rice Dishes in Taiwan

Another Style of Taiwanese Breakfast
另一種台式早餐

1. Clay oven roll with
   fried bread sticks 燒餅油條
2. Soy milk 豆漿
3. Taiwanese rice ball 飯糰
4. Salty soy milk 鹹豆漿
5. Radish cakes 蘿蔔糕
6. Steamed buns 饅頭
7. Steamed stuffed buns 包子

Rice Dishes

8. Minced pork congee with
   preserved egg 皮蛋瘦肉粥
9. Braised pork rice 滷肉飯
10. Rice with a chicken leg 雞腿飯
11. Fried rice 炒飯

36

01 | Listening

Listen to the statements and mark the information you get from each one.

1. ○ Taiwan offers visitors the chance to eat a variety of different dishes.
   ○ Noodles became popular in China because they were easy to store.

2. ○ There are plenty of food stalls in Taiwan's night markets.
   ○ There are many Western restaurants in Taiwan.

3. ○ Almost every meal in Taiwan includes rice or noodles.
   ○ Some noodles are made from rice flour.

4. ○ Families eat steamed rice with vegetables, fish, and meat.
   ○ Taiwanese people eat beef more now than they did in the past.

02 | Reading

Match the two halves of the sentences.

1. Chinese people are so interested in food _____

2. In the past, rice was _____

3. Rice and noodles in Taiwan _____

4. Congee is often eaten _____

(a) associated with prosperity.
(b) can be compared to potatoes in Ireland.
(c) because they feared famine and hunger in ancient times.
(d) with pickled vegetables.

03 | Writing

Fill in the blanks using the words provided.

1. *banquet, dishes, meat*
   With so many different _____ on the table, including _____, fish, and an array of vegetables, a Taiwanese dinner can look just like a _____.

2. *cows, eaten, agricultural*
   In the past, _____ were seen as important _____ animals and were therefore not _____.

3. *roadside, fried, stalls*
   If you have a taste for _____ rice noodles, you can eat your fill at many _____ food _____.

4. *paramount, disasters, suffered*
   The saying, "for people, food is _____," shows just how important food was to the ancient Chinese as they _____ through wars, famines, and _____.

Common Noodle Dishes in Taiwan

Rice noodles and thin noodles 米粉與麵線

1. Rice noodle soup 米粉湯
2. Fried rice noodles 炒米粉
3. Thin noodles with pig's intestines 大腸麵線

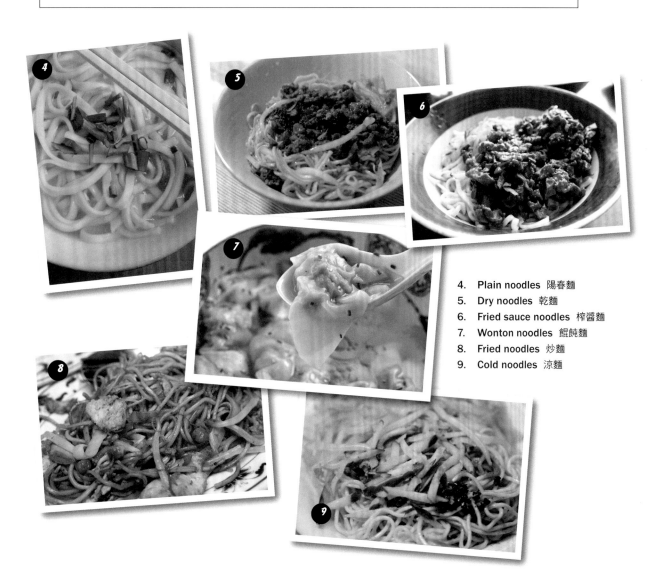

4. Plain noodles 陽春麵
5. Dry noodles 乾麵
6. Fried sauce noodles 榨醬麵
7. Wonton noodles 餛飩麵
8. Fried noodles 炒麵
9. Cold noodles 涼麵

Word Bank

mung bean 綠豆	**spicy** a. 辣的	**mug** n. 馬克杯	**burst** v. 流出
peanut n. 花生	**beerhouse** n. 啤酒屋	**quality** n. 品質	**terrain** n. 地勢;地形
steam v. 蒸	**basil** n. 九層塔	**renowned** a. 知名的	
stuffing n. 內餡	**sesame** n. 芝麻	**teahouse** n. 茶館	
	colleague n. 同事	**ethnic** a. 種族的	

37 **Reading Passage**

Small steamed dumplings
小籠包

Many Taiwanese dishes are similar to the ones that come from China, though most have a unique Taiwanese flavor. These include various snacks like **mung bean** cakes, **peanuts**, and tea eggs.

One of the most popular foods among tourists is "**steamed** dumplings." Steamed dumplings come from eastern China. They're also called *tangbao* or "soup dumplings" because of their juicy **stuffing**, made of pork, green onion, and ginger. Restaurants serving steamed dumplings often also offer other Chinese dishes like sour and **spicy** soup, chicken soup, steamed stuffed buns, fried rice, and so on.

Taiwanese people enjoy having food at local **beerhouses**. Stir-fried clams (with chili pepper and **basil**), three-cup chicken (made with a sauce of **sesame** oil, rice wine, and soy sauce), grilled fish, grilled squid, stir-fried

1. Tea eggs 茶葉蛋
2. Stir-fried clams 炒蛤蜊
3. Grilled squid 烤魷魚
4. Three-cup chicken 三杯雞

vegetables, and deep-fried tofu are common dishes on the menu. When people get off work, they usually get together with friends or **colleagues** at such restaurants to eat fried food and snacks, and drink **mugs** of cold beer!

Taiwanese people also love their drinks. Taiwan has an environment that is good for tea growing. Therefore, Taiwan's tea products are of very high **quality**. When it comes to tea, they enjoy drinking Chinese green tea or oolong tea without milk or sugar. Oolong tea is probably the most popular tea in Taiwan. The two **renowned** Taiwanese teas are Dongding oolong tea 凍頂烏龍茶 and Baozhong tea 包種茶. Taiwanese people will often have tea after their meals or with snacks. The island is full of **teahouses** where you can relax and enjoy anything from a hot pot of oolong tea to a glass of iced black tea with lemon. Maokong 貓空 in Taipei is well known for its numerous teahouses. They're always crowded with local people and visitors on weekends.

Quiz

1. What are some of the dishes served in Taiwan's beerhouses?

2. What are some of the ingredients used to make three-cup chicken?

3. What is the most popular kind of tea in Taiwan?

🎧(38) Conversation

Ethan   What's Taiwanese food like?

Laura   It's very different from the kind of Chinese food that you're used to eating in the West.

Ethan   I suppose there are different types of cooking due to all of the different **ethnic** groups in Taiwan.

Laura   Yes. The indigenous people, Hakka, and Taiwanese all have their own cuisine. They've probably influenced each other as well.

Ethan   Are there any special dishes?

Laura   Every city has its own special dishes, but if you mean throughout the whole island, there are lots. For example, beef noodles can be found everywhere.

Ethan   And what are these steamed dumplings that I keep hearing about?

Famous Taiwanese Tea

Dongding Oolong Tea
凍頂烏龍茶

Wenshan Baozhong Tea
文山包種茶

Oriental Beauty Tea
東方美人茶

Iron Guanyin
鐵觀音

High Mountain Tea
高山茶

Alishan Julu Tea
阿里山珠露茶

Black Jade Tea (TTES#18)
紅玉紅茶（台茶 18 號）

Longjing Tea
龍井茶

Longquan Tea
龍泉茶

Laura   They are dumplings stuffed with pork and green onion and they are very juicy inside. When you have a bite, the soup inside usually **bursts** out. So they're also called "soup dumplings."

Ethan   What kinds of drinks are popular on the island?

Laura   Oolong tea is Taiwanese people's favorite tea. Tea is not just a drink, but also a part of the culture.

Ethan   Does Taiwan produce its own tea?

Laura   Taiwan probably produces some of the best quality tea in the world. The mountainous **terrain** and climate here are good for growing tea.

Common Taiwanese Cuisine

Oysters in black bean sauce
蔭豉鮮蚵

Stir-fried vegetables
炒青菜

Stir-fried muttun in Shacha sauce 沙茶炒羊肉

pork leg
豬腳

Spicy pig's intestines
五更腸旺

Roast duck
烤鴨

Sour and spicy soup
酸辣湯

39

01 | Listening

Listen to the first part of each short dialogue. Match each one with the correct reply.

1. _____
2. _____
3. _____
4. _____
5. _____

(a) Of course. Taiwan has the perfect environment for growing great tasting tea.

(b) Teas like oolong tea and Chinese green tea are drunk without milk.

(c) It's cooked in soy sauce, sesame oil, and rice wine.

(d) It's made of pork, green onion, and ginger.

(e) Things like tea eggs, mung beans, and peanuts are popular snacks here.

02 | Reading

Circle the correct option in each sentence.

1. Indigenous, Hakka, and Taiwanese cuisines have all **influenced/stuffed** each other.

2. Getting together with friends or **colleagues/visitors** at the local beerhouse is a popular Taiwanese pastime.

3. For the Taiwanese, tea is a part of their **future/culture** rather than just a drink.

4. Taiwan's teahouses are great places to enjoy a hot **soup/pot** of the island's famous Baozhong tea.

5. Each city in Taiwan has its own special **restaurants/dishes**, but certain ones, like beef noodles, are loved all over the island.

03 | Writing

Use the following words to fill in the blanks.

ethnic   renowned   burst   beerhouses

1. Local _____ serve dishes like deep-fried tofu, three-cup chicken and stir-fried clams.

2. Maokong is _____ for its many teahouses, which are often crowded with visitors at the weekend.

3. Taiwanese cuisine is so various because of the many different _____ groups that live on the island.

4. Be careful when taking a bite of a soup dumpling, as the hot soup inside can _____ out and burn your tongue.

Common Taiwanese Snacks

Square cookies 方塊酥　　**Pineapple cake** 鳳梨酥　　**Egg yolk shortcake** 蛋黃酥

Mochi
麻糬

Preserved fruit
蜜餞

Ox tongue shaped pastry
牛舌餅

Glutinous rice sesame ball
芝麻球

Green onion cake
蔥餅

Donut
甜甜圈

Dried pork slices
豬肉乾

Unit 14 Night Markets 夜市

🎧40 Reading Passage

Another distinguishing feature of Taiwan is its night markets which are found all over the island in almost every city. There are various Taiwanese snacks sold in night markets.

Stinky tofu 臭豆腐

Stinky tofu frying in a pan 鍋中油炸的臭豆腐

Visitors to a Taiwanese night market should not miss out on stinky tofu. Tofu is made from soy milk just like cheese is made from cow's milk. It is a very popular **ingredient** in Chinese cooking. Sometimes you will smell something very strange when walking around the streets of Taiwan. It is a smell that often **puzzles** foreign tourists. Stinky tofu is **pungent** because it has been left in a **brine** of **fermented** milk and other ingredients such as vegetables and meat for up to several months.

Oyster omelets are another Taiwanese snack that every visitor should try. They are made of eggs, oysters, and vegetables that are fried in a pan, and are eaten with a specially-made sauce. Sometimes, oysters are **replaced** with shrimp or squid.

Food stall selling oyster omelets in the market 市場中販售蚵仔煎的小吃攤

Shaved ice 挫冰

For dessert, people enjoy eating **shaved** ice covered with fruit or other tasty **toppings**. Western-style ice cream is also available all over the island.

Pearl milk tea 珍珠奶茶

Bubble tea is one distinctive Taiwanese drink that is becoming popular around the world. It was first invented in Taichung, central Taiwan, in the 1980s when a tea shop owner decided to try something new. He mixed fruit syrup, tea, and other ingredients together until he **stumbled** upon a delicious new drink. Since then, the popularity of bubble tea has spread around the world and new types of the drink are being invented every day. One of the most famous examples is pearl milk tea made using black tea, milk, and **chewy tapioca** balls.

And if you still have room to try more snacks, get a grilled sausage! In Taiwan, grilled sausages can be eaten with **coriander**, garlic, or cheese. Taiwanese people have even created a snack called "small sausage in large sausage," which is a pork sausage wrapped in a sticky rice sausage.

Food stall selling grilled sausages and "small sausage in large sausage" in the Shilin Night Market
士林夜市販售烤香腸以及「大腸包小腸」的小吃攤

Quiz

1. Name some famous foods that can be found in Taiwan's night markets.
2. What is stinky tofu?
3. What distinctive drink was invented in Taiwan?
4. In what part of Taiwan was it discovered? When?

Spicy stinky tofu
麻辣臭豆腐

🎧 Conversation

Ethan	There are so many night markets in Taiwan. Almost every city has one or more!
Laura	Yes. I like to visit the stalls selling delicious snacks. Talk about great eating!
Ethan	Hanging around the night markets is such an amazing experience! You can taste a variety of Taiwanese snacks and do some shopping for clothes and crafts as well.
Laura	Have you tried stinky tofu yet?
Ethan	No. The smell is enough to keep me away. How is that stuff made, anyways?
Laura	They put the tofu in fermented milk along with some vegetables and meat and leave it for a month or two. Pretty strong, don't you think?
Ethan	It's a little too strong for me, especially when they fry it!
Laura	Some people love it, some don't! By the way, you must drink pearl milk tea while you are in Taiwan. It's a distinctive drink here.
Ethan	I already did! I love it. The tapioca balls in it are very chewy. What an invention!
Laura	It was invented in Taichung. Now it's becoming popular around the world.
Ethan	And what is the "small sausage in large sausage"?
Laura	It's pretty much like an American hot dog. They wrap a grilled pork sausage in a sticky rice sausage, which is larger. That's where it gets the name.
Ethan	I see. I'll definitely get fat if I stay in Taiwan for a month or two!
Laura	Haha, and don't forget to end a night market tour with a plate of shaved ice!

Taiwan's Night Markets

Shilin Night Market
士林觀光夜市

Ning Xia Rd. Night Market
寧夏觀光夜市

Raohe St. Night Market
饒河街觀光夜市

Hwahsi Tourist Night Market
華西街觀光夜市

Liouhe Tourist Night Market
六合夜市

Fengjia Night Market
逢甲夜市

Luodong Tourist Night Market
羅東夜市

Keelung Miaokou Night Market
基隆廟口夜市

Hsinchu Du Cheng Huang Temple Night Market
新竹城隍廟口夜市

Practice

01 | Listening

Listen to the dialogue and mark the things that are mentioned in the conversation.

1. ○   2. ○   3. ○   4. ○   5. ○

02 | Reading

Complete the following short paragraph by choosing which of the given sentences should go in each blank space.

Night markets are found all over Taiwan in almost every city. **1)** _____ One of the most popular Taiwanese snacks is "small sausage in large sausage." **2)** _____ As they walk through the night market, some visitors may find themselves holding their noses. **3)** _____ Stinky tofu is made by soaking tofu in a brine of fermented milk, meat, and vegetables for several months. **4)** _____ Night markets are also home to oyster omelets. They are very delicious!

(a) They sell food, snacks, clothes, and crafts and are popular with both locals and visitors alike.

(b) Many foreigners don't dare to try it, but those who do usually admit that it tastes a lot better than it smells.

(c) This is because Taiwan's night markets are the home of stinky tofu—one of Asia's most pungent snacks.

(d) This is a pork sausage wrapped in a larger sausage of sticky rice.

03 | Writing

Fill in the blanks using the words provided.

1. *distinctive, popular, Taichung*
   Bubble tea is a _____ drink which was invented in _____ in the 1980s and has become _____ around the world.

2. *dessert, shaved, toppings*
   _____ ice is often covered with fruit or other tasty _____, and is often enjoyed as _____.

THE SHOPPING EXPERIENCE

Taiwan has 7-11s, FamilyMarts, night markets, and many other businesses that are open very late. This makes it easy for people to do their shopping at any time. Taiwanese people are so used to this that they are surprised when they travel to other countries and discover that shops close early.

Taiwanese tourists might decide to go out shopping after dinner only to discover that after 6 p.m., all the shops are closed except for certain supermarkets. Sometimes, this difference in shopping habits is caused by differences in climate. For example, the extremely hot climate of southern Australia would turn night markets into a very uncomfortable experience.

Leipzig, Germany
德國萊比錫

Traditional markets are only open during the day in most Western countries. If you want to do some serious shopping when you're abroad, you must do it during the weekend. In places like Leipzig, Germany, shops stay open until around 8 p.m. on Thursday nights. Although the United States is more of a 24-hour society, other English speaking countries have more restricted opening hours. So make sure that you find out about when stores are open before you travel somewhere.

In some countries, even the restaurants close early. Fortunately, there will always be a few Chinese restaurants that stay open until midnight!

TAIWANESE SNACKS

Tofu pudding 豆花

Jelly figs with lemon 檸檬愛玉

Grass jelly 仙草

Oyster omelet 蚵仔煎

Oyster thin noodles 蚵仔麵線

Taiwanese fried chicken 鹽酥雞

Fried chicken cutlet 雞排

Lumpia 潤餅

Small sausage in large sausage 大腸包小腸

Taiwanese meatballs 肉圓

Salty chicken 鹽水雞

Taiwanese fried buns 水煎包

Black pepper cake 胡椒餅

Stewed food 滷味

Pan-fried green onion cakes 蔥油餅

Rice tube pudding 筒仔米糕

Grilled corn 烤玉米

Grilled squid 烤魷魚

Donshan duck head 東山鴨頭

Meat ball soup 貢丸湯

Fish ball soup 魚丸湯

Sugar-covered fruit on sticks 糖葫蘆

Red bean cake 車輪餅

Steamed sandwich 刈包

Pigs' blood cake 豬血糕

Deep-fried oyster with leeks 蚵嗲   Baoxin fenyuan 包心粉圓   Leek pastry 韭菜餡餅

Deep-fried sweet potatoes 炸地瓜   Deep-fried squid 炸花枝   Grilled sausage 烤香腸

Horse hooves 雙胞胎   Hemp flowers 麻花   Ice cream spring roll with peanuts 花生冰淇淋

Grilled bird's egg 烤鳥蛋   Takoyaki 章魚小丸子

Sweet potatoes coated with sugar 蜜地瓜

Braised pork ribs with herbs 藥燉排骨

Papaya milkshake 木瓜牛奶

Sugar cane juice 甘蔗汁

Chinese herbal tea 青草茶

Winter melon tea 冬瓜茶

Grass jelly tea 仙草茶

Plum juice 酸梅汁

Star fruit juice 楊桃汁

Frog egg (Tapioca balls in sweet sauce) 青蛙下蛋

Cumquat lemon juice 金桔檸檬

Bubble tea 泡沫紅茶

Fresh-made juice 鮮榨果汁

Chinese New Year
中國新年

🔊43 Reading Passage

Several festivals are celebrated in Taiwan every year. For visitors, festivals can be both an enjoyable and colorful experience. For Taiwanese people, it's a great way to keep Taiwanese culture alive in today's world and get a day off work! Most of Taiwan's festivals go by the **lunar** calendar and their Western calendar date changes every year.

Chinese New Year falls on January 1st on the lunar calendar, and it is the biggest event on the Chinese cultural calendar. It generally occurs around the end of January to early February on the Western calendar. During Chinese New Year, families come together, eat, and enjoy each other's company no matter how far

↙ **Chinese New Year's cake** 年糕

apart they live. Traditionally, special foods such as sticky rice and year cakes are prepared. The words for "year cake" are pronounced like "**rise** in the coming year" in Chinese. So, people eat the cakes to wish for a good year. Some of the cakes are sweet because the Chinese believe that having sweet food can **bring about** good luck in the New Year.

There are several unusual beliefs about Chinese New Year. People don't like to **sweep** the floor during Chinese New Year because they don't want to sweep away good fortune along with the **dirt**. They also don't take out the garbage until the fifth day of Chinese New Year.

During Chinese New Year, Taiwanese people visit relatives and pay respects to the god of wealth. On the second day of the New Year, married couples go to the wife's house and spend time with her parents.

At this time, houses are decorated with flowers and **couplets** or **congratulatory** speeches written on red paper. Red is considered lucky and white represents death. Therefore, red is **emphasized** and white is discouraged during the holiday. Children and elderly people often receive gifts of money in red **envelopes**. Eventually, firecrackers are **set off** and families go out into the streets to enjoy traditional folk activities such as lion dances.

↑ **Red envelopes** 紅包

Not so many people believe in old ideas about good or bad fortune nowadays. However, people still like to follow the old traditions.

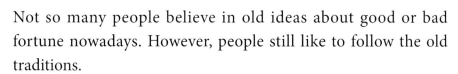
Quiz

1. What is the biggest yearly event for Taiwanese people?
2. Does Chinese New Year fall on the same day on the Western calendar every year?
3. What is one unusual belief about Chinese New Year?
4. What do some people do on the second day of the New Year?
5. Why won't people sweep their floors during Chinese New Year?

🎧 Conversation

⌐ Gold sycees 金元寶

Laura	It looks like you're going to spend Chinese New Year in Taiwan!
Ethan	Yes, I'm pretty excited about it. What's more, my parents just called to tell me they're coming here.
Laura	That's great! I'd love to meet them.
Ethan	Of course, I'd be glad to introduce you. They want to meet all my new Taiwanese and foreign friends.
Laura	Is there anybody else in your family coming to visit?
Ethan	My brother is thinking of coming with my parents. I was thinking it might be fun to take them to a traditional festival in Taiwan.
Laura	That's a great idea! Do you know how long they're planning on staying?
Ethan	They said they could stay for three weeks.
Laura	Well, if they're coming for three weeks that gives them the chance to stay for the entire Chinese New Year!
Ethan	I understand that this is an important family time in Taiwan.
Laura	That's right. Families try to get together just like for the Western New Year. Everyone **chats**, eats delicious food, and enjoys each other's company.
Ethan	Does everything **close down**? I'm worried that they may come to Taiwan and find that nothing is open.

← Spring Festival couplets 春聯

Laura	Not really. In fact, people are busy getting prepared during the week leading up to Chinese New Year, so the stores are open to **take advantage of** the season.
Ethan	So they can see all of the traditional decorations in the streets, and maybe some lion dances as well!
Laura	During Chinese New Year, some shops and restaurants are closed. However, the scenic spots are crowded with people. Various activities are held in the streets and temples to celebrate the New Year.

Practice

01 | Listening

Listen to the descriptions and check what you think is being referred to each time.

1. ○ Western New Year ○ Chinese New Year
2. ○ Year cakes ○ Couplets written on red paper
3. ○ Shops and restaurants ○ Scenic spots
4. ○ The god of wealth ○ Married couples

02 | Reading

Match the sentences to the pictures you think they best describe.

a b c d

_____ 1. During Chinese New Year, people wish for good fortune and success, so many people especially pay their respects to the god of wealth.

_____ 2. One of Chinese New Year's traditions is the giving of red envelopes full of money to children and elderly people.

_____ 3. During the holiday, families get together to eat lots of delicious food.

_____ 4. Chinese New Year is a great time for foreigners to visit Taiwan or join the celebrations around the world as they get to experience the sights and sounds of one of the most important holidays for the Chinese.

03 | Writing

Complete the sentences using the fragments given.

(a) each other's company **(b) before the holiday is over**
(c) considered an unlucky color **(d) eat sweet cakes**

1. White is _____ in Chinese tradition because it represents death, whereas red represents good fortune.

2. People _____ during the New Year as it is traditionally believed that sweet food can bring about good luck.

3. One strange belief is that if you sweep the floor _____, you'll sweep away the good fortune along with the dirt.

4. Chinese New Year is an important time for families in Taiwan, and people come together from far away to chat, eat, and enjoy _____.

Ready for the Big Event!

Taiwanese people start shopping for food, snacks and decorations several weeks prior to Chinese New Year. Candies and cookies are put into red candy boxes in every home.

Dihua Street 迪化街, Taipei, is the most famous place to shop for food and snacks, or "New Year supplies" in Chinese. It's also call the "New Year Supplies Avenue." When the Chinese New Year is approaching, Dihua Street is always packed with shoppers. Food materials such as dried mushrooms, dried shrimps, rice noodles, etc. are available as well as Chinese herbs, preserved fruit, and tea.

On Chinese New Year's Eve, people will go home to have dinner with their family. This is called a reunion dinner. People usually prepare lucky foods for the dinner, such as fish, which means "to have profit every year." The word "fish" and "profit" have the same pronunciation in Mandarin.

People also eat dumplings because they are shaped like the ancient gold sycee, or ingot, now a symbol of wealth.

Features for Chinese New Year

During Chinese New Year, firecrackers are set off to scare away the evil "year monsters." It is said that the year monsters are afraid of loud noise and anything red. That's why people hang red lanterns in front of their houses during this time of year.

Decorations such as lucky knots are hung around the house during Chinese New Year.

People like to wear red clothes during Chinese New Year because the color red represents good luck.

Black melon seeds are common snacks during Chinese New Year.

Unit 16

The Lantern Festival and Dragon Boat Festival
元宵節與端午節

(46) Reading Passage

The Lantern Festival

The **Lantern** Festival takes place on the fifteenth day of Chinese New Year. It is often known as the second New Year, or "little New Year," and it marks the end of the New Year season. During the festival, people make **elaborate**, beautiful lanterns. In the old days, only the rich were able to make these kinds of lanterns. In modern society, everyone can enjoy them, and it has become a special kind of art. Some lanterns are shaped like animals, people, or objects. There are even Taipei 101 lanterns! This is one tradition that has been modernized in a very successful way.

Nowadays, different parts of Taiwan hold public events to celebrate the Lantern Festival. They use modern technology to provide an exciting light display.

On the night of the Lantern Festival, people traditionally eat sweet **glutinous** rice balls. They are made of glutinous rice, sometimes with sweet stuffing, and served in syrup. Answering **riddles** is another traditional activity.

The Lantern Festivals around Taiwan 台灣各地燈會

Sweet glutinous rice balls 甜元宵

Sticky rice dumplings 粽子

The Dragon Boat Festival

Another important event is the Dragon Boat Festival. This festival falls on May 5th on the lunar calendar, and usually takes place in June on the Western calendar. In ancient China, summer was a time of **disease**, so this festival was created to drive away the evil spirits that cause sickness. As time passed, the story of Qu Yuan 屈原 was added. Qu Yuan was an ancient **minister** and poet who **drowned** himself when the king would not listen to his advice. After he jumped into the water, fishermen raced to try and save him. Although they were too late to save his life, they threw sticky rice dumplings into the river to keep the fish from eating his body. This is the story behind the tradition of racing dragon boats and eating sticky rice dumplings during the Dragon Boat Festival.

Dragon boat teams from different organizations are made up of students, businessmen, soldiers, and so on. The boats themselves are highly decorated and quite beautiful. This festival isn't just popular in Taiwan. Nowadays, dragon boat teams come from all over the world to **compete** in the races and celebrate this unique festival.

Dragon boat race 龍舟賽

Quiz

1. When is the Lantern Festival?
2. What kinds of lanterns do people make during the Lantern Festival?
3. Who was Qu Yuan?
4. Why did fishermen throw sticky rice dumplings into the river after Qu Yuan's death?
5. Which festival is growing in popularity all around the world?

🎧 47 Conversation

Ethan	What's the Lantern Festival?
Laura	It falls on the first full moon following Chinese New Year. It's a great end to the New Year **festivities**.
Ethan	Are there any interesting activities on this day?
Laura	You can experience the Lantern Festival in Taipei. It has become quite famous since it started in 1990. It's very modern, and there's an amazing light show.
Ethan	Sounds good.
Laura	Another special activity on Lantern Festival is the Yanshui 鹽水 **Beehive** Fireworks Festival held in Tainan. It's a little dangerous, though. Fireworks are shot into the crowds of people. So, you need to wear thick clothing and a **helmet**.
Ethan	Oh, that sounds dangerous! I think I'll skip that one.
Laura	If your family likes sports, then perhaps they should come to see the Dragon Boat Festival in June.
Ethan	Is this some kind of river god festival?
Laura	No. It **commemorates** an ancient poet, Qu Yuan, who drowned himself.
Ethan	Why did he do that?
Laura	He tried to give a king some advice that could save his **kingdom**, but the king **refused** to listen to him.
Ethan	So why is it called the Dragon Boat Festival? Is it some kind of race?
Laura	Yup. Teams of **rowers** in dragon boats race against each other. The tradition comes from fishermen **rushing** to save Qu Yuan. The boats are beautifully decorated. It's a festival that's becoming popular all over the world!

Qu Yuan
屈原

PINGXI SKY LANTERN FESTIVAL

Two important events accompanying the Lantern Festival are the Sky Lantern Festival in Pingxi 平溪, New Taipei City, and Yanshui 鹽水 Fireworks Festival in Tainan.

Pingxi Sky Lantern Festival is held annually. People write their wishes for the coming year on paper lanterns and release them into the sky. This festival is very popular among the young.

However, once the festival ends, the remains of the paper lanterns pollute the environment. The flames from the lanterns sometimes cause fires when they land on the ground. Thus, this activity is not encouraged as much nowadays.

01 | Listening

Listen to the statements and match each one with the picture that best illustrates it.

a

b

c

d

1. _____ 2. _____ 3. _____ 4. _____

02 | Reading

Choose the correct answer.

_____ 1. Why did the poet and minister Qu Yuan drown himself?
   (a) Because he had killed his best friend and felt guilty.
   (b) Because the king would not listen to his advice.
   (c) Because people did not like his poems.
   (d) Because he could not marry the girl he loved.

_____ 2. According to the passage, how was the Lantern Festival different in the old days?
   (a) Only rich people could make lanterns.
   (b) The lanterns were made out of animal skins.
   (c) It was held on the tenth day of Chinese New Year.
   (d) People ate nothing for the whole day.

_____ 3. Which of the following does NOT happen on the Lantern Festival?
   (a) People solve riddles.   (b) People eat glutinous rice balls.
   (c) People make lanterns.   (d) People race dragon boats.

_____ 4. Which of the following is NOT true about the Dragon Boat Festival?
   (a) People eat sticky rice dumplings.
   (b) People attend the Yanshui Beehive Fireworks Festival.
   (c) It's usually celebrated in June on the Western calendar.
   (d) People remember the death of Qu Yuan.

_____ 5. According to the story of Qu Yuan, why did fishermen throw sticky rice dumplings into the river?
   (a) To show respect to the river god.
   (b) To make their boats lighter.
   (c) To stop the fish from eating Qu Yuan's body.
   (d) To let the king know that they were angry.

03 | Writing

Use the words to complete the sentences.

disease   minister   rower   helmet   lanterns

1. To be a good dragon boat _____ you need to have strong arms and lots of stamina.

2. The _____ that people make during the festival are very beautiful and often shaped like animals.

3. People have gotten hurt at the Beehive Fireworks Festival because they didn't wear a _____.

4. Qu Yuan was a famous poet and a wise _____.

5. Summer in ancient China was often a time of _____ and sickness when many people would die.

YANSHUI BEEHIVE FIREWORKS FESTIVAL

A particularly crazy **fireworks** festival **takes place** around the same time as the Lantern Festival every year in Yanshui, Tainan. Rockets and fireworks are shot into the crowds and **explode** around them. The fireworks result in spectacular light and sound effects. People come from all around the world to experience this activity, because although it can be dangerous it is also very exciting. Participants have to wear a helmet and protective clothing. However, some people still get hurt. Thus, improvements are continually being made to the fireworks materials to reduce the danger.

Unit 17

Ghost Month and the Moon Festival
鬼月與中秋節

Reading Passage

Ghost Month

Taiwanese people believe that ghosts leave the underworld for one month every year. To **ensure** that these ghosts are happy and do not **bother** them, Taiwanese people **observe** certain traditions during "Ghost Month." This festival takes place in July on the lunar calendar. Ghost Month is a time when families pray for the ghosts of their ancestors. They will also leave food out to feed any "hungry ghosts" that might **wander** by.

Taiwanese people will also burn specially printed ghost money to make sure that their ancestors are comfortable in the **afterlife**. All in all, Ghost Month is seen as an unlucky time of year. Because of this, very few people get married, move into a new house, or open a business during this month. Going near water is also **forbidden**, because the wandering ghosts may drag you under to replace them, so that they can have another chance at life.

Ghost money 冥紙

Burning ghost money in Ghost Month 鬼月時燒冥紙

The Moon Festival

The last major event of the year is the Moon Festival, also known as the Mid-Autumn Festival. This festival takes place on the 15th of August on the lunar calendar. On the night of the full moon people get together with their family and eat "moon cakes" and **pomelos**. Since the festival is **in honor of** the moon, families often look up at the moon together.

↑ Pomelos 文旦
← Moon cakes 月餅

There are many different Chinese and Taiwanese legends about the moon. While Westerners may mention a man on the moon, Taiwanese people will talk about a woman called Chang-e 嫦娥 or the Jade Rabbit. Over time, it has become popular for people to give moon cakes to their relatives and friends during the Mid-Autumn Festival. Traditional moon cakes are made using egg **yolks** and flour. However, nowadays moon cakes come in many different flavors, including almond, chocolate, and pineapple. Some even come filled with ice cream!

Quiz

1. Why does no one want to get married or open a business during Ghost Month?
2. What do people eat during the Mid-Autumn Festival?

The puppets of Seventh Lord 七爺 **and Eighth Lord** 八爺 **in a parade during Ghost Month** 鬼月時出巡的七爺八爺人偶

🎧 50 Conversation

Ethan	Hmm, I don't know. My family isn't really into sports.
Laura	If they want something very Chinese that can be seen all over the island, they could come during "Ghost Month."
Ethan	What are you talking about?
Laura	They don't worry about bad luck, do they?
Ethan	No, they're not very **superstitious**.
Laura	Are they easily **frightened**?

Ethan	They aren't scared of ghosts, bad luck, **monsters**, or anything like that. Why do you ask?
Laura	The Chinese believe that the doors of the underworld are opened once a year and the ghosts get to take a break.
Ethan	So that's what you meant by ghosts, bad luck, and so on. So, what do people do during Ghost Month?
Laura	Not much. It's a very unlucky time of year.
Ethan	Let me guess—people don't get married or buy houses.
Laura	That's right. They won't do major things like get married or start a business. But, they will leave food out so that the ghosts won't bother them.
Ethan	Well, my family may not like such ghost stories!
Laura	If they want to avoid that time of year, the Moon Festival is also interesting.
Ethan	I heard it's a day for families to have a **reunion**.
Laura	That's correct. Families get together and eat moon cakes and pomelos. Usually, they will have a barbeque outdoors and watch the beautiful full moon.

Chinese Mythology About the Moon

There are many legends about the moon. In Chinese mythology, a story tells about a woman named Chang-e and her husband Houyi 后羿.

They were once immortals. One day, ten of the Jade Emperor's sons turned themselves into ten suns to scorch the earth and caused great pain. Being a great archer, Houyi shot down nine of them to save the earth. However, this enraged the Jade Emperor because nine of his sons had been killed. He drove Houyi and Chang-e out of heaven to become mortals.

Seeking to return to immortality, Houyi went to the goddess Xi Wangmu 西王母 and asked for an elixir. She agreed, but this elixir must be shared by Houyi and Chang-e because it was a dosage for two. However, Chang-e accidentally swallowed all of it and found herself floating into the sky until she landed on the moon. There she met a rabbit, named Jade Rabbit. The Jade Rabbit lives on the moon and grinds herbal medicine in a mortar. They keep each other company.

51

01 | Listening

Listen to the statements and mark the information you get from each one.

1. ○ People pray for their ancestors during Ghost Month.
   ○ People try to avoid getting married during Ghost Month.

2. ○ The Moon Festival is a time for families to get together.
   ○ The Moon Festival takes place on August 15th on the lunar calendar.

3. ○ The Taiwanese see the shape of a rabbit in the moon.
   ○ The moon is always full on the Moon Festival.

4. ○ You can get strawberry-flavored moon cakes.
   ○ People give moon cakes to relatives and friends.

5. ○ At the beginning of Ghost Month, the doors of the underworld are opened.
   ○ Going swimming during Ghost Month is considered dangerous by some.

02 | Reading

Put the dialogues in the correct order.

1. (a) Egg yolk and flour, but you can get different flavors too.
   (b) Yes, it's a moon cake. We eat them on the Moon Festival.
   (c) What's this? Is it a cake?
   (d) Oh, what are they made out of? They look tasty.
   → _____

2. (a) I'd like to buy a house in Taiwan. Any advice?
   (b) Is it considered unlucky, then?
   (c) Very unlucky. You shouldn't start a business either, or get married.
   (d) Well you certainly shouldn't buy one now. It's Ghost Month!
   → _____

3. (a) Well, we also have a barbecue.
   (b) Some people do, but most of the time people just barbecue on the sidewalk!
   (c) So apart from eating moon cakes, what else do you do on the Moon Festival?
   (d) Nice. Do you go to the park to cook? There aren't many gardens in Taipei.
   → _____

4. (a) Are there any times I should avoid visiting Taiwan?
   (b) Yeah, I do believe in ghosts. They really scare me.
   (c) Are you superstitious at all? I mean, do you believe in ghosts?
   (d) Then don't come to Taiwan during the seventh lunar month. That's Ghost Month.
   → _____

03 | Writing

Fill in the blanks using the words provided.

1. *ensure, observe, wander*

   During Ghost Month people _____ certain traditions to _____ that any ghosts that _____ by don't bother them.

2. *water, forbid, superstitious*

   Many _____ parents _____ their children from going near _____ during Ghost Month.

3. *reunion, pomelos, honor*

   The Moon Festival is held in _____ of the moon, and it's a day for families to have a _____, eat moon cakes and _____, and have a barbecue.

4. *underworld, frightened, monsters*

   If you're easily _____ by ghosts, _____ and other creatures from the _____, it's best to avoid Taiwan during Ghost Month.

5. *full, Chang-e, shapes*

   The moon is always _____ on the Moon Festival, so if you look closely at it, you might see the _____ of the Jade Rabbit and _____.

Having a Barbeque

The Moon Festival is also called the Reunion Festival. The country takes a day off on the fifteenth of August on the Chinese lunar calendar, allowing everyone to go home and enjoy a day with their family.

In Taiwan, people love to have barbeques under the full moon. A barbeque with family or friends on the night of the Moon Festival isn't a traditional activity, but it is very popular among families nowadays.

Unit 18

Local Festivals
地方節慶

52 Reading Passage

Wood carving 木雕

In addition to traditional festivals such as Chinese New Year and the Lantern Festival, there are many indigenous and modern cultural festivals held in Taiwan. Special industries, such as wood carving, have started to gain in **popularity** due to government **promotion**. Examples of industry-related events include the Sanyi Wood Carving Festival 三義木雕藝術節 and the Hsinchu City International Glass Art Festival.

Modern cultural festivals in Taiwan are quite **varied**. The Taiwan International Festival of Art and Spring Scream are very **representative** of this category. The Taiwan International Festival of Art began in 2009. It invites top performers, **producers**, actors, and **composers** from Taiwan and around the world to present dance, music, and drama performances. The festival

National Theater 國家戲劇院

Spring Scream
春天吶喊（春吶）

takes place at the National Theater and National Concert Hall in Taipei. It usually lasts for one and a half months.

Spring Scream is held in Kenting every April. It was begun in 1995 by two Americans living in Taiwan and is now the largest music festival in Taiwan. Hundreds of performing groups and artists **gather** in southern Taiwan to show their **passion** and **talent** for music. There are also stalls selling arts and crafts, clothes, and food. It's one of the most exciting festivals in Taiwan.

If you are traveling through an area where there are indigenous **communities**, such as the east coast, you may be lucky enough to see an indigenous ceremony. Harvest festivals are particularly important among the indigenous tribes as they express the tribe's **gratitude** to the **ancestral** spirits and tribal deities for giving them food. The Amis, Rukai, and Paiwan tribes all celebrate this traditional festival. Singing and dancing are **essential** parts of the festival. However, the Harvest Festival isn't just about being grateful for food. It is also a time to **unite** the tribal members and sometimes to carry out coming-of-age **rites**.

The Harvest Festival of the Amis Tribe—Singing and dancing form the core of this festival.
阿美族豐年祭──歌唱與舞蹈是慶典的核心。

cc by takunawan

Quiz

1. Where is the most likely place you will see an indigenous festival?
2. What is the Taiwan International Festival of Art? Where does it take place?
3. What is Spring Scream?

53 Conversation

Ethan If I want to take my parents and brother to a modern festival, are there any good choices?

Laura There are quite a lot. You can take them to the Sun Moon Lake Music Festival! It takes place every year in October.

Ethan Does that mean that there are many singers and bands playing by the lake?

Sun Moon Lake Music Festival
日月潭花火音樂嘉年華

by Yuyu

Yingge Old Street 鶯歌老街

Laura Yes, but there is more to this festival than that. You can see a fireworks show at night. There are also **symphony orchestra** and Taiwanese opera performances.

Ethan Sounds like fun!

Laura If they like arts and crafts, you can go to Yingge 鶯歌 in New Taipei City for the Ceramics Festival.

Ethan What is that? A display of ceramic works?

Laura There are shops and designers selling a variety of ceramic goods. Exhibitions are held to display ceramic **masterpieces**. And, there are food **vendors** along the street!

Ethan Wow. That sounds really interesting!

Laura You can even make your own ceramic cup as a **souvenir**.

Yenliao International Sand Sculpture Festival
鹽寮國際沙雕節

Yingge Ceramics Festival
鶯歌陶瓷嘉年華

Sailboat Season on the Northeast Coast
東北角帆船季

Yilan Green Expo
宜蘭綠色博覽會

Gongliao Rock Festival
貢寮海洋音樂祭

Shihmen International Kite Festival
石門國際風箏節

Hsinchu City International Glass Art Festival
竹塹國際玻璃藝術節

Sanyi Wood Carving Festival
三義木雕藝術節

Sun Moon Lake Music Festival
日月潭花火音樂嘉年華

Kenting Wind Chimes Festival
墾丁風鈴季

Kenting Spring Scream Festival
墾丁春天吶喊音樂季

Cultural Festivals

Yilan International Children's Folklore & Folkgame Festival
宜蘭國際童玩藝術節

Practice

01 | Listening

Listen to the short dialogues and fill in the blanks.

1. A: I'm going to travel down the _____. Do you think I'll be able to go to an indigenous festival?

    B: I'm sure you will. It's August, so the Amis will be _____ their _____ Festival.

2. A: We're going to Yingge today. I want to take you to the _____ Festival.

    B: Great! I can't wait to see all the beautiful pots on _____! Maybe I can buy one as a _____.

3. A: Have you heard about _____ Scream? It's this amazing music festival held in _____ every April.

    B: I know. Apparently hundreds of _____ play there, and people party all weekend on the beach.

02 | Reading

Circle the correct option in each sentence.

1. The Taiwan International Festival of Art is **held/representative** in Taipei each year.

2. Taiwan's indigenous tribes express their gratitude to the ancestral **dances/spirits** by holding harvest festivals.

3. At the Yingge Ceramics Festival, you can see many ceramic **masterpieces/shows** and even make your own.

03 | Writing

Unscramble the sentences.

1. Scream / living / two / Taiwan / was / started / by / Americans / Spring / in

    _____

    _____

2. see / can / indigenous / east / often / ceremonies / on / You / coast / the

    _____

    _____

3. Music / place / Sun / Lake / The / October / Festival / takes / year / every / Moon / in

    _____

    _____

Ear-Shooting Ritual of the Bunun Tribe
布農族打耳祭

Sea Ritual of the Amis Tribe
阿美族海祭

Adulthood Ritual of the Amis Tribe
阿美族成年祭

Harvest Festival of the Paiwan Tribe
排灣族豐年祭

Harvest Festival of the Amis Tribe
阿美族豐年祭

Sea-Howling Ritual of the Pingpu Tribe
平埔族嚎海祭

Harvest Festival of the Tao Tribe
達悟族收穫祭

Short Spirit Ceremony of Saisiat
賽夏族矮靈祭

Night Ritual of the Pingpu Tribe
平埔族夜祭

New Year Ritual of the Punuyumayan Tribe
卑南族跨年祭

Folk Culture Festival of the Atayal Tribe
泰雅族文化祭

Harvest Festival of the Rukai Tribe
魯凱族豐年祭

War Ritual of the Tsou Tribe
鄒族戰祭

Flying Fish Festival of the Tao Tribe
達悟族飛魚祭

Boat Ritual of the Tao Tribe
達悟族船祭

Unit 19
Taipei—Getting Around and Museums
台北：交通與博物館

🎧55 Reading Passage

Broadly speaking, the Taipei area includes Taipei City and New Taipei City (**formerly** Taipei County). Taipei is the **capital** of Taiwan. There are nearly 7 million people living there. It is a city that is alive with activity, day and night. You can always find something to do in Taipei's busy streets, night markets, parks, and mountains that surround the city. Getting around Taipei is easy. There are taxis and buses. Taipei's subway system is fast developing, too. It is called the **MRT** (Mass Rapid Transport) or "**Metro**." It opened in 1996 and **construction** of new **routes** and stations is still ongoing. Taipei's MRT offers several types of travel passes for visitors—one-day, two-day, three-day, and five-day passes.

Taipei MRT 台北捷運

On the MRT, **announcements** are made in four different languages: Chinese, Taiwanese, Hakka, and English. What's more, visitors carrying bicycles can get on and off the train at **designated** stations.

National Palace Museum
國立故宮博物院

Taipei has **abundant** art **galleries** and museums. When Chiang Kai-shek escaped from China, he and his followers took many ancient Chinese works of art with them in order to keep them safe. In spite of all of the danger, every single piece that was brought over arrived **intact** without any damage. The late 1940s and early 1950s were difficult times for Taiwan, so the works had to be stored in a safe place for several years. However, once the economy began to **expand**, the government got to work on building a suitable museum. The National Palace Museum was opened in 1965. It has since been a major attraction in Taipei. The National Palace Museum has such a massive collection that only part of it can be shown at one time. Some **artifacts** are always on display. Others are put away after a short time. Special exhibitions are held from time to time. The **Jadeite** Cabbage 翠玉白菜, Meat-Shaped Stone 肉形石, and Mao-Kung Ting 毛公鼎 are called the "Three Treasures" of the museum.

> **Quiz** →
>
> 1. How many people live in the Taipei area?
> 2. What is the most famous museum in Taipei?
> 3. Why was it built?
> 4. What kind of collection does it have?

🎧 Conversation

Laura	How are you finding life in Taipei?
Ethan	It's a very interesting place, but everyone is in such a hurry. Taipei can get a little crowded sometimes. On one hand, it's hard to find someplace to be alone. On the other, you never have to feel lonely.
Laura	Do you like museums?
Ethan	Yes, I do. I love seeing how people lived in the past. I also love old paintings, **pottery**, metal works, and other kinds of art works.
Laura	Then you must visit the National Palace Museum. You'll absolutely love it!
Ethan	Where is it?
Laura	It's in Shilin district in the northern part of Taipei. It displays the art that was taken from China for **safekeeping** in the 1940s.
Ethan	Wow! That sounds pretty risky to move **priceless** art around!
Laura	Definitely. What's more, they were moved around several times within China itself before coming to Taiwan. In the end, every piece got here without being damaged.
Ethan	That's pretty impressive. The collection must be massive. They don't show it all at once, do they?

Inside the National Palace Museum 國立故宮博物院內部 ‑‑‑‑‑‑‑‑‑‑‑‑‑‑‑‑‑ Photos by Yuyu

Viewing a modern
art display
參觀現代藝術作品

Laura	No. There's just too much. They only show a part of the collection. The rest of it is stored. They regularly change what is being displayed.
Ethan	Is it all in Chinese?
Laura	No, there are signs and tours in English as well.
Ethan	What other museums should I visit?
Laura	There are quite a few in Taipei. Another one that has been around for a while is the Fine Arts Museum. It displays art from Taiwanese and foreign artists.
Ethan	Does it display works from modern artists?
Laura	Well, it has artists from the last few hundred years. If you want to see newer works, you can try the Museum of **Contemporary** Art.

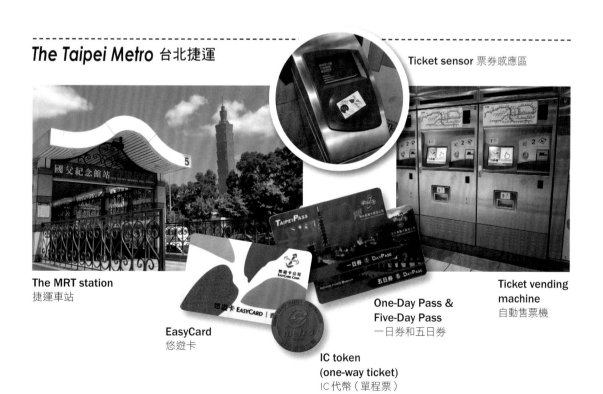

The Taipei Metro 台北捷運

Ticket sensor 票券感應區

The MRT station
捷運車站

EasyCard
悠遊卡

IC token
(one-way ticket)
IC 代幣（單程票）

One-Day Pass &
Five-Day Pass
一日券和五日券

Ticket vending
machine
自動售票機

Practice

01 | Listening

Listen to the dialogue and mark the things that are mentioned in the conversation.

1. ○

2. ○

3. ○

4. ○

02 | Reading

Match the two halves of the sentences.

1. The National Palace Museum displays _____

2. You can take bicycles onto the MRT, but _____

3. The "Three Treasures" of the National Palace Museum _____

4. If you want to see art by more modern artists, you _____

5. The Taipei area is incredibly crowded, with _____

(a) only at designated stations.

(b) a population of around seven million.

(c) are the Jadeite Cabbage, the Meat-Shapes stone, and the Mao-Kung Ting.

(d) should visit the Museum of Contemporary Art.

(e) the art that was taken from China in the 1940s.

03 | Writing

Use the following words to fill the blanks.

announcements   routes   abundant   artifacts   priceless

1. While some of the National Palace Museum's _____ are constantly on display, others are only shown during special exhibitions.

2. _____ on the MRT are made in Chinese, English, Hakka, and Taiwanese.

3. Taipei's MRT is constantly expanding, and new _____ are being planned and built as we speak.

4. The treasures in the National Palace Museum are considered to be _____ by lovers of Chinese art.

5. The Fine Arts Museum and the Museum of Contemporary Art are just two examples of Taipei's _____ museums and galleries.

Museums in Taipei

cc by Winertai

cc by Encyclopedist

National Taiwan Science Education Center
台灣科學教育館

Museum of Contemporary Art
台北當代藝術館

National Museum of History
國立歷史博物館

Taipei Fine Arts Museum
台北市立美術館

National Taiwan Museum
國立台灣博物館

Beitou Hot Spring Museum
北投溫泉博物館

Beitou is located near the Datun 大屯 Volcano Group. Thus, it has a rich hot spring resource and is one of the most famous hot springs in Taiwan.

Beitou Hot Spring Museum was once a public bathhouse. It was transformed into a museum in 1997.

北投鄰近大屯火山群，因此擁有豐富的溫泉資源，是台灣最知名的溫泉之一。

北投溫泉博物館過去是公共浴場，在1997年被改建為博物館。

Taipei Astronomical Museum
台北市立天文科學教育館

Unit 20

Taipei—Attractions
台北：熱門景點

Word Bank

combination n. 結合
skyscraper n. 摩天大樓
commemorate v. 紀念
memorable a. 難忘的

landscaping n. 景觀
commemorative a. 紀念的
atmosphere n. 氣氛
extend v. 延伸
underground adv. 在地下

elevator n. 電梯
landmark n. 地標
observatory n. 觀景台
preserved a. 保存的
prosperous a. 繁榮的

🔊58 Reading Passage

Chiang Kai-shek
Memorial Hall
中正紀念堂

Taipei has lots of temples, museums, old buildings, interesting shops, and other things to see. It's a **combination** of modern architecture and traditional buildings, Chinese and Western culture, green parks and **skyscrapers**, international restaurants and local night markets.

It is very possible that the first attraction you'll want to visit in Taipei is the Chiang Kai-shek Memorial Hall 中正紀念堂. It was built in 1980 to **commemorate** the former president of the Republic of China, and it is home to one of the most charming parks in Taipei. It is very **memorable** because of its traditional Chinese-style walls and buildings, sitting in the middle of a city of Western-style skyscrapers. The memorial grounds have beautiful Chinese-style **landscaping** and pools. The hall contains a large statue of the former president. It is guarded by armed soldiers. There are also exhibition rooms with displays that introduce his life and years as president. A visit to the National Concert Hall and the National Theater, both of which are next to the Chiang Kai-shek Memorial Hall, is recommended.

Dr. Sun Yat-sen
Memorial Hall
國父紀念館

The **Dr. Sun Yat-sen Memorial Hall** 國父紀念館 is another beautiful memorial in Taipei. It commemorates the life of Dr. Sun Yat-sen, the father of modern China. Although it is smaller than the Chiang Kai-shek Memorial Hall, it is still quite striking. You'll probably notice the grand golden Chinese roof of the main hall as soon as you enter the park. Inside the hall is a large statue of Dr. Sun Yat-sen, a **commemorative** museum, and a cultural center. You can see people walking their dogs, jogging, flying kites, or simply taking a walk on the grounds. It has a very relaxing **atmosphere**.

Taipei 101 opened in 2004 and is now the second tallest building in the world. It is 101 stories (508 m) tall, and **extends** another five stories **underground**. Its **elevators** are not only the fastest in the world, but are also some of the most technologically advanced. There are nice restaurants, offices, and a shopping mall inside the building. The building's New Year's Eve fireworks show is famous the world over.

The world-famous fireworks show
of Taipei 101 on New Year's Eve
世界知名的台北 101 大樓除夕煙火秀

Quiz

1. What are some of the attractions that can be enjoyed in Taipei?
2. Why was the Chiang Kai-shek Memorial Hall built? And when?
3. What do people usually do on the grounds of the Dr. Sun Yat-sen Memorial Hall?

If you need further information, you should contact the Tourism Bureau at (02) 2349-1500. There is also an information point in Taipei Railway Station. The English-speaking tourist hotline can be reached at 0800-011-765.

更多資訊請洽觀光局 (02) 2349-1500，台北火車站亦提供觀光資訊，英文語音觀光熱線請撥 0800-011-765。

Taipei 101
台北 101

Night scene of Taipei from Taipei 101
從台北 101 大樓俯瞰台北夜景

59 **Conversation**

Ethan	Taipei is the capital of this country. There must be a lot to see, right?
Laura	Right. I'm sure you've been to the Chiang Kai-shek Memorial Hall.
Ethan	I sure have. It's right in the center of Taipei, and it has such a nice park. I love the hall with those soldiers guarding the statue. It's the first place I'm bringing my parents to when they come and visit.
Laura	And, don't forget to take them to Taipei 101. It is also an important **landmark** in Taipei.
Ethan	It must be exciting to view Taipei City from up there.
Laura	Yes. The Taipei 101 **Observatory** is located on the 89th floor of the building. It is open from 9 a.m. to 10 p.m. every day. You can take your parents there to see Taipei at night.
Ethan	Are there any good restaurants around there?
Laura	There are some nice restaurants inside Taipei 101.
Ethan	That would be perfect. What about old houses and the like? I think they may also be interested in something other than the modern part of the city.
Laura	I suggest that you visit the Lin Antai Historical House 林安泰古厝. It's a **preserved** home that used to belong to a **prosperous** family in the late 18th century. The site was going to be destroyed in the 1970s, but it was saved at the last second. Inside, there is beautiful antique furniture.
Ethan	It sounds like my parents will have plenty to see in Taipei.

The North and Northeast of Taipei

Houtong
↖ 侯硐／猴硐

Jiufen
↗ 九份

Shifen Waterfall
↖ 十分瀑布

Yehliu Scenic Area
↑ 野柳風景區

Green Bay
↖ 翡翠灣

Coal Mine Museum
↖ 台灣煤礦博物館

Shenkeng Old Street
← 深坑老街

Practice

60

01 | Listening

Listen to the dialogue and mark the information that you hear.

1. ◯ The Chiang Kai-shek Memorial Hall was built in 1980.
2. ◯ Inside the Dr. Sun Yat-sen Memorial Hall is a commemorative museum.
3. ◯ The Dr. Sun Yat-sen Memorial Hall has a grand golden roof.
4. ◯ The Dr. Sun Yat-sen Memorial Hall is not as big as the Chiang Kai-shek Memorial Hall.
5. ◯ People like to walk their dogs and go jogging in the Dr. Sun Yat-sen Memorial Hall.

02 | Reading

Choose the correct answer.

_____ 1. Which of the following statements is TRUE about Taipei 101?
   (a) It's the world's tallest building.   (b) It was opened in 2003.
   (c) There is a movie theater inside.   (d) It has the world's fastest elevators.

_____ 2. What is the Lin Antai Historical House?
   (a) An antique furniture store.   (b) A preserved eighteenth-century home.
   (c) A memorial to Chang Kai-shek.   (d) A one-hundred-year-old temple.

_____ 3. Why was the Dr. Sun Yat-sen Memorial Hall built?
   (a) To remember the life of a famous painter.
   (b) To increase the amount of green space in Taipei.
   (c) To commemorate the father of modern China.
   (d) To celebrate the ROC's 50th anniversary.

03 | Writing

Use the prompts to write a sentence. You'll need to add necessary words or change the verb tenses to make correct sentences.

1. Taipei 101 Observatory / open / every day / 9 a.m. / 10 p. m.

_____

2. Lin Antai Historical House / use to / belong / prosperous/ family

_____

3. statue / Chiang Kai-shek / guard / armed /soldiers

_____

Taipei Famous SPOTS

Office of the President
↙ 總統府

National Concert Hall
↙ 國家音樂廳

Chiang Kai-shek Shilin Residence
↑ 士林官邸

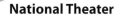

National Theater
↖ 國家戲劇院

Taipei World Trade Center
↗ 台北世貿中心

cc by Prince Roy

Taipei City Hall
↓ 台北市政府

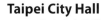

Maokong
↖ 貓空

Green Lake/Bitan
← 碧潭

by Yuyu

Grand Hotel
圓山大飯店

Taipei Arena
台北小巨蛋

Taipei Railway Station
台北車站

Lin Antai Historical Resident
林安泰古厝

Shuangxi Park and Chinese Garden
雙溪公園

by Yuyu

Taipei Zoo
台北市動物園

Red House Theater
西門紅樓

228 Memorial Peace Park
二二八和平紀念公園

Second-graded historical monument
二級古蹟

Taipei Water Park
台北自來水園區

Taipei Botanical Garden
台北植物園

The Lin's Family Mansion and Garden
板橋林家花園

Fishermen's Wharf
漁人碼頭

Martyrs' Shrine
忠烈祠

First-graded historical monument
一級古蹟

cc by Asimonlee

Fort San Domingo
淡水紅毛城

Former British Consulate
英國領事館

Huashan 1914 Creative Park
華山藝文特區

Unit 21

Hsinchu and Taichung 新竹與台中

municipal a. 市立的	**benefit n.** 獲利	**process v.** 加工	**culinary a.** 烹飪的
hub n. 中心	**expat a.**	**machinery n.**	**scientific a.** 科學的
stuff v. 填充	移居國外的	機械	**silicon n.** 矽
concentrate v.	**in turn** 依次；輪流	**textile n.** 紡織	**head v.** 前往
集中	**pace n.** 速度	**chemical a.** 化學的	**in addition to**
	crops n. 農作物	**malt n.** 麥芽	此外

61 Reading Passage

Hsinchu

Hsinchu is the oldest city in northern Taiwan. It's also one of Taiwan's most important industrial areas. It has lots of interesting things to see and it is easily reached from Taipei or Taichung. Some of the sites on offer are: the Hsinchu **Municipal** Glass Art Museum, Shibajian Mountain 十八尖山, and the Chenghuang Temple Night Market 城隍廟口夜市. Hsinchu is also an educational **hub**. It is home to National Chiao Tung University 國立交通大學, which is regarded as one of the island's best technical schools. Some of Hsinchu's specialty foods include rice noodles (*mifen*), meat ball soup, and **stuffed** meatballs.

National Chiao Tung University
(NCTU) 國立交通大學

Although Hsinchu is much smaller than Taipei, it is still very important to Taiwan's economy. This is because Hsinchu has a science park in which several hi-tech industries are **concentrated**. Science parks are being built all over Taiwan, including in Tainan and Taichung, and another one is planned for Kaohsiung. As a visitor, the **benefit** of these science parks is clear. More science parks mean more **expat** workers which **in turn** means more delicious international restaurants!

Taichung

Taichung is the biggest city in central Taiwan. It has a population of over two million people, making it the third largest city in Taiwan after Taipei and Kaohsiung. It is a city that is rich in culture. There are many museums and other attractions. It is also home to many well-known colleges and universities. While Taichung is still a big city, it is far slower and more relaxed in **pace** than Taipei. Many important **crops** are grown in the area surrounding Taichung, such as bananas, sugarcane, and rice. These crops are taken to Taichung for industrial **processing** before they are sent on to other places. Taichung also has some other important industries, such as **machinery**, **textiles**, and **chemical** production.

Night scene of Taichung
台中夜景

Quiz

1. What are some of the foods of Hsinchu?
2. What is one of Taiwan's best technical schools? Where is it located?
3. What is the third largest city in Taiwan?
4. What is Taichung famous for?
5. Which Taichung specialty foods make good gifts?

When it comes to food and drink, Taichung is the place to be. We already know that it's where the world-famous bubble tea was invented. However, it is also the birthplace of "sun cakes," a sweet cake with a **malt** sugar filling. Taichung is also the origin of **culinary** inventions like "chicken feet jelly" and "fengren shaved ice 豐仁冰." On the streets of Taichung you'll find "yixin dried tofu 一心豆干" as well. Taiwanese tourists will often buy these delicious foods when visiting Taichung and take them back home to give as gifts.

Shibajian
Mountain
十八尖山
cc by Weihao Chiu

🎧 62 Conversation

Ethan	I have heard of a city of **scientific** and technological importance in Taiwan. Is it near Taipei?
Laura	There are a few cities known for their scientific development, but I think you're talking about Hsinchu, which is south of Taipei.
Ethan	Are there many hi-tech people working there?
Laura	Yes. That's where the Hsinchu Science Park is located. It's similar to the **Silicon** Valley in the United States. Workers with scientific and technological backgrounds mostly go there to find a job.
Ethan	Are there any delicious local foods like in other cities?
Laura	Of course. If you visit the Chenghuang Temple Night Market, you can taste delicious rice noodles and meat ball soup.
Ethan	My mouth is watering again!
Laura	You may want to **head** for Taichung after visiting Hsinchu.
Ethan	Where is Taichung?
Laura	It's south of Hsinchu. It is the largest city in central Taiwan and the third largest in Taiwan.
Ethan	Oh, I remember that it is home to the world-famous bubble tea.
Laura	That's right. **In addition to** that, there's also a famous snack called sun cakes. Visitors to Taichung usually buy these cakes to take back home as gifts for family and friends. Other delicious snacks like shaved ice and dried tofu are also worth a try.
Ethan	Wow! I can't wait to go!

Chenghuang
Temple
城隍廟
by Yuyu

Attractions and Food in Hsinchu

The East Gate (Ying Xi Gate)

東門（迎曦門）

Big City

巨城購物中心

Photo provided by Leofoo Village Theme Park

Leofoo Village Theme Park

六福村主題遊樂園

cc by mingwangx

Hsinchu City Hall

新竹市政府

National Tsing Hua University

國立清華大學

Fried rice noodles 炒米粉
by yuyu

Meat ball soup 貢丸湯

Taiwanese meatballs 肉圓
by yuyu

01 | Listening

Listen to the descriptions and check the thing that you think is being referred to each time.

1. ◯ Hsinchu   ◯ Shibajian Mountain
2. ◯ Sun cakes   ◯ Meatball soup
3. ◯ National Chao Tang University   ◯ Taichung
4. ◯ Bananas, sugarcane, and rice   ◯ Machinery, chemicals, and textiles
5. ◯ Chicken feet jelly   ◯ Chenghuang Temple Night Market

02 | Reading

Choose the correct caption for each picture.

_____ 1.

(a) Science parks are important for Taiwan's economy.
(b) A worker at the Hsinchu Science Park
(c) Science parks are being built all over Taiwan.
(d) The Hsinchu Science Park is similar to Silicon Valley.

_____ 2.

(a) An important crop grown near Taichung
(b) A tasty gift from Hsinchu
(c) Traditional night-market food
(d) Taichung's textile industry

03 | Writing

Complete the sentences using the fragments given.

(a) plans to build   **(b) in a hi-tech industry**
(c) to Taiwan's economy   **(d) fengren shaved ice**

1. Hsinchu is much smaller than Taipei, but it's still very important _____.

2. There are _____ a science park in Kaohsiung similar to the one in Hsinchu.

3. Sun cakes, chicken feet jelly, and _____ are just some of Taichung's famous snacks

4. Hsinchu is a hub for those wanting to get a job _____, and many people move there after they graduate to find work.

Attractions and Food in Taichung

Sun cake
太陽餅

Pearl milk tea
珍珠奶茶

Guguan hot springs 谷關溫泉
Wuchi Fish Harbor 梧棲漁港
Tiezhen Mountain Scenic Area 鐵砧山風景區
Lishan Scenic Area 梨山風景區

Guoxing Well 國姓井 **(Sword Well** 劍井 **) in Tiezhen Mountain Scenic Area**
位於鐵砧山風景區的國姓井
（又稱劍井）

Cingjing Farm

清境農場

Wuling Farm

武陵農場

Unit 22

Taichung— Attractions

台中：熱門景點

Word Bank

bamboo **n.** 竹
hustle **n.** 忙碌
bustle **n.** 喧囂
wetland **n.** 濕地
Black-Faced Spoonbill
　　黑面琵鷺

Chinese Egret
　　唐白鷺
thrill **v.** 刺激
windmill **n.** 風車
dam **n.** 水壩
boardwalk **n.**
　　木板人行步道

boast **v.**
　　以有……而自豪
venue **n.** 場所
stroll **n.** 漫步
sculpture **n.**
　　雕像
theme **v.** 主題

metropolitan **a.**
　　大都會
facility **n.** 設備
interactive **a.**
　　互動的
clip **n.** 短片

🎧 Reading Passage

Taichung is a great place to see some traditional Taiwanese culture. If you head to Folk Park, you can experience a whole range of traditional activities, including paper cutting, **bamboo** weaving, and traditional dancing. If you go during a festival, you will find even more activities that are taking place. Folk Park also has a house built in the southern Chinese-style and a gallery with folk art and antiques. If you get tired you can go to a teahouse and rest while you enjoy a traditional tea ceremony.

If you need a break from the **hustle** and **bustle** of the city, then it might be a good idea to visit the Gaomei Wetlands 高美濕地. It's one of the last major wetlands in

Gaomei Wetlands
高美濕地

National Museum of Natural Science
國立自然科學博物館

cc by Jimmyarch8118

Taiwan. It's also home to several rare bird species like the **Black-Faced Spoonbill** and the **Chinese Egret**. If you aren't **thrilled** by bird-watching, don't worry. There are plenty of other things to do at the Gaomei Wetlands. You can visit local sites like the **windmill** or the **dam**, or explore the **boardwalk** and biking trails.

For people who love learning about the world around us, there's the National Museum of Natural Science. It is Taiwan's first science museum and it **boasts** an impressive six **venues**, including the Science Center, Life Science Hall, and Global Environment Hall. It also organizes special exhibitions so that visitors have something new to enjoy whenever they come back. The museum has six different theaters where you can view IMAX or 3-D movies.

There are lots of things to do in Taichung other than eating, drinking, and connecting with nature. The beautiful campus at Tunghai University 東海大學 is great for a **stroll**. On top of that, there's the National Taiwan Museum of Fine Arts, Fengle **Sculpture** Park 豐樂雕塑公園, and Tea Street, as well as Tunghai Art Street 東海藝術街 with its art shops and **themed** cafés. Taichung **Metropolitan** Park and the Fengjia Night Market 逢甲夜市 also shouldn't be missed. There's so much to see in Taichung that it can be a bit exhausting but always exciting!

Black-Faced Spoonbill 黑面琵鷺

If you are staying in Taipei or Kaohsiung, a weekend visit to Taichung is a tempting possibility. You can easily get around Taichung by bus. The city's tourism bureau can be reached at (04) 2221-2126. It can provide detailed information about bus routes and places to see.

從台北或高雄要前往台中來一趟週末旅遊並不成問題，在台中也可以輕鬆搭乘公車趴趴走，台中的觀光局聯絡電話為 (04) 2221-2126，並有提供公車路線與觀光景點的詳細資料。

Quiz

1. What activities does Taichung Folk Park offer?
2. What are some interesting places to visit in Taichung?
3. How many theaters does the National Museum of Natural Science have?

🎧65 Conversation

Ethan	I remember you said something about how easy it is to travel in Taiwan now. How long does it take to get down to Taichung?
Laura	It takes about three hours by train or bus from Taipei, but it's only about 50 minutes if you take the High Speed Rail. You could make it a day trip if you wake up early enough. But, as for Taichung, you do know that there's no MRT, right? You have to get around by bus, taxi, bike, or motorcycle.
Ethan	That's no problem for me.
Laura	Taichung is a city that's known for its educational and cultural **facilities**. There's plenty to see and do.
Ethan	What kinds of things?
Laura	There are plenty of museums. One of the most interesting is the National Museum of Natural Science. It has lots of **interactive** exhibits.
Ethan	Hmm, learning is good and everything, but I prefer to go to the movies.
Laura	The National Museum of Natural Science has its own movie theaters! In fact, it has six of them. Different theaters show **clips** about different scientific subjects.
Ethan	What is there to see other than museums?

Luce Memorial Chapel 路思義教堂

Laura	You can go for a nice walk at the Sculpture Park, or maybe go check out the Tunghai Art Street with its cafés and shops. You could also visit Tunghai University. Its campus is so lush and beautiful that it's more like a park than a school! If you go, be sure to visit the Luce Memorial Chapel. It was built in honor of a 19th century American missionary named Henry Luce and it has a very unique shape.

Attractions in Taichung

Dongfong Bikeway
東豐自行車綠廊 &
Houfong Bikeway
后豐鐵馬道

cc by nnice

Night streets of Taichung

cc by Yoxem

Taichung Metropolitan Park
台中都會公園

cc by EssO

National Taiwan Museum of Fine Arts
國立台灣美術館

Fengle Sculpture Park
豐樂雕塑公園

Jingming 1st Street
精明一街

Taichung City Seaport Art
Center
臺中市立港區藝術中心

Folk Park
民俗公園

Practice

01 | Listening

Listen to the statements and match each one with the picture that best illustrates it.

1. _____   2. _____   3. _____   4. _____   5. _____

a

b

c

d

e

cc by Mingwangx

02 | Reading

Complete the following short paragraph by choosing which of the given sentences should go in each blank space.

1) _____ It is only around 50 minutes from Taipei by high-speed rail. **2)** _____ However, getting around Taichung can be tricky. **3)** _____ Therefore, it is recommended that visitors rent a scooter while visiting as the bus system can be a little complicated. There is a wide range of things for visitors to do while in Taichung. **4)** _____ It has six theaters where visitors can watch 3-D movies about science. After exploring the museum, why not take a coffee break on Tunghai Art Street? **5)** _____

(a) Taichung is a very easy city to get to.

(b) Apart from the usual eating and drinking, tourists can visit the National Museum of Natural Science—Taiwan's first science museum.

(c) This makes it possible to visit Taichung as a day trip from Taipei.

(d) There are enough stylish cafés and shops there to keep you entertained for hours.

(e) There is no MRT like there is in Taipei.

03 | Writing

Use the following words to complete the sentences.

boardwalk **bamboo** **stroll** **Sculpture** **windmills**

1. You can try many traditional activities like paper cutting and _____ weaving in Taichung's Folk Park.

2. Walking along the _____ in the Gaomei Wetlands is a great way to appreciate the area's natural beauty.

3. At the Fengle _____ Park visitors can see many interesting statues on display throughout the grounds.

4. The stunning campus of Tunghai University is the perfect place for taking an afternoon _____.

5. The sun setting behind the _____ in the Gaomei Wetlands makes for a great photo opportunity.

Taichung City Hall
台中市政府

cc by Ludahai

Taichung Railway Station
台中車站

cc by Essolo

Taichung Historical Sites

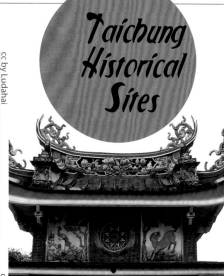

Wufeng Lin Family Mansion and Garden
霧峰林家宅園

cc by Fcuk1203

Unit 23

Sun Moon Lake
日月潭

🎧67 Reading Passage

Not too far from Taichung, you'll find the famous Sun Moon Lake. The lake is located in Nantou County. It is the largest **freshwater** lake in Taiwan. It is a **combination** of two lakes, one of which is shaped like the sun and the other shaped like the moon. That's how it was given the name Sun Moon Lake. This lake and the **surrounding** area are very beautiful. What's more, the weather is pleasant all year round. It is home to the Thao tribe. It's not too surprising that indigenous people established communities here. Nowadays, you can enjoy the natural beauty of Sun Moon Lake and experience some indigenous culture at the same time.

In recent years, new hotels have been built to replace the old ones. Walking and cycling paths have also been constructed along with new boating facilities. Boating is a popular activity for tourists. Boats can be rented in Shuishe Village 水社. Visitors can also explore Lalu Island 拉魯島 in the center of the lake. If going

solo isn't your thing, it's possible to take organized tours of the lake. Most tours visit all the sights and some of them even include bird-watching. It is possible to travel around by bus, but it can be a little slow sometimes. Other travel options include renting a car or bicycle.

Swimming in Sun Moon Lake is **forbidden**. It is only allowed once a year for the Sun Moon Lake Swimming Festival. Every September, people from all around Taiwan jump in and try to swim to the other side. Of course, you have to be a very good swimmer to make it across.

If you want to see how Taiwan's indigenous peoples used to live, then visit the Formosan Aboriginal Cultural Village. It offers an opportunity to learn about traditional buildings, folk art, customs, and tribal dancing. It also gives visitors the rare opportunity to taste traditional indigenous food.

There are several other interesting places to see around Sun Moon Lake, such as **Peacock** Garden, the indigenous Dehua Community 德化社, Cien **Pagoda** 慈恩塔 and many beautiful temples.

If you visit during the summer, you may get a chance to see the Thao tribe's Full Moon Harvest Festival. This event takes place over the **course** of several days.

View of Lalu Island, which lies in the center of Sun Moon Lake. The scenery is a mix of beautiful mountains and water.
日月潭中央的拉魯島，湖上呈現融合山光水色的美景。

Quiz

1. Where is Sun Moon Lake?

2. Why is it called Sun Moon Lake?

3. What is the weather like at Sun Moon Lake?

4. What are some interesting things to do at Sun Moon Lake?

5. When is swimming allowed in Sun Moon Lake?

Sun Moon Lake Ropeway 日月潭纜車

cc by Josephjong

Conversation

Ethan	I'm really interested in visiting Sun Moon Lake. Every Taiwan travel guide mentions this beautiful lake.
Laura	Yes. You can't travel to Taiwan without paying a visit to Sun Moon Lake. It is one of the most important **scenic** spots in Taiwan.
Ethan	Why is it called Sun Moon Lake?
Laura	It is **composed** of two lakes actually. One of them has the shape of the sun, and the other the shape of a **crescent** moon.
Ethan	Interesting! I guess boating is one of the activities I can do on the lake?
Laura	Yes. Cycling and walking around the lake are really nice, too.
Ethan	Yeah, I can already imagine **cycling** by the lake, while taking in the beautiful mountain **scenery**, and maybe listening to birds singing. What a wonderful day! But, what about swimming?
Laura	Swimming is not allowed in Sun Moon Lake, **except for** the **annual** Swimming Festival.
Ethan	Can you tell me more about the festival?
Laura	Once a year, tens of thousands of people from all over Taiwan gather there to swim across Sun Moon Lake.
Ethan	Sounds exciting.
Laura	It sure is. If you are not so much into sports, you can explore the indigenous culture there. It is home to the Thao tribe.
Ethan	Is it possible that I can stay there **overnight**? It looks like I need more than one day to **appreciate** the scenery along with the local culture.
Laura	Of course. There are a lot of nice hotels around the lake.

The 921 Earthquake

cc by Takoradee

On the 21st of September 1999, an earthquake measuring 7.3 on the Richter scale hit Taiwan. Its epicenter was in Jiji 集集, Nantou County. The main tremor lasted for 102 seconds and was followed by 12,911 aftershocks in the following month. One of the aftershocks even reached an intensity of 6.8 on the Richter scale.

The 921 Earthquake caused serious damage to the entire island. Some 2,415 people were killed and 11,305 injured. Lots of buildings collapsed.

All of Taiwan suffered from serious electric power cuts and hampered transportation and communications. Rescue teams came from all over the world to help find survivors and rebuild the disaster areas. It was the most serious earthquake in Taiwan since 1945.

The Jiji Station was destroyed in the 921 Earthquake. It was rebuilt in 2001 and is now a popular tourist spot.
集集火車站在 921 大地震時被摧毀，2001 年歷經重建，如今成為熱門的觀光景點。

The Wuchang Temple 武昌宮 in Jiji collapsed during the earthquake. The remaining temple structure was kept in place and a new temple was built elsewhere.
集集的武昌宮在大地震中倒塌，寺廟殘跡仍被保留於原址，並另覓地點重建寺廟。

Damaged road being repaired after the earthquake
地震之後搶修毀壞的道路

cc by Asiir

01 | Listening

Listen to the statements and fill in the blanks.

1. Visitors can learn about indigenous folk art, _____, and tribal _____ at the Formosan Aboriginal Cultural Village.

2. _____ around the lake is a very popular activity for tourists because it allows them to take in the beautiful mountain _____.

3. Tours visit all the major _____ on the lake and may even _____ a little bird-watching.

4. Sun Moon Lake is so named because it is _____ of two lakes, one in the shape of the sun and another in the shape of a _____ moon.

02 | Reading

Put the dialogues in the correct order.

1. (a) Are there any indigenous tribes living around Sun Moon Lake?
   (b) Will they be holding any festivals while we're here?
   (c) Yes. The lake is home to the Thao tribe.
   (d) I think we're too late. It's October now and their harvest festival is held in the summer.   → _____

2. (a) Definitely. It's a long way from one end of the lake to the other!
   (b) I bet you have to be a good swimmer to take part.
   (c) It's held in September. And tens of thousand of people usually come from all over Taiwan.
   (d) So tell me more about the Swimming Festival. When is it held? → _____

03 | Writing

Use the following words to fill the blanks.

<u>freshwater</u>   <u>annual</u>   <u>solo</u>

1. The Thao tribe's Full Moon Harvest Festival is an _____ event held during the summer months.

2. Sun Moon Lake is located in Nantou County, near Taichung, and is the largest _____ lake in Taiwan.

3. For those of you who don't like to explore the lake _____, tours of the lake can be organized by your hotel.

Maolan Mountain Trail
貓囒山步道

Wenwu Temple 文武廟

Formosan Aboriginal Cultural Village 九族文化村
[Photo provided by the Formosan Aboriginal Cultural Village]

Peacock Garden 孔雀園

Meihe Gardens
梅荷園

Church of Christ
耶穌堂

Lalu Island 拉魯島

Ita Thao 伊達邵
This was formerly known as the Dehua Community 德化社. It is a small indigenous Thao village located along the banks of Sun Moon Lake.
原稱德化社，是位於日月潭湖岸的小型原住民邵族村落。

Xiangshan Visitor Center
向山行政暨遊客中心

Xuanguang Temple
玄光寺

Xuanzang Temple
玄奘寺

Cien Pagoda 慈恩塔

cc by forgemind

Attractions Around
Sun Moon Lake

Unit 24 Tainan—History
台南：歷史

70 Reading Passage

Tainan is a very old city with a rich history. Located in southern Taiwan between Taichung and Kaohsiung, Tainan has a population of over 1.8 million, making it Taiwan's fourth largest city.

After the Portuguese discovered Taiwan, other European nations quickly learned of the island's **existence** and tried to take it over. The Dutch built a fort (Fort Anping 安平古堡) in what is now Tainan. A Ming dynasty **warlord** named Zheng Chenggong (also known as Koxinga) **drove** the Dutch **off** the island to establish a base from which to fight those **seeking** to **overthrow** the Ming **emperor**. Soon after, the Qing dynasty **defeated** the Ming and took over China. An **influx** of Chinese **immigrants** came to Tainan and it became Taiwan's most important city.

Therefore, Tainan offers a rare opportunity in Taiwan to see old European buildings. **Fort Anping** (originally called Fort Zeelandia 熱蘭遮城) was built by the Dutch in 1624. Although there isn't much of the original fort left except for sections of brick wall, the Japanese built some impressive buildings where the fort used to stand. It's definitely worth a visit, if only to climb the tower and watch a beautiful sunset.

Fort Anping 安平古堡

Statue of Shen Baozhen at the Eternal Golden Castle
億載金城內的沈葆禎像

Statue of Zheng Chenggong (Koxinga) at Anping Fort 安平古堡內的鄭成功（國姓爺）像

There is another important **military** structure in Anping called the "**Eternal Golden Castle.**" It was first built by the famous Qing official Shen Baozhen 沈葆禎 in 1874 to **defend** against the possibility of a Japanese **invasion**. Thus, its original purpose was sea defense. After Japan conquered Taiwan in 1895, most of the Eternal Golden Castle's cannons were sold off to help pay for the war.

Zheng Chenggong had a big influence on Taiwan before he died. The **Koxinga Shrine** was built to honor his **contributions**. It is the only official shrine to Koxinga on the island. You'll find the Taiwan Cultural Museum next to the Koxinga Shrine. It tells the history of Koxinga, Fort Anping, traditional clothing, puppetry, and more. Thankfully, the descriptions have all been translated into English!

The city has a wonderful mix of Taiwanese, Chinese, European, and indigenous history. It has a warm and comfortable climate all year round. Life is also slower in Tainan, and its people are well known for being friendly and outgoing. It can be a nice place to visit for people who don't speak Chinese, as there are many signs and much information in English.

Quiz

1. Why did Tainan continue to develop even after the death of Koxinga?
2. What is the population of Tainan?
3. Who built Fort Anping? When did they build it?
4. Why did Koxinga drive the Dutch out of Taiwan?

Conversation

Ethan	So tell me a little about the history of Tainan.
Laura	In a way, it's where Chinese Taiwan was born.
Ethan	But the indigenous people were there first, right?
Laura	Yes, but just like in America and Australia, once new people with better **weapons** arrived, everything changed.
Ethan	Are you talking about the Chinese?
Laura	No, I'm talking about the Europeans.
Ethan	Really? What do you mean?
Laura	The first Europeans to discover Taiwan were the Portuguese. Then, the Spanish came along. After that, the Dutch **landed** and took over most of the island.
Ethan	The Dutch built the first buildings in Tainan, right? I bet they were mostly military buildings.
Laura	Yeah. If you want to take over, you've got to build your forts first. So, we can visit the sites of the old Dutch forts in Tainan. One of them was rebuilt by the Japanese after they took over Taiwan.
Ethan	Didn't Tainan used to be the capital of Taiwan?
Laura	Yes, it was used by both the Chinese and the Europeans.
Ethan	When did the Chinese come to Taiwan?
Laura	Some came very early, but more came after Koxinga turned Taiwan into a base to **attack** the Qing dynasty in China. He drove the Dutch off the island in 1662 and established a new government on Taiwan. However, he died soon after his victory.
Ethan	So, this is how the Chinese way of life came to Taiwan and it has been here ever since. I suppose Tainan has a few firsts then?
Laura	Yes, it has the oldest Confucius and god of war temples in Taiwan. Some people even **refer** to Tainan as the city of temples because of all of the beautiful and historic architecture. It has a lot of **rural** scenery as well.

Tainan is home to world-famous film director Ang Lee and Major League Baseball pitchers Wang Chien-ming and Guo Hong-chih.
世界名導李安和美國職棒大聯盟投手王建民、郭泓志都是台南人。

cc by Cbl62

cc by Keith Allison

Historical Sites in Tainan

Chihkan Tower

赤崁樓

First-graded historical monument 一級古蹟

Fort Anping

安平古堡

First-graded historical monument 一級古蹟

Eternal Golden Castle

億載金城

First-graded historical monument 一級古蹟

Grand Matsu Temple

大天后宮

Anping Former Tait & Co.

德記洋行

Bushido Hall

武德殿

Koxinga Shrine

延平郡王祠

Great East Gate

大東門城

Great South Gate

大南門城

Duei Yue Gate

兌悅門

cc by Pbdragonwang

cc by Pbdragonwang

01 | Listening

Listen to the descriptions and check the thing that you think is being referred to each time.

1. ◯ The Portuguese   ◯ The Chinese
2. ◯ The Taiwan Cultural Museum   ◯ The Eternal Golden Castle
3. ◯ The Japanese   ◯ The Dutch
4. ◯ Fort Zeelandia   ◯ Zheng Chenggong
5. ◯ Taiwan's indigenous people   ◯ Chinese immigrants

02 | Reading

Choose the correct ending for each sentence.

_____ 1. The famous Qing general Shen Baozhen built the Eternal Golden Castle to . . .

(a) overthrow the Qing emperor.   (b) defend against a Japanese invasion.

_____ 2. Zheng Chenggong was a Ming dynasty warlord who . . .

(a) drove the Dutch out of Taiwan.   (b) built Fort Anping in 1624.

_____ 3. Tainan is sometimes referred to as the city of temples . . .

(a) because it is the fourth largest city in Taiwan.

(b) because of its many beautiful and ancient buildings.

_____ 4. The buildings built by the Dutch in Taiwan were . . .

(a) originally inhabited by indigenous tribes.

(b) mostly military structures like forts.

03 | Writing

Unscramble the sentences.

1. used / attack / Taiwan / as / a / Koxinga / to / dynasty / the / base / Qing

_____

_____

2. Koxinga / a / Taiwan / government / on / afterward / established / but / soon / died

_____

_____

3. Confucius / oldest / The / Tainan / temple / in / Taiwan / is / in

_____

_____

Salt farms

Tainan is noted for its beautiful salt farms.
台南美麗的鹽田頗為知名。

cc by Erik

Fishing Industry

Fishing and farming are two important industries in Tainan.
漁業、農業為台南的兩大產業。

cc by Hao-wei Paul Hsu

Tsengwen Reservoir

The Tsengwen Reservoir 曾文水庫 stretches across Chiayi and Tainan. It was completed in 1973 and is the largest reservoir in Taiwan.

曾文水庫跨嘉義、台南兩縣，於1973年竣工，是台灣最大的水庫。

cc by Mk2010

The Eye of Tsengwen 曾文之眼 serves as the Tsengwen Reservoir visitor center.

「曾文之眼」是曾文水庫的遊客服務中心。

Guanziling Hot Springs

The hot springs at Guanziling 關仔嶺 are mud springs, which are very rich in minerals. The temperature of the springs is around 75°C.

關仔嶺溫泉屬於泥漿溫泉，富含礦物質。泉水溫度可達攝氏75度。

Unit 25

Tainan—Attractions
台南：熱門景點

73 ## Reading Passage

Since Tainan was the first capital of Taiwan, it's not surprising that it has many historic sites. Tainan has more Buddhist and Taoist temples than any other place in Taiwan. Two important temples are those **devoted** to the worship of Confucius and the god of war. The Confucius Temple is the oldest in Taiwan. It was originally a Confucian school, which is why people call it the "first school in Taiwan." It still has some of the original stones with rules for students **carved** on them. One stone tells us that students were not allowed to drink **alcohol**. If you visit on September 28th you will be treated to interesting ceremonies to honor Confucius.

The first Confucian temple in Taiwan is located in Tainan. It has been designated a first grade historical monument.

台南孔廟是全台第一間孔廟，現為一級古蹟。

Much like Tainan's Confucius Temple, the Martial Temple is also the oldest of its kind in Taiwan. This temple is home to a **striking** statue of Guan Gong riding a horse and holding his **legendary** "green dragon crescent **blade**." Guan Gong was

Guan Yu and the Sacrificial Rites Martial Temple 祀典武廟 **in Tainan**
關羽像與台南祀典武廟

originally a Chinese general. Government officials and business people have been coming to this temple for hundreds of years to offer **sacrifices**. They do this out of the hope that Guan Gong will reward them with good luck. Over the years, people have **donated** new decorations and **lavish** gifts to the temple, making it a particularly **vibrant** structure. Legend has it that women were stopped from entering the temple in the past because of its high step.

Tainan is a city that is **teeming** with wonderful things to see. Some notable sites include the Great South Gate, National Museum of Taiwanese Literature, and the Chihkan Tower 赤崁樓 —and that's just to name a few. The area along the west coast highway just outside the city is also known for its natural beauty. It's a great place to do some bird-watching!

Quiz

1. Why is the Confucius Temple in Tainan known as "first school in Taiwan"?
2. Who was the god of war?
3. Why is the Martial Temple so vibrant?
4. Name two kinds of food from Tainan.

Tainan has lots of delicious traditional foods. **Coffin** sandwiches are one of the more popular ones. The bread is **hollowed** out and stuffed with tasty filling like **curried** chicken. Pig's **trotters** and shrimp cakes are two other popular dishes from Tainan. While in Tainan, also try a dessert called Anping bean jelly and a special noodle dish called danzai mian 擔仔麵. Just like any other Taiwanese city, you can find these special dishes and other delicious cuisine in restaurants, food stalls, night markets, and even in **alleyways**. Tasty food is never too far away!

Laura	Have you considered checking out Tainan? It's totally worth visiting, and right on the way to Kaohsiung.
Ethan	What's so good about it?
Laura	It's the oldest and most historic city in Taiwan.
Ethan	Sounds like a place my parents would have liked. What a pity they didn't have more time.
Laura	It's got such great food too. Just thinking about it makes me hungry.
Ethan	I'm always up for discovering something new to eat! As long as the food isn't too strange.
Laura	Don't worry, Tainan's food is loved by both Taiwanese and foreigners alike.
Ethan	Oh really? Do tell.
Laura	The most famous food in Tainan is coffin sandwiches.
Ethan	Uh, didn't you say that Taiwanese people don't like hearing about death?

Common Tainan Food

Shrimp cakes
蝦餅

cc by Guan-Hwa Huang

Eel noodles
鱔魚意麵

Pig's trotters
豬腳

by Yuyu

Steamed rice cake
米糕

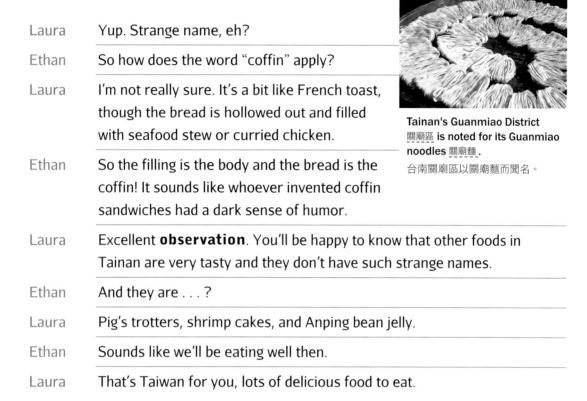

Tainan's Guanmiao District 關廟區 is noted for its Guanmiao noodles 關廟麵.

台南關廟區以關廟麵而聞名。

Laura	Yup. Strange name, eh?
Ethan	So how does the word "coffin" apply?
Laura	I'm not really sure. It's a bit like French toast, though the bread is hollowed out and filled with seafood stew or curried chicken.
Ethan	So the filling is the body and the bread is the coffin! It sounds like whoever invented coffin sandwiches had a dark sense of humor.
Laura	Excellent **observation**. You'll be happy to know that other foods in Tainan are very tasty and they don't have such strange names.
Ethan	And they are . . . ?
Laura	Pig's trotters, shrimp cakes, and Anping bean jelly.
Ethan	Sounds like we'll be eating well then.
Laura	That's Taiwan for you, lots of delicious food to eat.

Danzi noodles/ Danzai mian
擔仔麵

Shrimp rolls
蝦捲

cc by 回憶

Coffin sandwich
棺材板

Anping bean jelly
安平豆花

75

01 | Listening

Listen to the first part of each short dialogue. Match each one with the correct reply.

1. _____

2. _____

3. _____

(a) Ah yes! It's called a coffin sandwich. It's one of Tainan's signature snacks.

(b) Well it is now. But originally it was a Confucian school.

(c) Because Guan Gong, the god of war, is said to be able to give them good luck.

02 | Reading

Complete the following short paragraph by choosing which of the given sentences should go in each blank space.

1) _____ Coffin sandwiches, Anping bean jelly, and shrimp cakes are all examples of some of Tainan's most popular dishes. Good food is never far away in Tainan. As well as being rich in good food, Tainan is also full of historical sites. 2) _____ The Tainan Confucius Temple, for example, is the oldest of its kind in Taiwan. 3) _____ Guan Gong is also the god of businessmen. 4) _____

(a) Tainan was the first capital of Taiwan, so there are many buildings there which are centuries old.

(b) And this temple is particularly vibrant because many rich people have donated expensive gifts over the years.

(c) The Martial Temple dedicated to Guan Gong, the god of war, is also an important historical site.

(d) Tainan's delicious food is famous all around the island.

03 | Writing

Use the following words to complete the sentences.

blade   alleyways   donate

1. Guan Gong is a god who is very easy to recognize. He has a red face, a long black beard, and is often pictured holding his legendary "green dragon crescent _____."

2. Tainan's special dishes can be found in almost every corner of the city. You might even come across tasty snacks being sold in the some of the city's narrow _____.

3. If someone experiences good luck after praying for it in a temple, they will usually _____ money or a lavish gift to the temple to give thanks to the god.

Famous Spots in Tainan

First-graded historical monument
一級古蹟

Tainan Confucius Temple
台南孔廟

Martyrs' Shrine
忠烈祠

National Museum of Taiwan Literature
國立台灣文學館

Anping Lighthouse
安平燈塔

Tsou Ma Lai Farm
走馬瀨農場

Barclay Memorial Park
巴克禮紀念公園

cc by Koika

Lin Moniang Park
林默娘公園

Unit 26 Kaohsiung—General 高雄：概述

(76) Reading Passage

Kaohsiung is located in the southern part of the island. Its population of over 2.7 million people makes it Taiwan's second largest city. Unlike in Taipei, **residents** are much more likely to speak Taiwanese than they are Mandarin.

Kaohsiung is one of the busiest **container** ports anywhere in the world. Most of Taiwan's heavy industry has traditionally been located close to this port. However, there is more to Kaohsiung than just **manufacturing**. There's the famous Love River that runs through the city. It's very pleasant to walk along the water's **edge** because of all the new shops and boardwalks. Going for a boat

Night Scene of Kaohsiung City
高雄夜景

Love River 愛河

cruise along the Love River offers a great opportunity to **admire** the city lights in the evening.

The city government has been hard at work building more attractions, turning the city into a relaxing and romantic place. Nine artists were invited to work together to complete the Urban Spotlight Arcade in 2001 to offer lighted decorations in the evening, giving the city a touch of romance. Having dinner at another famous spot, the True Love Harbor, is also recommended. Kaohsiung doesn't have many famous local foods. However, sitting inside one of the restaurants along the Love River or at the True Love Harbor, you will have the opportunity to enjoy delicious **exotic** foods.

Kaohsiung is a great place to visit for anyone who lives in the north. Although it is a little industrialized in certain areas, there is no **shortage** of surrounding countryside to enjoy. Kaohsiung is also a good place to stay while you take day trips to surrounding **destinations** such as Kenting or Pingtung. If you want to go even farther, you can take a boat or plane to the Penghu Islands that lie between Taiwan and China. A visit to these islands can be like going back in time to the way life used to be in Taiwanese fishing villages.

Quiz

1. What is the population of Kaohsiung?
2. What is the Love River like? What can you do there?
3. Where is someplace that you can take a boat or an airplane to?

🎧77 Conversation

Ethan	What's the deal with Kaohsiung? Is it worth seeing?
Laura	Well, in the past, tourism and Kaohsiung didn't go together. But, it really has improved over the last few years. The city government has turned Kaohsiung into a tourist destination.
Ethan	It's south of Taichung, right?
Laura	Yes, it's about five to six hours away from Taipei by train. If you are coming from Taichung, it's a **fairly** easy visit.
Ethan	So what does the city have to offer?
Laura	The city's Love River is one of the main attractions that visitors may notice.
Ethan	**Judging** by the name, I suppose that it is mostly married couples and lovers that visit this place.
Laura	Ha, not only married couples and lovers. In fact, the city government has built new walking paths, restaurants, and shops, so it is very pleasant to walk along the river.
Ethan	Are there boat cruises on the Love River?
Laura	Yup, and they're quite nice. I went on one last year.
Ethan	Are there any nice islands nearby?
Laura	How near is nearby? You can take a boat to the Penghu Islands if you want. It's a nice place to stay for a few days.
Ethan	I don't think we'll have the time for that. Do you know of anywhere closer? Maybe somewhere for a day trip?
Laura	You can take a day trip to Kenting National Park.
Ethan	That sounds great!

城市光廊
URBAN SPOTLIGHT

Urban Spotlight Arcade
城市光廊

cc by Jnlin

Beautiful Harbors and Wharfs in Kaohsiung

Kaohsiung Harbor
高雄港

True Love Harbor
真愛碼頭

Fisherman's Wharf
漁人碼頭

Xinguang Ferry Wharf
新光碼頭

Practice

01 | Listening

Listen to the statements and match each one with the picture that best illustrates it.

1. _____
2. _____
3. _____
4. _____

a

b

c

d

02 | Reading

Circle the correct option in each sentence.

1. Even though Kaohsiung is an important industrial city, there's still no **destination/ shortage** of countryside to enjoy.

2. Kaohsiung is a good base for people to take **day trips/boat cruises** to places further south like Kenting or Pingtung.

3. Due to the hard work of Kaohsiung's **heavy industry/city government**, the city is now a relaxing and romantic place for tourists to visit.

4. Walking along the Love River or taking a boat cruise after dark is a great way to **judge/admire** the city lights.

5. Kaohsiung is around 250 km away from Taipei, but Taiwan's High Speed Rail has made it **fairly/likely** quick and easy to get to.

Taiwan's High Speed Rail
台灣高鐵

03 | Writing

Some of the information in the following sentences is incorrect. Write the sentences out again with the correct information.

1. The boardwalks along the edges of the Love Port are a great place for taking romantic swims.

   _____

   _____

2. From Kaohsiung you can take a train to the Penghu Islands, which lie behind Taiwan and China.

   _____

   _____

3. In the past, Kaohsiung was not considered a good destination for tourists, but over the last few months it has improved a lot.

   _____

   _____

4. In 2001, nine writers were invited to work on lighted decorations for the Urban Daylight Arcade.

   _____

   _____

All of Kaohsiung City is bathed in colorful lights at night.
夜晚的高雄市沐浴在一片燈火輝煌中。

Kaohsiung—Attractions (1)
高雄：熱門景點

79 Reading Passage

Since the Kaohsiung MRT opened in 2008, people's lives have gotten a lot more convenient. Before then, tourists had to use taxis or buses to get around the city.

You may take one look at the wide roads in Kaohsiung and think about renting a car. However, many foreigners may find that it is not so easy to drive in Taiwan. Therefore, it is recommended that you don't rent a car unless you have at least a little experience driving in Taiwan.

For many people, Kaohsiung's main attraction is nearby Fokuangshan 佛光山. Fokuangshan is a famous Buddhist **monastery**. It is possible to stay in the monastery overnight either as an ordinary tourist or for **spiritual** reasons. The monastery can teach visitors a lot about how Buddhism is practiced in Taiwan. For example, it runs **meditation**

The Central Park entrances and an inside view of the Kaohsiung MRT
高雄捷運的中央公園車站及捷運內部

The Buddha Memorial Center 佛陀紀念館 **on Fokuangshan**
佛光山的佛陀紀念館

classes that anyone can join. There is a wonderful garden on the monastery grounds with several statues of **Buddha**. The largest statue is over 40m high. The monastery was closed to visitors in 1997, but it opened again in 2000.

A visit to Qijin Island 旗津 can be a great way to relax, and the island is very conveniently located. By boat, the trip only takes about five minutes. You can also get there by going through an underwater **tunnel**. When exploring Qijin Island, you'll come across plenty of delicious seafood restaurants. There's also a Matsu temple and a **lighthouse**.

Kaohsiung's Hakka Cultural Center is full of old photographs that **detail** the traditional way of life of the Hakka people. The city used to have many old Hakka-style houses that were built according to strict feng shui principles. Unfortunately, many of these houses have been **torn** down over the past few decades. The **citizens** of Kaohsiung have been coming together in an effort to save the few remaining Hakka-style houses that are still standing in Meinong 美濃 and Qishan 旗山.

Qijin Island lighthouse
旗津燈塔

- Quiz

1. What has made transportation more convenient?

2. Name some of the main attractions in Kaohsiung.

3. Where's Fokuangshan? How would you describe Fokuangshan?

4. Talk about the Hakka culture in Kaohsiung.

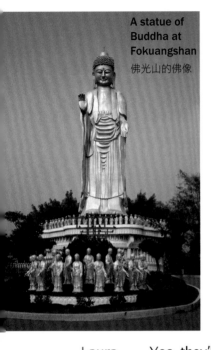 Conversation

A statue of Buddha at Fokuangshan
佛光山的佛像

Ethan	What about getting around the city? Is it just buses like Taichung?
Laura	Nope. Thankfully, the Kaohsiung MRT opened in 2008.
Ethan	What a **relief**! That means I don't need to rent a car.
Laura	Yes. Driving in Taiwan may not be a good idea for foreigners.
Ethan	What's the main attraction in Kaohsiung?
Laura	A **favorite** place for visitors is Fokuangshan. It's a famous Buddhist monastery near Kaohsiung.
Ethan	Is it possible to stay there overnight?
Laura	Yes, they'll take you in for a few days. Of course you have to **abide by** all of their rules and only eat **vegetarian** food.
Ethan	Is there anything else worth checking out?
Laura	There are lots of museums, a Hakka cultural center, and beautiful countryside outside the city.
Ethan	That sounds good. We'll probably need to see some nature sooner or later. Do you know of any place that is close? Maybe somewhere we could take a day trip?
Laura	How about Qijin Island? It's only about five minutes away from the city by boat. Or, you can take an underwater tunnel to get there.
Ethan	Can it be much of an island if it's that close to Kaohsiung.
Laura	It definitely has the feel of an island. There is a lighthouse, plenty of seafood restaurants, and a Matsu temple.
Ethan	Who's Matsu? Is she the folk goddess of the sea that you mentioned before?
Laura	Right! You remembered!

Famous Spots in Kaohsiung

National Stadium
國家體育場

**Vision for Kaohsiung
(Old station building)**
高雄願景館

Dream Mall
夢時代購物中心

British Consulate at Takao
打狗英國領事館

The Dome of Light 光之穹頂
**at Formosa Boulevard Station of the
Kaohsiung MRT** 位於高雄捷運美麗島站

**Gaoping River
Cable-Stayed Bridge**
高屏溪斜張橋

Gaoping River Cable-Stayed
Bridge crosses the Gaoping
River. It is an asymmetrical
single-pylon bridge with a
main span of 330 meters.

高屏溪斜張橋橫跨高屏溪，為
非對襯單塔型的設計，主跨徑
330 公尺。

**85 Sky Tower/
Tuntex Sky Tower**
高雄 85 大樓

cc by 揚威 企鵝

Kaohsiung Central Park
中央公園

81

01 | Listening

Listen to the dialogue and mark the things that are mentioned in the conversation.

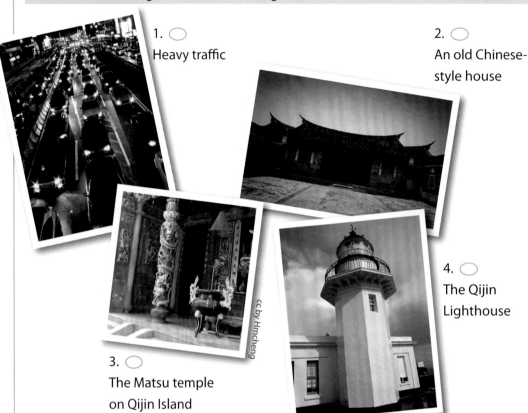

1. ◯
Heavy traffic

2. ◯
An old Chinese-style house

3. ◯
The Matsu temple on Qijin Island

4. ◯
The Qijin Lighthouse

cc by Hmcheng

02 | Reading

Match the two halves of the sentences.

1. Kaohsiung's MRT opened in 2008 and has _____

2. Renting a car in Kaohsiung is not a good idea if _____

3. In the grounds of Fokuangshan there is _____

4. Many of Kaohsiung's old Hakka-style houses _____

5. If you would like to stay at Fokuangshan, remember that _____

(a) a garden with several statues of Buddha.

(b) made people's lives much more convenient.

(c) you must abide by the strict rules of the monastery.

(d) have been torn down over the last few decades.

(e) you don't have any experience of driving in Taiwan.

03 | Writing

Use the following words to fill in the blanks.

<u>vegetarian</u> <u>tunnel</u> <u>lighthouse</u> <u>spiritual</u> <u>citizen</u>

1. One of the conditions of staying the night in Fokuangshan is that you must eat a _____ diet.

2. There are two ways of getting to Qijin Island—by boat or via an underwater _____ .

3. Visitors to Kaohsiung looking for a more _____ experience can join one of Fokuangshan's meditation classes.

4. Kaohsiung's new MRT means that its _____ no longer have to rely entirely on buses and taxis to get around.

5. Even though it's not very big, Qijin Island has plenty of things for visitors to see, such as a _____ , a Matsu temple, and many seafood restaurants.

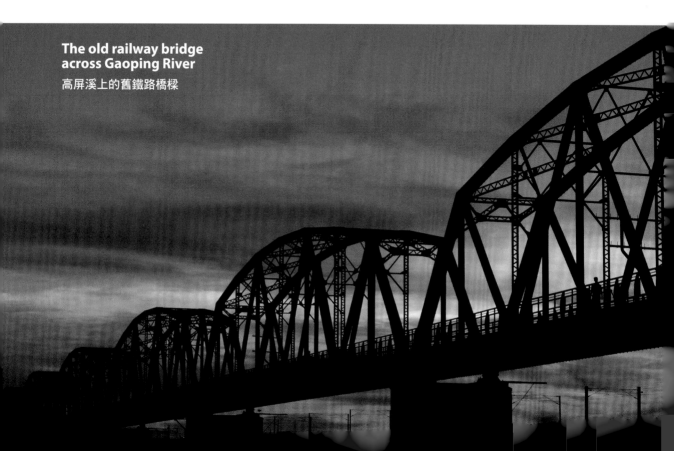

The old railway bridge across Gaoping River
高屏溪上的舊鐵路橋樑

Unit 28

Kaohsiung—Attractions (2)
高雄：熱門景點

Word Bank

lotus n. 蓮花
pavilion n. 涼亭
dedicate v. 奉獻
appear v. 出現

urge v. 力勸
deed n. 行為；行動
punishment n. 懲罰
await v. 等待
magnificent a. 雄偉的

imposing a. 壯觀的
biotechnology n. 生物科技
dinosaur n. 恐龍

82 Reading Passage

Lotus Lake 蓮池潭

If you take the train to Zuoying Station 左營車站, you will find yourself near **Lotus Lake**, one of the most beautiful places in the city. Here, there is a large park lined with beautiful buildings and temples. These buildings are based on traditional Chinese beliefs and stories. If you walk around the lake, you will come across the **Spring and Autumn Pavilions**. They are **dedicated** to Guan Gong, a famous soldier of ancient time. In front of these pavilions there is a statue of Guanyin, the goddess of mercy. She is riding a dragon. It is said that she **appeared** in the clouds one day and made the request that the statue be built like this.

Guanyin riding a dragon 乘龍的觀音菩薩

Further down the road are two tall Chinese-style buildings called the **Dragon and Tiger pagodas**. One represents the tiger and the other represents the dragon. If you go in through the dragon's mouth and come out the tiger's mouth, it is said

Dragon and Tiger Pagodas 龍虎塔

that you'll be rewarded with good luck. The pagodas have many paintings inside them. Some of these paintings **urge** visitors to do good **deeds**, and others warn of the **punishment** that **awaits** them if they do bad deeds. All of these paintings are based on traditional Chinese religion.

Other attractions of note are Shou Shan Zoo 壽山動物園, Xiziwan Scenic Area 西子灣風景區, and Ban Ping Mountain 半屏山 in the northern part of the city. There is also a **magnificent** Confucius Temple that can't be missed. This temple is the largest one of its kind in Taiwan, and there is an **imposing** statue of Confucius nearby.

Kaohsiung has opened quite a few museums over the years. The main ones are the National Science and Technology Museum, the Kaohsiung Museum of Fine Arts, and the Kaohsiung Museum of History.

Quiz

1. If you take the train to Zuoying Station, what attraction is nearby?
2. If you visit Lotus Lake, what should you do so that you may be granted good luck?
3. Name some of the museums in Kaohsiung.

Bureau can be reached at (07) 2155-100.
觀光局請洽 (02) 2155-100。

Kaohsiung Museum of History
高雄市立歷史博物館

cc by Taiwan Junior

83 Conversation

Kaohsiung Confucius Temple 高雄孔廟

Ethan	Are there any other sights near the city?
Laura	Well, you'll definitely want to visit Lotus Lake.
Ethan	That sounds pretty. Is it some kind of park?
Laura	It sure is. To be exact, it's a lake that's surrounded by a large park that has several temples and other interesting buildings. It's very popular with tourists.
Ethan	Let me guess. Those temples are devoted to the sea goddess you told me about?
Laura	Not that I know of. There is however the biggest Confucian temple in all of Taiwan. There are also two pavilions dedicated to the god of war, and a beautiful statue of Guanyin, the goddess of mercy.
Ethan	What is your favorite thing to do at Lotus Lake?
Laura	That would have to be the two dragon and tiger pagodas. A lot of people go into the dragon's mouth and come out of the tiger's mouth. It's supposed to bring good luck.
Ethan	I can always use some good luck. Are there any museums or galleries like other cities in Taiwan?
Laura	Of course. Maybe you'll be interested in the National Science and Technology Museum.
Ethan	What does it display?
Laura	There are lots of exhibitions taking place around the year. For example, there are exhibitions about **biotechnology**, water resources, and the food industry. There's even a special exhibition on **dinosaurs**!
Ethan	Wow, sounds interesting! I'll definitely go and take a look!

Famous Spots in Kaohsiung

cc by vegafish

Kaohsiung Museum of Fine Arts
高雄市立美術館

cc by micro-playground

National Science and Technology Museum
國立科學工藝博物館

Spring and Autumn Pavilions
春秋閣

cc by Bizmac

Cheng Ching Lake
澄清湖

cc by shaufu27

Xiziwan Scenic Area
西子灣風景區

cc by Peellden

Ban Ping Mountain
半屏山

cc by Jessepylin

Fongshan Longshan Temple
鳳山龍山寺

01 | Listening

Listen to the statements and fill in the blanks.

1. In front of the Spring and Autumn Pavilions is a _____ of Guanyin, the goddess of mercy, riding a _____.

2. Paintings inside the Dragon and Tiger Pagodas show people the _____ they will suffer if they do bad _____.

3. Kaohsiung's National Science and Technology Museum has _____ on biotechnology, water _____, and the food industry.

4. Lotus Lake, near Zuoying Train Station, is _____ by a large park and is very popular with _____.

5. Kaohsiung's magnificent _____ temple is the _____ of its kind on the island.

02 | Reading

Choose the correct ending for each sentence.

_____ 1. Nearby the Kaohsiung Confucius Temple . . .
   (a) is an imposing statue of Confucius.
   (b) are two Chinese-style pagodas.

_____ 2. It is said that the statue of Guanyin in Lotus Park . . .
   (a) is the oldest statue of the goddess in Taiwan.
   (b) was asked to be built by the goddess herself.

_____ 3. The Spring and Autumn Pavilions are . . .
   (a) dedicated to Guan Gong, an ancient Chinese soldier.
   (b) filled with paintings urging people to do good.

_____ 4. It is said of the Dragon and Tiger Pagodas that you will receive good luck if you . . .
   (a) walk around the lake until you see the statue of Guanyin riding a dragon.
   (b) walk into the dragon's mouth and come out of the tiger's.

_____ 5. Visitors who are interested in science . . .
   (a) will probably enjoy climbing Ban Ping Mountain.
   (b) may want to visit the National Science and Technology Museum.

03 | Writing

Complete the dialogue using the fragments provided.

(a) dedicated to any particular god or goddess   **(b) that statue in front of**
(c) there are many interesting temples and buildings
(d) appeared out of the clouds   **(e) other side of the lake**

A Lotus Lake is very pretty isn't it? The scenery is so beautiful, and **1)** _____ in the surrounding park.

B Yes, you're right. I think it's one of the most beautiful places in the city.

A So what shall we go and see first? How about the Spring and Autumn Pavilions?

B OK. They're on the **2)** _____, so we'll have to walk a bit to get there.

A No problem. We can enjoy the view while we walk. Are the pavilions **3)** _____?

B Yes, they're dedicated to Guan Gong. He's the god with the red face and long black beard.

A I see. Here we are. Wow, look at **4)** _____ the pavilions. Is that a goddess riding a dragon?

B Yes! It's the goddess Guanyin. Actually there's a cool story behind this statue.

A Oh Really?

B Yeah. People say that the goddess herself **5)** _____ and asked for the statue to be built like this.

The Gangshan District 岡山區 of Kaohsiung is famous for doubanjiang 豆瓣醬, a tasty spicy sauce.
高雄岡山區盛產一種味辣的豆瓣醬。

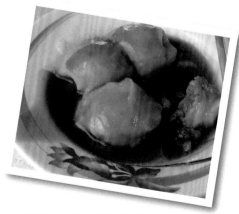

The meatballs produced in Kaohsiung differ from those produced in other places in Taiwan. They're steamed instead of deep-fried and are thus less greasy.
高雄肉圓與台灣其他地方的肉圓不同，是用蒸的而非油炸的，因此較為清爽。

Unit 29 Kenting 墾丁

Word Bank

resort n. 名勝	**reef** n. 礁	**Grey-Faced Buzzard** 灰面鷲	**chime** n. 風鈴
southernmost a. 最南端的	**landform** n. 地形	**shrike** n. 伯勞鳥	**formation** n. 形成
tableland n. 台地	**erosion** n. 侵蝕	**sperm** n. 抹香鯨	**indeed** adv. 的確
coral a. 珊瑚的	**erode** v. 侵蝕	**surfboard** n. 衝浪板	**tan** n. 曬成的棕褐膚色
	crouch v. 蹲伏	**surf** v. 衝浪	
	migratory a. 遷移的		

🎧 Reading Passage

Kenting National Park is one of the most famous summer **resorts** in Taiwan. It lies in Pingtung County, in the **southernmost** part of Taiwan, and is the first national park on the island. The park was established in 1984. It measures 333 square kilometers, covering land and sea.

Kenting National Park is composed mostly of hills and **tablelands**. The park's **coral reefs** and other peculiar **landforms** are the result of the earth's crust movements and **erosion** caused by the sea. There are a lot of unique landscapes inside the park. For example, located at the southern tip of the park, Maobitou 貓鼻頭 (Cat Nose Rock) is a typical **eroded** coral reef landform. It was named because it is shaped like a **crouching** cat. Other well-known landscapes include Nanwan Beach 南灣, Chuanfan Rock 船帆石, and Cape Eluanbi 鵝鑾鼻, etc.

Chuanfan Rock (Sail Rock) 船帆石   Cape Eluanbi 鵝鑾鼻

↑ **Kenting National Park** 墾丁國家公園
← **Kenting Street** 墾丁大街

Due to the tropical climate, there are a variety of animal and plant species. It is the winter resort of many **migratory** birds, such as the **Grey-Faced Buzzard** and **shrikes**. **Sperm** whales and many kinds of dolphins are commonly seen in the sea.

Kenting is very warm throughout the year. For Taiwanese people, it is a place of beaches and sunshine. Young people from all over the island come to Kenting to enjoy the various exciting water sports during the summer. The beaches and streets are full of men in casual trunks and women in bikinis! You may see young people carrying their **surfboards**, either heading for the sea or taking a rest after **surfing** for many hours! Kenting is certainly a place of youth, passion, and energy!

Kenting is home to many large-scale activities, including the famous Spring Scream, which takes place in April every year, and the Wind **Chimes** Festival. There are plenty of tourist spots in the park.

There is also the Kenting Street Night Market. It has a lot of hotels, shops, food stalls, and bars. Visitors can also shop for swimming and water sports gear on this street.

Quiz

1. Where is Kenting National Park located?
2. How were Kenting's landscapes formed?
3. Is Kenting rich in animal and plant species? Why?
4. Name some popular tourist spots in Kenting National Park.

🎧 86 Conversation

Ethan	You mentioned that Kenting National Park is near Kaohsiung. Is it very popular among tourists?
Laura	Of course. It is definitely one of the favorite spots among Taiwanese people and foreign tourists.
Ethan	Can you tell me about it?
Laura	Sure. Kenting was formed by the earth's crust movements. After being eroded by wind and sea for so many years, it finally has the various landforms that we see today.
Ethan	What kinds of landforms?
Laura	Mainly small hills, rock **formations**, and coral reefs!
Ethan	Amazing! So, it is located in the south of Taiwan. I suppose it must be very hot!
Laura	Very hot **indeed**! It is warm all year round due to the tropical climate.
Ethan	That must make it the perfect place for water sports!
Laura	Right, especially a place called Nanwan Beach. Many people crowd onto the beach every summer to enjoy the sunshine!
Ethan	Wow! I can imagine the busy beach crowded with young people and their surfboards or diving equipment, or simply lying on the beach while getting a **tan**! But, my parents aren't into water sports.
Laura	Don't worry. There are so many tourist spots in the park, such as the Eluanbi Lighthouse, which is the southernmost lighthouse in Taiwan. They can also take a look at Chuanfan Rock, a rock shaped like a sailboat, and Maobitou, a rock shaped like a crouching cat!
Ethan	Wow, I think they'll be interested! What about dinner? Any good restaurants?
Laura	You can take them to the famous Kenting Street Night Market. There are lots of food stalls and international restaurants and bars on that street.

Famous Spots in Kenting

Maobitou
貓鼻頭

Jialeshui
佳樂水

Baisha Bay
白沙灣

by Yuyu

Nanwan Beach (South Bay Beach)
南灣

Nanwan Beach is perfect for water activities.
南灣最適合從事水上活動。

by Yuyu

Shadau (Sand Island)
砂島

Eluanbi Lighthouse
鵝鑾鼻燈塔

Eluanbi Lighthouse is located in Cape Eluanbi. It is the southernmost lighthouse in Taiwan. It is also a historic monument dating back more than 100 years. It has the most powerful light source among all of the lighthouses in Taiwan, and thus has earned the nickname "the light of East Asia."

鵝鑾鼻燈塔位於鵝鑾鼻，是台灣最南的燈塔，同時也是超過 100 年的古蹟。此燈塔光力之強為全台之最，因此被稱為「東亞之光」。

by Yuyu

Small Bay
小灣

Practice

01 | Listening

Listen to the statements and mark the information you get from each one.

1. ○ Kenting National Park has been established for more than 25 years.
   ○ Kenting National Park is in the southernmost part of Taiwan.

2. ○ Maobitou is a coral reef landform.
   ○ Maobitou is shaped like an animal.

3. ○ Kenting stays warm throughout the year.
   ○ You can see sperm whales in the waters around Kenting.

02 | Reading

Choose the caption that best describes each picture.

_____ 1.
   (a) You may get a chance to see dolphins near Kenting.
   (b) Kenting is a great place for fans of water sports.
   (c) It is one of Kenting National Park's many tourist spots.
   (d) You can buy swimming gear at the Kenting Street Night Market.

_____ 2.
   (a) Kenting Street Night Market
   (b) The lighthouse at Eluanbi
   (c) The sailboat-shaped Chuanfan Rock
   (d) One of Kenting's coral reefs

03 | Writing

Fill in the blanks using the words provided.

1. *landforms, movements, wind*
   The earth's crust _____ along with erosion from the sea and _____ caused many of Kenting's peculiar _____.

2. *surfboards, heading, months*
   During the summer _____ you're likely to see many visitors to Kenting carrying _____ and _____ for the sea.

3. *buzzard, weather, migratory*
   The grey-faced _____ and other _____ birds make Kenting their winter home because of the constant warm _____.

Around Kenting

Guanshan 關山
Guanshan is noted for its beautiful sunset.
[Photo by Yuyu]

by Yuyu

Old city gate of Hengchun—West Gate
恆春古城──西門

by Yuyu

Old city gate of Hengchun—South Gate
恆春古城──南門

National Museum of Marine Biology and Aquarium
國立海洋生物博物館

Fire From the Earth
出火

The Southernmost Point
最南點

The East Coast— General 東海岸：概述

Word Bank

consequently adv. 結果
pristine a. 原始的；純樸的
mere a. 僅僅
lack a. 缺乏

hectic a. 忙亂的
take advantage of 利用
participate v. 參加
toughness n. 堅強；強韌
raft v. 乘筏

rubber a. 橡膠
breathe v. 呼吸

🎧 Reading Passage

Taiwan's east coast is cut off from the rest of the island by the Central Mountain Range. **Consequently**, there is not much industry on the east coast and much of the countryside remains **pristine** and untouched. There are no large cities on the east coast and it is far less crowded than western Taiwan. Hualien City, for example, has a population of just over 110,000 people. In fact, the whole of Hualien County has a **mere** 340,000 people.

The countryside, coastline, and **lack** of industry make the east coast one of Taiwan's most scenic and relaxed areas. There is much more room here and life is much less **hectic**. Many visitors **take advantage of** this relaxed lifestyle by **participating** in outdoor sports such as diving, cycling, and hiking. Summer is the high season on the east coast because of all the Taiwanese tourists taking vacations with their families.

The Tropic of
Cancer Marker
in Ruisui 瑞穗
位於瑞穗的
北回歸線標

cc by Dodd

The east coast was not fully modernized until the 1960s when new roads were built connecting it to other parts of Taiwan. The people who live on the east coast are well known for their **toughness** and passion for life. Another fun fact about the east coast is that the sun goes down early because it is cut off by the massive mountain range in the west.

The two biggest cities on the east coast are Hualien and Taitung. While both of them are relatively quiet places at present, the government is planning to turn them into tourist destinations.

After the longest tunnel in Taiwan, the Xuehshan Tunnel 雪山隧道, was opened in 2006, the traffic between the eastern and western parts of Taiwan has improved a lot. The travel time has been greatly cut down from two hours to a mere 40 minutes from Taipei to Yilan. This has helped attract more visitors to the east coast.

Quiz

1. What's the population of Hualien City and Hualien County?
2. What are the people living on the east coast well known for?
3. What is a fun fact about the east coast?

↑ Xuehshan Tunnel
雪山隧道
← Qingshui Cliff
清水斷崖

Conversation

Ethan	I was thinking of trying one or two outdoor sports while I'm here. Where's a good place to go for this?
Laura	You should check out the east coast. There are many outdoor sports to participate in there. And, while you're on the east coast, you can enjoy all of the open space!
Ethan	What sports can I try?
Laura	Have you ever tried white water **rafting**?
Ethan	Whoa, that might be a little too exciting! Is that the one where you go down a fast river on a **rubber** raft?
Laura	Yup, there are lots of rivers on the east coast. It's the most undeveloped part of Taiwan, so it's very natural and clean. It was the last area of Taiwan that Chinese people settled.
Ethan	So there are no big cities?
Laura	No. There is Hualien City with 110,000 people and Taitung with 109,000.
Ethan	Are there any opportunities for hiking, swimming, or diving?
Laura	Yes, but you need to make plans before you go. The east coast is also popular with Taiwanese tourists.
Ethan	Is it because it's less industrialized?
Laura	That is one reason. The east coast offers lots of natural spots to enjoy.
Ethan	I'll get to planning it right now! Looks like I can get an opportunity to escape from the big city and **breathe** some fresh air!

← The beautiful mountain view of the
   east coast in Taiwan
   台灣東岸的美麗山景

↓ The flower field in the Huatong Valley
   花東縱谷的花田

Practice

01 | Listening

Listen to the dialogue and mark the information that you hear.

1. ○ The population of Hualian County is 340,000 people.
2. ○ The east coast and west coasts of Taiwan are very different.
3. ○ Before 1960 it was difficult to get to the east coast from the west coast.
4. ○ The Xuehshan Tunnel was built in 2006.
5. ○ Rafting is one the activities you can do on the east coast.

02 | Reading

Put the dialogues in the correct order.

1. (a) But why is it so underdeveloped?
   (b) Because the east coast was the last place to be settled by the Chinese.
   (c) The east coast is far less industrialized than the west coast, isn't it?
   (d) Yes. It's very natural and clean. Tourists love it.
   → _____

2. (a) I agree. The lifestyle here on the east coast is much more relaxed.
   (b) Hualien is a lot less crowded than Taipei, isn't it?
   (c) Yes, definitely. Hualien City has a population of just over 100,000 people.
   (d) It's nice. In fact, I think Taipei is a little too crowded. The lifestyle is too hectic.
   → _____

03 | Writing

Use the following words to complete the sentences.

toughness **pristine** **rafting** **breathe**

1. Many people visit the east coast in order to escape the crowds and pollution of the cities and _____ some fresh air.

2. The people who live on the east coast are known for being very friendly and passionate, but also for their _____.

3. One of the most exciting outdoor activities you can try on the east coast is white-water _____.

4. Travelling down the east coast on the train or by car is a great way to take in the area's _____ scenery.

Attractions in Hualien

Guangfu Sugar Factory
光復觀光糖廠

Liyu Lake
鯉魚潭

Huatong Valley
花東縱谷

Ruisui Pasture
瑞穗牧場

Qixingtan Scenic Area
七星潭

Mount Qilai
奇萊山

Taroko National Park
太魯閣國家公園

cc by Prattfora

Xiuguluan River

秀姑巒溪

by Yuyu

Luoshan Recreation Area

羅山休憩區

Tropic of Cancer Marker

北回歸線地標

Liushidan Mountain

六十石山

Saoba Stone Pillars

掃叭石柱

cc by Mnb

Lintienshan Forestry Cultural Park

林田山林場

Hualien County Stone Sculptural Museum

花蓮縣石雕博物館

Pine Garden

松園別館

Shihtiping Rest Area

石梯坪

Hongye Hot Springs

紅葉溫泉

Matai'an Wetland

馬太鞍濕地

Antong Hot Springs

安通溫泉

Jiqi Beach

磯崎海水浴場

Farglory Ocean Park

海洋公園

Unit 31

The East Coast— Hualien and Taitung
東海岸：花蓮與台東

🎧 91 Reading Passage

Hualien

Hualien City is famous for its stone carvings. Every year, it holds an international stone carving festival. This festival has become famous worldwide. Traditionally, visitors have bought **marble** when they came to Hualien. Unfortunately, marble cutting has begun to have a negative effect on the environment in local mountainous areas. So if you visit, it might be a better idea to buy some jade instead.

Taroko National Park 太魯閣國家公園

It also has pleasant parks, temples, Japanese-style buildings, and coastline. If you go to Hualien, you must visit Taroko National Park, named after Taroko **Gorge**. The word Taroko means "magnificent and beautiful" in the local tribe's language. The park is full of magnificent gorges and **cliffs**. It is one of Taiwan's national parks and it's a great opportunity to experience some of the island's untouched natural beauty.

Hualien also has some famous foods and snacks, such as **mochi** (rice cake) and wonton.

Taitung

Taitung is the other main city on the east coast. It has a population of around 109,000 people. Visitors should be sure to visit Taitung's National Museum of Prehistory and Peinan Cultural Park 卑南文化公園 . The Peinan Cultural Park is an **archeological** site that was discovered by accident during the construction of a railway station in 1980. The park shows how prehistoric peoples used to live thousands of years ago.

cc by Benson KC Fang

Peinan Cultural Park 卑南文化公園

If you're interested in local art, then the Taitung Railway Art Village shouldn't be **overlooked**. The Taitung government **converted** several of the city's old railway station buildings into exhibition halls for local artists. The end result is a comfortable space that mixes modern art with local history.

There are so many things to see in Hualien and Taitung. They are also noted for their hot springs resources. Zhiben Hot Springs 知本溫泉 in Taitung County is one of the most famous hot springs in Taiwan. It is a **sodium bicarbonate** spring and the temperature of the water can reach as high as 85°C.

Zhiben Hot Springs 知本溫泉

Taiwan's east coast offers cultural experiences as well as natural resources. You can also head for one of the offshore islands, Green Island or Lanyu (**Orchid** Island), from here. You will never be bored when visiting the east coast of Taiwan! Just be sure to go slow and take it easy!

Quiz

1. Which national park is located in Hualien?
2. What are some famous foods and snacks of Hualien?
3. What are some attractions in Taitung?
4. What kind of spring is Zhiben Hot Springs?

🎧92 Conversation

Ethan	Are there any museums in these cities so I can learn more about indigenous culture?
Laura	Taitung has the National Museum of Prehistory and its Peinan Cultural Park. They can teach you a lot about ancient history and culture in Taiwan.
Ethan	What are other attractions in Taitung?
Laura	You can take a look at the Taitung Railway Art Village.
Ethan	Does it have exhibits of Taiwan's railway culture?
Laura	Not really. The 80-year-old Taitung Railway Station has been turned into an exhibition hall for local artists.
Ethan	Sounds interesting! Are there lots of natural spots on the east coast?

The Beauty of Taroko National Park

Changchun (Eternal Spring) Shrine
長春祠

Shakadang	Yanzikou (Swallow Grotto)	Baiyang Waterfall	Cimu Bridge
砂卡礑	燕子口	白楊瀑布	慈母橋

Laura	Of course! Don't miss out on the well-known Taroko National Park in Hualien. You'll be **astonished** by its beauty!
Ethan	What does the word "Taroko" mean? It doesn't sounds like Mandarin.
Laura	It comes from the local indigenous tribe's language. "Taroko" means "magnificent and beautiful."
Ethan	Is it a place of hills and sea like Kenting National Park?
Laura	Not at all. Because the Liwu River 立霧溪 cuts through the park, it is full of gorges and cliffs.
Ethan	I bet the east coast **reserves** much of Taiwan's natural scenery. It must be a good place for visitors to get to know the natural Taiwan.
Laura	That's right. That's because the east coast is less industrialized. It is very popular among Taiwanese people as a vacation destination. So, it can be crowded on weekends and holidays!

Common Food in Hualien and Taitung

Mochi, Hualien
花蓮麻糬

by Jingguo

Peeled chili, Hualien
花蓮剝皮辣椒

by Yuyu

Chihshang lunch box 池上飯包, Taitung
台東池上飯包

Steamed bun, Taitung
台東包子

Sugar apples, Taitung
台東釋迦

Lilies, Taitung
台東金針花

Practice

01 | Listening

Listen to the statements and match each one with the picture that best illustrates it.

1. _____
2. _____
3. _____

cc by Benson KC Fang

a Taroko National Park   **b** Stone carving   **c** Peinan Cultural Park

02 | Reading

Match the two halves of the sentences.

1. Buying jade from Hualien is _____
2. The local indigenous tribe named Hualien's famous gorge "Taroko," _____
3. For Taiwanese people, the east coast is a popular place to take a vacation _____
4. The east coast is a good place to start if you _____

(a) want to visit one of Taiwan's outlying islands.
(b) which means "magnificent and beautiful."
(c) because it's much less industrialized than the west coast.
(d) better for the environment than buying marble.

03 | Writing

Complete the sentences using the fragments given.

(a) sodium bicarbonate   **(b) natural beauty**   **(c) local history**
(d) take it easy   **(e) exhibition hall**   **(f) return astonished**

1. The east coast is the perfect place to go in order to experience Taiwan's _____, and many people _____ by what they've seen.
2. The hot springs at Zhiben are some of Taiwan's most famous and draw visitors from all over island with their _____ waters.
3. The Railway Art Village is a special kind of _____ , which mixes modern art with _____.
4. The most important thing to remember while travelling the east coast is to go slow and _____!

Attractions in Taitung

Dulan Mountain

都蘭山

Zhinzen Mountain

金針山

Chu Lu Ranch

初鹿牧場

Water Running Up

水往上流

Sansiantai

三仙台

Baisha Bay

白沙灣

The First Light of Millennium Year Memorial Park

千禧曙光紀念園區

National Museum of Prehistory

台灣史前文化博物館

Human Rights Memorial Park, Green Island

綠島人權紀念公園

Zhaori Hot Springs, Green Island

綠島朝日溫泉

The East Coast— Indigenous Culture

東海岸：原住民文化

Word Bank

celebrate **v.** 慶祝
rite of passage
　人生大事及其慶祝儀式
grand **a.** 盛大的

millet **n.** 小米
emphasize **v.** 強調
hunt **v.** 狩獵
pottery **n.** 陶器
concrete **a.** 混凝土

Austronesian **a.** 南島的
bridge **v.** 把……連結起來
prehistory **n.** 史前時代史
apparently **adv.** 顯然地
basement **n.** 地下室

🎧94 Reading Passage

One of the main attractions of Hualien and Taitung is its indigenous culture that has managed to survive to this day. Unfortunately, there is also a danger that increasing tourism may end up destroying this culture.

There are several indigenous tribes on the east coast: the Paiwan, Amis, Puyuma, Bunun, Rukai, Sakizaya, Kavalan, Truku, and Tao. These ancient cultures are still influencing life to this day. Their festivals are widely **celebrated**, especially the Amis Harvest Festival that is held in July or August. It is celebrated in each Amis village and represents a cultural **rite of passage** where boys become men. The festival itself is a **grand** celebration with dancing, singing, drinking, and eating.

To this day, the Bunun people still speak their own language. They were the only tribe to develop a calendar using icons. They too celebrate a harvest festival that includes the singing of the Pasibutbut

The Bunun Tribe 布農族 ↓

The Tao Tribe 達悟族 ↑

or "prayer for an abundant **millet** harvest." The Bunun also hold an "ear-shooting ceremony" which **emphasizes** the teaching of **hunting** skills to young boys. It takes place every April.

The Tao live on Lanyu 蘭嶼 (Orchid Island) in Taitung County. They are well known for their carved boats, silver items, and **pottery**. Since they live on an island that is fairly far away from Taiwan, it has been easier for their culture to survive. However, they are still affected by the modern world. The Tao people traditionally lived in underground houses until the government started a program to move them into **concrete** houses in the 1960s. Unfortunately, a concrete house is not as well suited to the climate as the traditional houses. Traditional houses were very good at keeping out the heat in summer and the cold in winter.

There are many ways to enjoy indigenous culture on the east coast. Hualien is home to an indigenous woodcarving museum. In Taitung, there is the annual Festival of **Austronesian** Cultures which tries to **bridge** the gap between local indigenous and Austronesian cultures. There is also the National Museum of **Prehistory** in Taitung. This museum explores early indigenous and Taiwanese prehistory before the arrival of the Europeans and Chinese.

Quiz

1. What is one of the main attractions of Hualien and Taitung?
2. Which indigenous tribes live on the east coast?
3. Describe the Bunun culture.
4. Describe the Tao culture.

95

Conversation

Laura	The east coast is home to many indigenous people. If you're lucky, you might get to experience one of their festivals.
Ethan	Tell me a little about the indigenous people. Do they have much cultural influence in Taiwan?
Laura	Well, they definitely have more of a presence on the east coast. So much so that indigenous festivals are often celebrated in schools there.
Ethan	I imagine that these festivals include coming-of-age rites.
Laura	Yes. It is interesting to note that there are several tribes on the east coast. The Bunun were the only tribe to develop icons for marking important events during the year.
Ethan	Really? You mean that they had their own calendar?
Laura	That's right. They had their own calendar long before the Chinese came. They also have a festival with a strange name. It's called the "ear-shooting ceremony."
Ethan	Does it have any particular purpose?
Laura	It's meant to teach boys how to become good hunters.
Ethan	Are there any islands off the east coast? I want to go on a boat ride.
Laura	Yes, Lanyu is in Taitung County. That is where the Tao tribe is from.
Ethan	A tribe that lives on a small island? That must mean that their culture has survived better than some of the tribes from the main island.
Laura	That was true for a long time, but it's hard to fight off the modern world nowadays.
Ethan	You're right of course. It's the same story everywhere now.
Laura	Yeah. **Apparently** the government even made the Tao people live in concrete houses above ground. They traditionally lived in underground houses that were better suited to the climate.
Ethan	I bet they have deep **basements**! They must have managed to keep that part of their culture.

INDIGENOUS CULTURE
of the East Coast

cc by Benson KC Fang

House of the Puyuma tribe
卑南族房屋

cc by Benson KC Fang

The place where Puyuma males aged 12 to 18 years traditionally received training in warring skills and tribal legends.
卑南族文化傳統中 12 到 18 歲的男子接受戰鬥訓練與與認識部落神話的地方。

cc by Benson KC Fang

House of the Paiwan tribe
排灣族房屋

cc by Benson KC Fang

A monument on which is written "the origins of the Amis"
寫有「阿美族發源地」之紀念碑

cc by A-giâu

Traditional houses (right) and modern buildings (left) of the Tao people
達悟族傳統住屋（右）與現代建築（左）

Practice

96

01 | Listening

Listen to the short dialogues and fill in the blanks.

1. A: Why is the Amis Cultural Festival so important to the _____ people in the Amis tribe?

    B: It's important to them because the festival is a _____ rite of _____ where the boys of the tribe become men.

2. A: I know that the Tao live on _____ Island, which is quite far from Taiwan. But what else are they well known for?

    B: They're best known for making beautiful _____ boats, as well as pottery and items made from _____.

3. A: How difficult is it for Taiwan's indigenous people to keep their culture and traditions _____?

    B: It can be difficult, especially with increased _____. But there are also plenty of festivals and _____ which try to help keep indigenous culture alive.

4. A: Why did the Tao people use to build their houses _____?

    B: Because those houses were much better at _____ the heat out in summer and the cold out in winter.

02 | Reading

Complete the following short paragraph by choosing which of the given sentences should go in each blank space.

The culture and traditions of the Tao people are probably the best preserved of all Taiwan's indigenous tribes. **1)** _____ While Taiwan's other indigenous tribes were being influenced by Chinese immigrants and Japanese invaders, the Tao remained largely undisturbed. **2)** _____ These houses were designed to be especially suited to the climate of Orchid Island. They would keep out the heat in summer and the cold in winter. However, in the 1960s, the Taiwanese government decided to move the Tao into concrete houses. But despite this, the Tao still have a very strong attachment to their island life and culture. **3)** _____

(a) This is because the Tao live on Orchid Island, which is far away from the main island of Taiwan.

(b) For example, until 1960, the Tao people still lived in their traditional underground houses.

(c) They still build beautiful carved boats and celebrate the Flying Fish Festival each year.

03 | Writing

Unscramble the sentences.

1. ear-shooting / good / Bunun's / The / boys / teaches / to / ceremony / young / be / how / hunters

   _____

   _____

2. The / developed / tribe / Bunun / a / for / calendar / during / events / marking / important / year / the

   _____

   _____

3. can / visiting / about / National / indigenous / history / You / by / the / Museum / learn / Prehistory / of

   _____

   _____

4. cultures / still / indigenous / this / The / of / Taiwan's / people / ancient / influence / day / life / to

   _____

   _____

Traditional indigenous houses were built mainly from straw, bamboo or stone. 傳統原住民居屋以稻草、竹子或石頭搭建而成。

Indigenous Arts and Architecture

Indigenous wood carving 原住民木雕

Indigenous tapestry 原住民織錦

Indigenous ornaments 原住民飾物

TRANSLATION

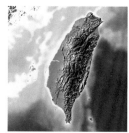

1 地理

Page 6 ## Reading Passage

台灣是個島嶼，位處東亞，介於菲律賓與日本之間。台灣鄰近中國大陸，中隔台灣海峽，海峽最寬處僅 220 公里，最窄處則為 130 公里。台灣的面積是 36,000 平方公里，與荷蘭相當。台灣由一個大島與其他幾個小島組成，這些小島包含澎湖群島、蘭嶼和綠島。一般人提到「台灣」時，指的通常是這些島嶼的總稱，其中最主要的大島又名福爾摩沙。將近五百年前，葡萄牙水手最早發現這個島嶼時，把這個島取名為「福爾摩沙」，意思就是「美麗的島嶼」。

台灣島山巒起伏，玉山高達 3,952 公尺，是東北亞第一高峰。貫穿全島中央的則是綿長的中央山脈，全長 340 公里。台灣的山路風景優美，但駕駛經過這些路段時，要小心謹慎，因為有時會有土崩的狀況出現。

台灣的山川大都林木蓊鬱，林中有許多有趣的動植物。其中蛇類就有很多種，有些蛇有毒，但遊客不容易看見這些蛇。要想瞥見台灣黑熊的身影也很困難，比較容易看見的，應該是鳥類。許多鳥類是台灣特有品種，例如台灣藍鵲現在經常現身觀光景點，牠的尾巴有 40 公分之長。這些美麗的鳥類因為不怕人，遊客可能有機會遇到牠們。

數百萬年前，台灣有許多活火山，而今都成了死火山或休火山，但是它們仍然是台灣溫泉的來源！台灣大多數溫泉都在山裡，這裡的人也喜歡泡溫泉，因為這對健康有益。

Page 8 ## Conversation

伊森 為我介紹一下台灣吧。

蘿拉 台灣是位於中國大陸外海的一座島嶼，位於東亞。

伊森 台灣有多大？

蘿拉 有 36,000 平方公里，大約和荷蘭一樣大。

伊森 為什麼台灣被稱為「福爾摩沙」？

蘿拉 大約五百年前，葡萄牙水手發現台灣時，就這樣稱呼它，這個詞在葡萄牙文中是「美麗」的意思。

伊森 台灣現在還美麗嗎？我聽說那裡現在有很多工廠。

蘿拉 山脈還是很美麗，平地也還有很多好地方。大多數工廠都集中在某些區域。你去過陽明山國家公園嗎？

伊森 我一直想找時間去，聽說那裡很漂亮。

蘿拉 是很漂亮。我們運氣很好，那裡離台北很近。

伊森 說說看那裡是什麼樣子。

蘿拉 呃，那是個可以親近大自然的地方，很適合走走，有很多步道和遊客中心。

伊森 聽說還有幾個溫泉，水永遠是熱的。

蘿拉 沒錯，幾百萬年前，這個區域到處都是火山，現在這些火山沒什麼在活動了，但仍然可以提供熱泉。記得在週一到週五去體驗看看喔。

伊森 我猜最好要早點去是吧。這些溫泉會很多人，對不對？

蘿拉 對，陽明山的溫泉總是吸引許多遊客前往。

2 氣候

中譯

Page 12 Reading Passage

台灣的氣候炎熱多雨，適合植物生長，每年雨量約 2,500 公釐。北回歸線橫越台灣中部，因此台灣的氣候一半是熱帶，一半是亞熱帶。

台灣夏季酷熱，溫度很少低於攝氏 30 度，濕度又高，適合享受涼爽的山林和各種水上活動。遊客最好戴上帽子和太陽眼鏡，同時塗上防曬油。

七月到十月是颱風季。每年這個時期都會有好幾個颱風侵襲台灣，或者從旁經過。颱風的風雨可能很強烈，引發嚴重的災害。颱風來襲時，遊客必須遠離沿岸地區與外島。

春天的天氣通常溫和宜人，是走訪城市郊外景點，欣賞各種花朵的好時機。

梅雨季從五月中開始，直到六月為止。在這段時間裡，很容易碰上陣雨，遊客在這段雨季期間一定要帶傘。

秋天天氣涼爽，濕度開始下降，就和春天一樣舒適宜人。

台灣雖然天氣炎熱，但北部地區到了冬季依然會很冷，尤其台灣一些高山的峰頂更是寒冷，不但溫度可能降至攝氏零下十度，地面還會積雪。人們會到合歡山等山上賞雪。所以，如果你要在這個季節造訪台灣，別忘了帶些禦寒的衣物。

台灣有很多事物值得欣賞，幾乎每個城市都有美麗的廟宇和擁擠的夜市。城市外圍就是鄉間，通常美麗壯觀，有優美的山川與森林。台灣還有好幾個花季，每個花季都獨具特色，非常吸睛。每年在櫻花盛開的季節，人們往往闔家前往阿里山、陽明山、烏來等地，欣賞這些雅緻的粉紅色花朵。

Page 14 Conversation

伊森	天氣呢？很熱，對嗎？
蘿拉	大多數時候很熱，但不一定都如此。北部冬天往往很冷，有時候更是凍得不得了。
伊森	真的嗎？那人們在家裡如何取暖？
蘿拉	台灣很少有中央暖氣系統，因為天氣冷的時間並不長。一般人通常就用小小的電暖爐，然後多穿一點衣服。
伊森	那山上呢？冬天山上有多冷？
蘿拉	冬天山上可能出奇的冷。我有個朋友有一年到山上露營，他說那裡的溫度降到攝氏零下 10 度。
伊森	我想台灣人應該很珍惜山林，那些山林給了他們遠離塵囂、享受自然的大好機會。
蘿拉	沒錯，山區變得越來越重要。人們會到山上避暑，欣賞美麗的花朵與植物。
伊森	所以夏天真的很熱囉！
蘿拉	絕對是。夏天還會有颱風。
伊森	颱風的風雨會很大嗎？
蘿拉	對，颱風通常伴隨著強風豪雨，破壞力可能十分強大。

台灣天氣二三事

Page 17

台灣橫跨熱帶與亞熱帶，一般氣候以亞熱帶為主，同時濕度也高。北台灣屬於亞熱帶氣候，平均溫度約攝氏 22 度；南台灣屬於熱帶氣候，平均溫度為攝氏 24 度。

六月到八月是夏季，氣溫可高達攝氏 38 度。冬季雖然相對溫和，高山地區仍有可能結霜或降雪。雨季期間，特別是五、六月時，午後經常有短暫的大雨。

3 人口

Page 18 Reading Passage

　　台灣人口超過兩千三百萬。由於台灣多山，大部分人口都居住在西部的平原，每平方公里的人口超過640人。台北無疑是全台人口密度最高的城市，居民超過680萬。

　　原住民是島上最早的居民，現在官方認定的有14族。原住民約佔台灣人口的2%，阿美族是最大的一族，大多居住在花蓮和台東。原住民多從事農耕和捕魚為生。

　　外來族群開始抵達台灣並試圖掌權之後，台灣的原住民就再也無法享有平靜的生活。1623年，荷蘭人接管了台灣，統治全島大部分地區，直到1661年中國第一批大軍抵達為止。這支軍隊由中國將領「國姓爺」鄭成功率領，當時他和中國滿清皇帝對抗，逃至台灣。他抵達台灣後不久便過世，隨後又有許多中國人移居台灣，大多數原住民於是逃往山上，但還是有些原住民留在平地，留下來的人就和中國移民通婚，因此大多數台灣人實際上都是不同族群的混血。

　　如今，台灣人口包括台灣人（又稱福佬人或河洛人）、外省人和原住民。還有一群來自中國的客家人，努力保存自己的語言和習俗。大多數外省人都是在1949年時，由於中國的政治問題來到台灣。目前台灣人口有70%是福佬人或河洛人，14%是客家人，14%是外省人，還有2%是原住民，也有很多外國人住在台灣。

原住民文化

Page 23

在台灣的文化多元性中，原住民文化佔有重要角色。雖遭政府打壓多年，原住民文化仍在1990年代開始復甦，如今原住民歌手阿妹等十分走紅，不過要近距離接觸傳統原住民文化依然不易。況且原住民文化本身更是包羅萬象，島上共有14個官方認定的原住民種族，各有其獨特習俗與生活方式。

還好台灣有許多博物館與村落可供民眾瞭解原住民文化。原住民社區遍佈全台各地，多數位於花蓮、台東和南投縣。原住民的藝術多元，包含音樂、舞蹈、木雕、編織和籃簍手工藝。甚至也有原住民的電視台。

Page 20 Conversation

伊森　這裡人真的很多。

蘿拉　是啊，城市都生氣蓬勃。

伊森　我就連到鄉下或山上，有時都很難找到完全安靜的地方。

蘿拉　我明白你的意思。有時你爬山要到山上看夕陽，卻發現山頂上早就有一群人在等你！

伊森　台灣有多少人？

蘿拉　超過兩千三百萬人，而且大都住在西部的平原。

伊森　我想原住民是此地最早的居民吧？

蘿拉　對，就和美國一樣。

伊森　有沒有人知道他們是從哪裡來的？

蘿拉　沒人說得準，但有人認為他們來自中國南部。

伊森　那中國人又是何時來到台灣的？

蘿拉　大約四百年前，但他們得先驅逐荷蘭統治者。

伊森　當時征戰不休嗎？

蘿拉　對，他們征戰數月，有一位人稱國姓爺的中國將領，想把台灣當作反清基地，因此驅逐了荷蘭人。

伊森　「客家」是什麼意思？

蘿拉　客家是中國的族群之一，遍佈全中國。

伊森　他們人口很多嗎？

蘿拉　他們約佔台灣人口的14%。客家人以勤奮聞名，還有獨特的習俗與飲食。

伊森　那河佬人呢？

蘿拉　他們約佔人口的70%。

4 語言

Page 24 Reading Passage

台灣由於族群眾多，使用的語言也有很多種，不過國語是唯一的官方語言，政府刊物與活動都使用國語，兒童在學校上課也用國語教學。過去幾年來，其他語言也開始受到重視，80%的人會説台灣話（又稱福建話或閩南話），電視和廣播也有台語節目。台灣話最早源自福建省的一種語言。大多數的台灣人都會講國語和台灣話，有些人還會講客家話，但是這樣的人越來越少了，於是出現一些設法挽救客家話的措施，例如2003年推出了客家電視台。

華語和歐洲語言差異很大，華語有聲調，因此非華人很難正確發音。同一個字可能依聲調的不同而有好幾個意思，例如「ma」這個音，隨著聲調的不同，就至少有四種不同的意義。正因如此，西方人學華語更是費心。另外由於中國方言差異很大，只會説客家話的人也聽不懂閩南語。好在幾乎每個人都會講國語，再不然靠書面文字也可以彼此溝通。國字是每個人都會學的，如果聽不懂彼此的話，也可以寫下來用看的，因為各種方言都使用相同的文字。

日本曾經統治台灣50年，因此有些老一輩的人會説日語。很多年輕人也開始在大學時學習日語。日語在台灣僅次於英語，是第二受歡迎的外語。

大多數台灣人都懂一點英語，聽不懂英語的人通常也看得懂。很多老一輩的台灣人一生沒有機會學英語，年輕一輩的卻從小學開始就要學英語。政府努力建立英語環境，例如在台灣各處設立英語路標，現在外國人要在城市和鄉鎮中找路就容易多了。

客家文化

Page 27

台灣約有450萬客家人，他們最早來自中國大陸，擁有自己的語言、習俗和飲食。部分客家人聚居於南部美濃等小村落，保存著客家文化。

客家人向以勤奮和節儉聞名，客家飲食也和其他中國飲食有點不同。薑絲炒大腸、客家小炒、福菜湯等都是有名的客家菜。

油紙傘是傳統的客家手工藝品之一。美濃所產的油紙傘是以竹子製作傘骨，尤其使用孟宗竹。接著再上柿子油並繪製圖畫，完成一把油紙傘。

Page 26 Conversation

伊森 國姓爺打敗荷蘭人之後，中國人開始湧入台灣，就因為這樣，國語才成為此地官方的語言嗎？

蘿拉 不完全是，國語的普及要比這晚很多。但你要知道，國語不是台灣唯一使用的語言喔。

伊森 還有其他的語言嗎？我是説，除了原住民的語言之外？

蘿拉 有，還有台灣話和客家話。

伊森 這些語言和國語很像嗎？

蘿拉 他們有關係，但差異性還是很大。

伊森 不過台灣官方的語言還是國語，對不對？

蘿拉 對，大多數人都説國語，不過南部人更常講台灣話。

伊森 台灣話源自哪裡？

蘿拉 台灣話和中國南部福建省所使用的語言很像。

伊森 電視和廣播節目會使用這些語言嗎？

蘿拉 會，使用台灣話的節目越來越多，還有客家電視台也成立了，越來越多人開始對這些語言感興趣。

伊森 還有其他的語言嗎？

蘿拉 呃，不算正式的語言，不過有不少人還會説日語。

伊森 聽説多半是老一輩的人是嗎？

蘿拉 沒錯，也有些年輕人在大學裡選修日語，甚至去日本留學。

伊森 英語一定是最受歡迎的外語，對不對？

蘿拉 我不知道英語算不算「受歡迎」，但這裡很多人都知道他們必須學英語。

許多台灣人都會講台灣話（閩南話），台語的發音非常接近中國古音，許多中國古音雖已隨著時間消失，但仍保存於台語中。也因此出現了一個有趣的現象，當我們用台語來朗讀唐詩或宋詞時，發音會發現比用國語朗讀來得正確！ Page 29

5 宗教

Page 30 Reading Passage

Page 32 Conversation

佛教與道教是台灣兩大宗教。還有一種重要哲學稱為儒家思想，和一些民間信仰一樣廣泛流傳。多數台灣人的信仰都是結合了宗教與民間信仰。

傳統民間宗教綜合了神、鬼、祖先與命運之說。有些台灣人在做出重大決定之前，會先問過算命師，也是時有所聞。台灣各地有不同風俗和信仰，以漁村為例，那裡的居民多拜媽祖，祂是民間流傳的海上之神；其他地區的人可能會拜觀音（慈悲之神）或關羽（中國的名將）。另一方面，農民則愛拜土地公，因為祂對豐收之事更為瞭解。台灣的民間信仰真是多采多姿，種類繁多。

台灣許多本地的節慶都是宗教活動，其中一個最大的宗教節慶就是每年農曆三月的「國際媽祖文化節」。信眾的隊伍從台中大甲鎮瀾宮出發，沿路停駐於台灣中、南部好幾個不同的地點，九天後才回到鎮瀾宮。媽祖的神像、其他神像、舞龍舞獅、表演團體，再加上沿路燃放的鞭炮，形成了聲勢驚人、活潑熱鬧的遊行隊伍，路旁則擠滿了圍觀的群眾。來自全國各地的信徒跟著隊伍前進，希望能獲得媽祖的庇佑。

另外一個重要的本地節慶和城隍爺有關。舉例而言，每年農曆五月都會慶祝台北城隍爺的壽誕，其他神明的壽誕也會在廟前慶祝，有各種表演活動，吸引眾多民眾圍觀。

伊森	為我介紹一下台灣的宗教吧。
蘿拉	佛教和道教是台灣最重要的宗教，不過大多數台灣人的信仰都結合了這兩種宗教，他們也信奉儒家思想和其他民間信仰。
伊森	信仰不同的人能夠和諧共處，真是好事。
蘿拉	的確如此。台灣人也很重視祭祖。
伊森	你們真的拜好多神啊！你可以為我介紹一下這裡的民間信仰嗎？
蘿拉	舉例而言，台灣人普遍會拜海神媽祖，有很多關於媽祖的傳說，據說祂是漁民和水手的守護神，民眾通常會拜媽祖，祈求好運和平安。
伊森	這裡的民間信仰很生動有趣！
蘿拉	對啊，你可能聽說過八家將吧。
伊森	他們是誰？
蘿拉	是來自地獄的八位使者，負責逮捕或驅逐邪靈和鬼怪，同時也是主神的護法，因此你經常可以看到他們擔任朝聖隊伍的前導。
伊森	那中國人又是何時來到台灣的？
蘿拉	大約四百年前，但他們得先驅逐荷蘭統治者。
伊森	當時征戰不休嗎？
蘿拉	對，他們征戰數月，有一名人稱國姓爺的中國將領，想把台灣當作反清基地，因此驅逐了荷蘭人。
伊森	「客家」是什麼意思？
蘿拉	客家是中國的族群之一，遍佈全中國。
伊森	他們人口很多嗎？
蘿拉	他們約佔台灣人口的14%。客家人以勤奮聞名，還有獨特的習俗與飲食。
伊森	那河佬人呢？
蘿拉	他們約佔人口的70%。

6 廟宇

中譯

Page 38 Reading Passage

第一次到台灣的人首先會注意到的事物之一，就是廟宇，這些廟宇和西方的教堂很不一樣。台灣各地都可以看到廟宇，從大廟到小廟都有。許多廟宇的裝飾繽紛華麗，非常引人注目。

你可能廟宇各式各樣都有，讓人眼花撩亂，這是因為所有廟宇都依照「風水」的特殊規則而建造。當然，每個廟宇有其本身獨特的故事與所供奉神明的歷史，建造方式也會有些許差異。

有些廟宇總是香火鼎盛，例如台北的龍山寺，不管你什麼時候去，都有人在那裡點香拜拜。所謂「拜拜」指的是雙手合十，經常手上也會握香，然後向神壇鞠躬。這個儀式可以用來拜神或拜祖先。

道廟通常由地方人士管理，外觀往往比佛寺更加華麗。道廟不只是宗教場所，更是社區中心，作為民眾聚會的場所，甚至在廟外的廣場還會有老人下棋或打牌。

台灣許多民間藝術都和廟宇息息相關，例如音樂、舞蹈、布袋戲和歌仔戲。廟宇的建築和裝飾為各類文化表演增添活力，非但如此，雕刻作為裝飾的神像、龍、神靈和其他各種傳奇珍獸，以及這些作品背後饒富教育意義的故事內容等，本身就是一種傳統的藝術形式。碰上農曆新年等重要的節日，民眾經常會到廟裡觀賞表演，有些廟甚至一連兩週，每天都推出不同的表演。

Page 40 Conversation

伊森	台灣有好多廟！
蘿拉	對，這是本地的一大特色。
伊森	那我們今天要去哪一間？
蘿拉	我要帶你去龍山寺，那是台北人潮最多的寺廟之一。
伊森	我幾乎無法分辨佛寺和道廟。
蘿拉	一般而言，台灣的廟宇都有點混在一起了，一間廟往往同時供奉佛教、道教、民間信仰等的各種神明，龍山寺也不例外。

（伊森和蘿拉抵達龍山寺）

伊森	這是什麼時候建造的？
蘿拉	龍山寺建於兩百多年前，已正式列為二級古蹟，是很典型的寺廟建築。
伊森	哇，你看這建築四處古老的雕刻！
蘿拉	龍山寺曾經幾度毀壞又重建，這裡有全台灣僅見的銅鑄蟠龍檐柱。來，我帶你去看。
伊森	這真是驚人！我可以照相嗎？
蘿拉	可以啊。
伊森	這裡拜的是哪些神明？
蘿拉	有大慈大悲的、掌管海事的、文的，還有其他神明。你可能會對管婚姻的有興趣喔，據說祂可以幫助人們找到合適的另一半！
伊森	難怪這裡每天都擠滿了信徒！我也要向月下老人許願，說不定我會在這裡找到真命天女！

7 儒家思想

Page 48 Reading Passage

　　儒家思想、佛教與道教對台灣社會的影響都很大。即使到了今天，一般人的生活與想法依然遵循著儒家思想。孔子是一位偉大的哲學家，他生逢戰時，最大的目標就是希望有朝一日人們能和平共處。他希望改變人與人之間的關係，以創造一個和平的社會。

　　他認為每個人在社會上都有自己的位置。社會上各個部分都要能夠和諧共處，這點很重要。人人須盡本分，舉例而言，父親要照顧家庭，兒子要敬愛父母，並在父母年老時照顧他們。

　　孔子也是個偉大的教師。他相信人只要接受教育，行事自然能夠正確。「有教無類」是孔子強烈的信念。

　　如今，很多城市都建有孔廟，以向這位中國偉大的老師致敬。台北孔廟最早建於 1879 年，並於 1925 年重建，這是北台灣最大的孔廟，每年的 9 月 28 日都會舉行祭孔大典，以慶祝孔子的壽誕。傳統的舞蹈和儀式均遵照古禮進行。

　　台北孔廟擁有典型的傳統中國式建築，有莊嚴的大門、宏偉的紅柱、華麗的屋頂、五彩繽紛的繪畫與裝飾。大門前半月形的池塘稱為泮池，是根據風水原則所設計，同時也具有防火和調節溫度的功能。

　　工業化始於西方，因此西方國家也是最早被工業衝擊傳統習俗的地方。西方過去一直是農業社會，各國均有其傳統的價值觀，與世界各地其他農業社會差不多。家庭、國家與宗教都是很重要的觀念。人民也會服從於更高的權威當局，例如教會（天主教）和政府。然而，隨著科學進步，人們對宗教開始產生懷疑，宗教在人們生活中的重要性逐漸降低。

Page 50 Conversation

伊森　我上星期去拜訪了一個台灣家庭，他們把祖父母照顧得真好。

蘿拉　那是因為儒家思想對台灣社會還是有很大的影響。

伊森　可是我想台灣的生活應該也在改變吧！

蘿拉　沒錯。台灣老一輩的人過去通常和長子同住，但過去幾年來，這種狀況漸漸改變。

伊森　什麼樣的改變呢？

蘿拉　有時家中沒有長子，可能就由女兒來照顧他們。非但如此，現在有時女兒的工作反而比較好。

伊森　所以孔子認為家庭很重要，對不對？

蘿拉　沒錯。不過別忘了，他對社會也有整體的規劃。

伊森　什麼樣的規劃？

蘿拉　呃，他認為社會上人人都有其應遵循的行為方式，人人都該適得其所。

伊森　對中國人來說，他一定是一位偉大的導師。

蘿拉　沒錯，他是公認中國歷史上最偉大的老師。你在很多中國和台灣的城市裡，都可以看到孔廟。

伊森　我有機會在台北參觀到孔廟嗎？

蘿拉　有啊，台北的孔廟很大，建築和裝飾都依照傳統，並遵循風水的原則。你一定會大開眼界！

Page 53

現在更強調個人自由，孩子一到 18 歲便早早離家，他們對工作自主、對信仰自主，更自己決定結婚對象，200 年前是不可能這樣的。

有些人認為這些改變是壞事，因為家庭的聯結變弱，人們不重視倫理。現代人的生活變得孤獨，壓力更大，人們不懂得互相尊重。

但也有人認為自由使社會更加美好，人們可以做自己的主人，生活也更加快樂。也許，解決之道便是在傳統思維與現代之間取得一個自在的平衡點。

8 傳統藝術

Page 54 Reading Passage

　　台灣有許多傳統藝術，主要可以分為兩大類傳統工藝與表演藝術。傳統工藝包括繪畫、雕刻、編織與製陶等，表演藝術則包括民俗音樂、民俗舞蹈、民俗歌劇、雜技表演與布袋戲等。

　　台灣人雖然不再過著傳統的生活，卻仍對傳統工藝深感興趣。如果你到台灣人的家裡，可能會看到傳統繪畫或木雕作品，也可能會看到傳統陶器，像是杯子、碟子、茶壺等，這些都兼具實用與裝飾的功能。

　　台灣本土就有許多不同的歌劇，台灣的「歌仔戲」實際上結合了幾種不同的中國歌劇，再融入原住民音樂與台灣民謠。歌仔戲常在廟外演出，有時整個社區的民眾都會到戶外來欣賞。近年來，有許多嶄新形式的歌仔戲被創作出來，這是一種仍在蓬勃發展的藝術。

　　這種表演藝術描繪的通常是人們的生活與民間傳說，往往與民間宗教相關，而且會在許多宗教場合演出。

　　其他的民俗藝術，例如紙雕，在現代的台灣還是存在。比較需要技巧的藝術，例如布袋戲、舞獅、民俗歌劇和雜技等則是越來越少了。政府和各種社區團體致力於保存這些民俗藝術，就像其他國家一樣，台灣政府也大力提倡各種節慶，以協助振興文化活動。有些這類節慶辦得十分成功。

　　傳統藝術的創新在存續上扮演了重要的角色。例如，台灣布袋戲利用嶄新的燈光科技，創造絢爛奪目的視覺效果，布袋戲偶的服裝多采多姿，旨在吸引年輕人。

Page 56 Conversation

伊森　我注意到台灣有許多傳統民俗藝術。

蘿拉　的確是，包括繪畫、雕刻、舞蹈等等。

伊森　可是有了電視、網路各種新的玩意之後，是不是有些傳統藝術形式逐漸式微？

蘿拉　有些藝術形式，例如布袋戲和舞獅，確實是面臨了危機。但是過去幾年來，城市裡的文化生活已經有很大的改善。

伊森　這裡指的是當代文化，像是劇場、音樂等等，對不對？

蘿拉　我指的是所有的文化，包括中國的和西方的、傳統的和現代的。

伊森　有沒有人採取什麼措施來挽救逐漸消失的藝術形式？

蘿拉　政府試著在台灣各地提倡藝術活動，包括建造許多文化中心、支持新興的藝術團體，並且舉辦許多節慶和展覽等。

伊森　我聽說傳統藝術也接納了現代化的想法，有了嶄新的面貌。

蘿拉　沒錯，表演藝術運用現代科技，甚至取材於西方，以吸引年輕人，其中有些十分成功呢。

伊森　我還聽說許多有趣的節慶活動和傳統藝術有關。

蘿拉　對啊，舉例而言，東海岸宜蘭的國際童玩節就是。

9 傳統與現代建築

過去數十年來，台灣的建築歷經很大的變化。五十年前，台灣許多建築都有特殊的中國式屋頂，如今台灣人多半住在西式的大樓裡。台灣人口太多，沒辦法每個人都一直住在中國式建築裡，不過，有好幾棟公共建築仍然採用老式的中國風，其中一棟就是台北火車站。

傳統建築遵循風水的原則。風水是中國古老的信仰，說明建築的方位如何安排。如果建築的方位和山、水和各種地形的相對關係，沒有調整正確，就可能招來厄運。有時在建造住家、寺廟、甚至是公共或商業建築時，也會用到風水。

日本曾經統治台灣五十年，因此台灣各處依然可見到日本的影響，這點不足為奇。舉例而言，台灣的語言仍使用很多日語詞彙，日本料理在台灣很受歡迎，而且很多人學習日語，偶爾也可以看到老式的日式建築。如果你對這類建築有興趣，國父史蹟紀念館、一滴水紀念館和臨濟護國禪寺都很適合走訪。

荷蘭人和西班牙人抵達台灣的時間比日本更早，他們在十六世紀初期入侵台灣，留下了一些歷史建築。荷蘭式建築的主要特色就是使用磚塊，台南安平古堡外圍的幾座紅磚牆，就是一個例子。另外還有一些英式建築，像是位於高雄、1865 年所建的打狗英國領事館。

伊森	西化對台灣社會有什麼影響？
蘿拉	這裡有很多漢堡店，也看得到西方電影、電視節目等，可是這種現象在其他地方也有，不只在台灣。
伊森	我看到台北有一些日式建築，這是因為日本曾經統治過台灣一段很長的時間嗎？
蘿拉	台灣被日本統治了五十年，有很多建築都是在那個時候蓋的，有些當代的建築也採取日式風格。
伊森	我聽說過新北市的「一滴水紀念館」，我知道那是日式建築。
蘿拉	對，那是在 2009 年搬到淡水、重新組建的，2011 年正式對外開放。
伊森	還有哪些日式建築是值得一看的？
蘿拉	桃園的忠烈祠、台北的臨濟護國禪寺和宜蘭設治紀念館，都是典型的日式建築。
伊森	我還知道有一些荷蘭、西班牙和英國所留下的古蹟。
蘿拉	對啊，台灣的殖民背景導致各式各樣的建築風格與特色。

10 傳統禮儀

Reading Passage
Page 66

　　台灣和其他國家一樣，有自己的傳統風俗與禮儀。很多外國人對這些風俗禮儀並不熟悉，因此有時無意之間冒犯了台灣人卻不自知，這對外國人來說有時難以理解。在台灣社會，讓人感覺良好總是好事，因此台灣人經常會稱讚自己的客人，並對自己和所提供的食品很謙卑，這種時而讚美時而謙卑的狀況，有時會讓外國人摸不著頭腦。舉例而言，台灣人可能會稱讚一位外國人國語說得很好，但當被問起的時候，他們又會說自己的英文很爛，就算他們的英文講得比外國客人的國語還要好，他們也會這樣說！

　　台灣人在處理工作和日常生活上的種種問題時，常仰賴深厚的人際關係。舉例而言，一個正在找工作的人，如果剛好有朋友認識想找新員工的人，那麼他找到工作的機會就比較大。這是因為台灣人十分重視家庭和朋友，「互相幫助」是台灣社會的美德。即使不認識你，台灣人往往也樂意提供協助，所以如果你在台灣迷路的話，儘管請台灣人幫你，你會發現他們都很友善。

　　最後，千萬不要和台灣人討論死亡這件事，談論死亡可能會帶來厄運，這也是台灣觀光客到美國去玩時，往往會略過「死亡谷」的原因。

Conversation
Page 68

伊森　在這裡好像很容易在無意之間犯錯，傷害到別人。

蘿拉　你只要熟悉這裡的禮儀就可以了。台灣人對人總是以禮相待，所以你和人說話時也不要太直接。

伊森　所以我應該小心，不要讓人在大家面前出糗。

蘿拉　沒錯。

伊森　喔，還有，為什麼就算我只會說「你好」，大家還是覺得我的中文很好？

蘿拉　一般而言，我們很重視讓人感覺良好，所以讚美在台灣社會是很常見的。

伊森　所以他們只是想讓我開心而已？

蘿拉　他們只是希望表現得有禮貌。可是誰知道呢？說不定你的「你好」真的是他們聽過說得最好的。

伊森　不太可能啦，不過他們能這樣說真好。

蘿拉　你也可以考慮讚美他人呀。雖然台灣人很謙虛，大家偶爾還是喜歡聽些好話。

伊森　這是當然的啊，我剛好可以練習國語！

蘿拉　你也可以交些台灣朋友。這裡的人相信人際關係很重要，有需要時應該互相支持。

伊森　我正學習在這裡建立人際關係，很多台灣人都很友善，就算不認識我，也很樂意幫我，很不錯！

西方習俗
Page 69

過去兩百年來，西方生活有了相當的改變。與 50 年前相比，現代社會也大大不同了。1950 年代時，人們謹言慎行，希望給人彬彬有禮的好印象。例如，男士和陌生人交談時都會舉帽。男人表現紳士風度，會幫女士開門，讓女士優先。公車上如果有女士或身障人士，男士都會讓座。

西方社會和台灣一樣，到別人家拜訪時應該帶個小禮物，像是鮮花、巧克力、酒等等。現在儘管大家都不講究收禮了，準備個小禮物還是一個貼心的舉動。

為何習慣改變了？其中一個原因可能是女權運動。女人希望男女平等，所以她們自立自強，開始自己開門。1960 年代的嘻皮運動也有影響，那時人們主張獲得更多自由，不再遵守死板的禮儀，行為也不再那麼正式。然而，說「請」和「謝謝」仍是西方重視的禮貌。

台灣的飲酒文化
Page 71

飲酒在台灣文化中佔有一席之地，朋友聚會時，許多台灣人總是要小酌啤酒或紅酒，放鬆一下。

喝紅酒或啤酒時，台灣人喜歡互相敬酒，慶祝最近發生的好事。他們喜歡一口氣喝完一杯，展現義氣。

台灣人會先說「乾杯！」再一飲而盡。「乾杯」就是英文裡的「cheers」。還有一句說法是「杯底不可養金魚」，所以，杯底可別剩下沒喝完的酒。

時至今日，「乾杯」文化逐漸消失。政府呼籲「開車不喝酒、喝酒不開車」，因此當今比較流行的作法是敬酒淺嘗即止，不要求對方乾杯了。

11 送禮的文化

Page 72 **Reading Passage**

送禮在台灣是一種普遍的行為，很多場合都會送禮，諸如結婚、搬家、生子、開幕等等，通常都會收到朋友送的禮物。

過農曆新年時，兒童和長輩會收到錢作為禮物，新婚夫婦在結婚當日也會收到禮金。就連參加喪禮，也必須致贈慰問金給往生者家屬。在台灣，除非是喪禮，否則送錢時一定會放在紅包袋裡，喪禮時則改用白包。在台灣文化裡，紅色代表好運，白色則和死亡有關。送禮時，外國人要小心金額的數字不能包括4，因為這個數字代表了死亡。在國語裡，「死」和「四」發音相似，因此，台灣人通常會避開這個數字。即使是今日，台灣的醫院仍然沒有四樓，如果有也沒有人願意住進去。

在台灣，到別人家裡拜訪帶伴手禮是很重要的，水果、巧克力、蛋糕、酒之類的東西，都可以當作禮物。送禮時要用雙手奉上，並且謙虛表示這份禮物只是一點心意。如果對方收下禮物後先放著，沒有馬上打開，不要感到訝異，台灣人通常不會當著送禮的人面前把禮物打開，你在收禮時最好也這樣做。如果你送的是貴重禮物，最好慎重包裝。台灣人認為送禮是個人誠意的表現，不過，時鐘和刀子千萬不能當作禮物送給台灣人，時鐘因為「鐘」的發音在國語裡與表示死亡的「終」字相同，而刀子則代表「斷情」。

台灣人進到別人家裡一定會脫鞋。主人或許會說不用脫鞋，可是你最好還是把鞋子脫下來。之後主人通常會遞上一雙拖鞋讓你在屋裡穿。

還有一個實用的小提醒，每次到別人家裡，一定要先向年紀最長的長輩打招呼，以示尊敬。

> 台灣人生子時會收到賀禮，而在小孩出生滿月時，父母親則要準備禮物致贈親友，慶祝孩子的「彌月」。Page 77彌月禮通常是蛋糕、紅蛋和油飯加雞腿，象徵著吉利、繁衍子孫和將來可以升官。

Page 74 **Conversation**

（伊森和蘿拉在麵包店買鳳梨酥）

伊森　你買這麼多鳳梨酥要幹什麼？

蘿拉　我明天要去我阿姨家，想帶一些禮物去，鳳梨酥再適合不過了。

伊森　台灣文化也包含送禮嗎？

蘿拉　對啊，台灣社會很重視送禮，蛋糕、水果、酒和茶葉等，都可以當作禮物，有些場合我們還會送錢呢。

伊森　什麼場合會送錢？

蘿拉　大多是婚宴和喪禮，我們會送錢表示祝福或安慰。

伊森　我聽說農曆過年有送裝了錢的紅包給小孩和老人的習俗。

蘿拉　一點都不錯。

伊森　那妳明天要參加的是什麼樣的場合？

蘿拉　哈，什麼都不是！我只是很久沒去看我阿姨了，我想在台灣社會，探訪親朋好友的時候，送禮就是一種禮貌和誠意，尤其是到長輩家裡，沒帶禮物是很失禮的。

伊森　我懂了。所以什麼東西都可以當作禮物嗎？

蘿拉　不，不。送時鐘、刀子、鞋子和雨傘就很不妥。時鐘暗示送終，刀子是斷情啊。

伊森　那鞋子和雨傘怎麼會有負面的意義？

蘿拉　鞋子暗示請人離開，雨傘則代表分離，因為國語發音裡，「傘」等同「散」。

伊森　哇！還好你有告訴我，我選禮物的時候可要格外小心才是。

12 飲食文化

Page 78 **Reading Passage**

　　台灣文化十分重視飲食。台灣人連見面都要問「吃飽了沒？」遊客一到台灣映入眼簾的其中一件事，恐怕就是好多的餐廳和小吃店，而且路邊和傳統夜市還有好多小吃攤。

　　在台灣，你可以吃到各種不同的中國菜，台灣自己也有百年而來的本土料理。你甚至可以吃到傳統原住民飲食。現代化的台灣城市有許多餐廳，提供來自全球各地的異國料理，包括印度料理、泰國料理、韓國料理、法國料理和墨西哥餐廳等等。在台北，你甚至可以品嚐希臘、伊朗和俄羅斯料理。當然，美國速食到處都有，也有台式的速食餐廳，這些餐廳對外國人而言有點怪怪的，卻又有一種說不上來的熟悉感。

　　台灣的主食是米飯和麵食。既然米飯如此重要，台灣有很多美味的米飯料理也不足為奇。台灣人早餐有時會吃稀飯配醬菜，稀飯在英文裡稱為「congee」。晚餐的話，台灣一般家庭會吃煮熟的白米飯，配上蔬菜和魚、肉。有時台灣人的晚餐會弄得像辦桌一樣豐盛呢！

　　麵食是台灣的另一種主食。麵條因為容易攜帶與保存，所以自古便是中國很普遍的食物。「湯麵」和「牛肉麵」是台灣兩種很受歡迎的麵點。牛肉麵愈來愈受歡迎。過去人們不吃牛肉，因為牛是重要的農耕動物，不過大多數台灣人現在都吃牛肉了。

　　還有一些麵是用米磨成的粉做的，夜市和路旁的小吃攤都有美味的炒米粉和米粉湯。

Page 80 **Conversation**

伊森	你知道嗎？很奇怪喔，一般人不是問我吃過了沒，就是問我吃飽了沒，這是為什麼？
蘿拉	這只是禮貌而已啊。你也知道，台灣人熱愛美食，中國甚至有句古老的諺語說：「民以食為天。」
伊森	從全世界有這麼多美味的中國餐廳看來，這點倒是不足為奇。可是他們為什麼這麼熱衷飲食呢？
蘿拉	有人說，這是因為古代的中國人老是擔心食物不夠，會餓到家人。
伊森	我想當時有很多飢荒吧？
蘿拉	飢荒、乾旱與戰爭，這些災難都會讓人挨餓，米飯因此變得非常重要。
伊森	聽來就像愛爾蘭人對馬鈴薯的感覺一樣，馬鈴薯是他們的主食，只要有馬鈴薯就能活下去。
蘿拉	沒錯，中國人也把米飯、食物和富裕聯想在一起，有錢人想吃多少就能吃多少。
伊森	所以，即使今天台灣人人有飯吃，這種想法還是沒有變。
蘿拉	沒錯。
伊森	台灣人每一餐都會吃飯嗎？
蘿拉	多多少少都會，不管他們是在家吃飯，還是出去參加豪華宴會，白飯幾乎配什麼都好吃。
伊森	那所有主要的中國菜在台灣都有嗎？
蘿拉	對啊，所以說這裡是饕客的天堂！大都市裡還有各式各樣的外國料理，像是泰國菜、越南菜、法國菜，還有印尼菜。

13 受歡迎的食物與飲料

Page 84 **Reading Passage**

很多台灣菜和中國菜很像，只是多半有一種獨特的台灣味，各式各樣的點心像是綠豆糕、花生和茶葉蛋都是這樣。

觀光客最愛的一項美食就是「小籠包」了。小籠包來自中國東部，又稱為「湯包」，因為用豬肉、青蔥和薑製成的內餡湯汁飽滿而得名。有賣小籠包的餐廳，通常也會有其他的中國菜，像是酸辣湯、雞湯、包子、炒飯等等。

台灣人喜歡在當地的啤酒屋吃飯。炒蛤蜊（加上辣椒和九層塔）、三杯雞（使用麻油、米酒加醬油調製的醬料）、烤魚、烤魷魚、炒青菜和炸豆腐，都是常見的菜色。一般人下班後常和三五好友或同事到這類餐廳聚餐，吃吃熱炒和點心，配上一杯又一杯的冰啤酒！

台灣人愛喝飲料。台灣的環境很適合茶樹生長，因此，台灣茶的品質非常好。說到茶，台灣人喜歡喝中式綠茶或烏龍茶，不加牛奶也不加糖。烏龍茶應該稱得上是台灣最受歡迎的茶。台灣茶最出名的就是凍頂烏龍茶和包種茶。台灣人經常在飯後喝點茶，或者一邊喝茶一邊配點心。台灣處處都有茶館，這裡的氣氛輕鬆，你可以好好享受一壺熱熱的烏龍茶到一杯冰涼的檸檬紅茶什麼的。台北的貓空以茶坊林立聞名，到了週末總是擠滿了當地人和外來的遊客。

Page 86 **Conversation**

伊森　形容一下台灣料理吧？

蘿拉　和你在西方習慣吃的那種中國菜很不一樣喔。

伊森　我想台灣有這麼多不同的族群，一定也有不同的料理方式。

蘿拉　對啊，原住民、客家人和台灣人都有自己的料理，他們也會互相影響。

伊森　有什麼特別的料理嗎？

蘿拉　每個城市都有自己特有的飲食。不過如果你指的是普遍都有的話，也有很多喔，像牛肉麵就到處都吃得到。

伊森　那人家一直說的那個小籠包是什麼？

蘿拉　那是包了豬肉和青蔥的小包子，內餡非常多汁，一咬下去，裡面的湯汁就會流出來，所以又稱為「湯包」。

伊森　台灣人喜歡喝些什麼？

蘿拉　台灣人最愛喝烏龍茶了。茶已經不只是飲料，也是文化的一部份。

伊森　台灣本身有產茶嗎？

蘿拉　台灣茶的品質可稱得上全球數一數二的，這裡多山的地形和氣候很適合種茶。

14 夜市

中譯

Page 90 Reading Passage

　　台灣另一個特色就是夜市，幾乎每個城市都有。夜市裡販賣各式各樣的台灣小吃。

　　走訪台灣夜市一趟絕不能錯過臭豆腐。豆腐是用豆漿做的，就像乳酪是用牛奶做的一樣。豆腐是中國料理常用的食材。有時走在台灣的街道上，你會聞到一股怪味，外國人常常搞不清楚這是什麼味道。臭豆腐的味道會這麼重，是因為豆腐在發酵的滷汁裡浸泡了好個月，滷汁裡還加了一些原料像是青菜和肉等等。

　　蚵仔煎是另一道遊客必吃的台灣小吃，是把蛋、蚵仔加蔬菜用平底鍋煎成的，吃的時候還要淋上特製醬料。有時蚵仔也可以換成蝦仁或花枝。

　　在甜點方面，一般人喜歡吃刨冰，上面加上水果和各種可口的配料。西式冰淇淋在台灣各處也都找得到。

　　泡沫紅茶是一種台灣獨特的飲料，現在世界各地都越來越受歡迎。這種茶最早是在 1980 年代，在台灣中部的台中發明的，當時有位茶店老闆決定要試試新產品，他把水果糖漿、茶和其他原料混合在一起，無意間便創造出一種好喝的新飲料。從那時起，泡沫紅茶開始普及到全世界，而且每天都有人研製出創新的泡沫紅茶，其中最知名的一個例子，就是用紅茶、牛奶和很有嚼勁的粉圓所做成的珍珠奶茶。

　　如果你還吃得下，就來根烤香腸吧！在台灣，烤香腸可以和香菜、大蒜或乳酪一起吃，台灣人還發明出一種「大腸包小腸」，在糯米腸裡面包一條香腸來吃。

Page 92 Conversation

伊森	台灣好多夜市，幾乎每個城市至少都有一個夜市！
蘿拉	對啊，我喜歡去那些賣美味小吃的攤子，那才是真正的美食！
伊森	逛夜市真的是很有趣的體驗！可以吃到各種台灣小吃，還可以買買衣服和手工藝品之類的。
蘿拉	你吃過臭豆腐沒？
伊森	沒有，光是那道就足夠讓我退避三舍了。那東西到底是怎麼做的？
蘿拉	他們把豆腐和一些蔬菜、肉類等，一起浸泡在發酵的滷汁裡，泡上一、兩個月，那味道很重，你不覺得嗎？
伊森	對我來說有點太重了，尤其他們在炸的時候！
蘿拉	有人很愛，有人不愛啊。對了，你在台灣的時候一定要喝珍珠奶茶，那可是這裡的一絕啊。
伊森	我已經喝過了，我超愛的，裡面的粉圓很有嚼勁，真是一種偉大的發明！
蘿拉	那是在台中發明的，現在全世界都很受歡迎。
伊森	那「大腸包小腸」是什麼？
蘿拉	很像美國的熱狗，他們把烤香腸包在一根更大的糯米腸裡，那名稱就是這樣來的。
伊森	原來如此。如果我在台灣待上一、兩個月，一定會變胖！
蘿拉	哈哈，還有，逛夜市逛到最後別忘了來一盤刨冰！

台灣的 7-11、全家便利商店、夜市和一些店家都開到很晚，方便大家隨時買東西。台灣人習慣了這樣的購物方式，因此到了國外發現商店早早關門，總是很訝異。

台灣觀光客到了國外，想在晚餐後逛逛街，往往發現除了部分超市之外，其他商店一過六點就打烊了。有時候購物的習慣是隨著當地氣候而有所不同，例如澳洲南部氣候炎熱，如果晚上還要逛夜市可叫人吃不消。

Page 95

多數西方國家的傳統市場也只有白天營業，如果你在國外想要好好地逛個街，還是選在週末吧。而像德國的萊比錫，商店在週四晚上會開到八點左右。美國比較多 24 小時營業的商店，其他英語國家則對營業時間多所限制，所以出國前，別忘了打聽一下當地商店的營業時間。

有些國家連餐廳都早早關門，還好，總是可以找到幾家營業到深夜的中國餐廳！

15 農曆新年

Page 100 Reading Passage

　　台灣每年有好幾個節日。對觀光客而言，節慶不但好玩，而且是一種多采多姿的經驗；對台灣人而言，節日在現代社會有助於文化保存，還能放一天假！大多數台灣節慶都是看農曆，因此每年的國曆日期都不一樣。

　　農曆一月一日開始是中國新年，這是漢文化裡的大日子。這天的國曆日期通常落在一月底到二月初。農曆新年間，家人無論相隔多遠，都會團聚吃飯、相伴。傳統上會準備一些特別的食物，像是糯米和年糕。「年糕」這個詞的中文發音像是「年年高升」，因此，人們吃年糕祈求來年一切順利。有些年糕做成甜的，因為中國人相信「吃甜甜，過好年」。

　　農曆新年有一些特殊的習俗。人們在過年期間不喜歡掃地，因為不想把好運跟著灰塵一起掃掉，而且要等到大年初五才會把垃圾拿出去倒。

　　台灣人在過年期間會拜訪親戚，也要拜財神。大年初二時，已婚夫婦要回娘家，和妻子的父母一起過年。

　　此時，家家戶戶裝飾著花卉，並且貼上寫著賀辭的紅聯。紅色被認為是幸運的顏色，白色則代表死亡。因此過年期間會多用紅色，而避用白色。小孩和長輩通常會收到裝了壓歲錢的紅包。最後，大家會放鞭炮，全家人一起上街觀賞舞獅之類的傳統民俗活動。

　　如今已沒有那麼多人相信好運厄運的老觀念，不過大家還是喜歡遵循這些老傳統。

準備大過年囉！

農曆新年前幾週，台灣人就會開始採買食物、點心和裝飾品。家家戶戶會用紅色的糖果盒裝著糖果和餅乾，在過年期間招待所有來訪的親朋好友。

台北的迪化街是購買食物點心（或稱「辦年貨」）最有名的地方。這裡稱為「年貨大街」，每當農曆新年將近時，迪化街總是人潮擁擠。這裡有賣許多食材，像是乾香菇、蝦米、米粉等，也可以買得到中藥、蜜餞和茶葉。

農曆的除夕，人人都會返鄉與家人共進晚餐，也就是所謂的「團圓飯」。

Page 104

大家通常會準備一些象徵福氣的食物，例如過年要吃魚，才能「年年有餘」，國語的「魚」發音同「餘」（盈餘）。

過年還要吃餃子，因為餃子形狀像古代的元寶，是財富的象徵。

Page 102 Conversation

蘿拉	看來你要在台灣過農曆年了！
伊森	對啊，我可興奮了。而且我爸媽剛才打電話來說他們要過來呢。
蘿拉	太好了！我很想見見他們。
伊森	那當然，我很高興介紹你給他們認識。他們想看看我新認識的所有台灣和外國朋友。
蘿拉	你家還有其他人要來嗎？
伊森	我哥正在考慮和我爸媽一起來，我想，帶他們去參加台灣傳統的節慶活動，應該會很好玩。
蘿拉	這個主意真不錯！你知道他們打算待多久嗎？
伊森	他們說可以待三個星期。
蘿拉	嗯，如果他們可以待上三個星期，就有機會過完整個農曆新年！
伊森	我瞭解新年在台灣是很重要的闔家團圓時刻。
蘿拉	沒錯，就像西方過新年一樣，全家人都要團聚。大家會聊聊天、享用美食，享受彼此陪伴的時光。
伊森	那所有商店都會關門嗎？我很擔心他們來到台灣的時候，發現沒有一家店是開著的。
蘿拉	不一定。事實上在農曆過年前一週，大家忙著辦年貨，所以商店都會開，趁此機會多賺點錢。
伊森	那他們就可以看到街上所有傳統的裝飾，說不定還能看到舞獅！
蘿拉	過年期間有些商店和餐廳不會營業。不過風景區一定擠滿人，街上和廟宇會舉辦各種慶祝活動。

中國新年的特色

- 中國新年期間會放鞭炮來趕走邪惡的「年獸」，據說年獸害怕巨大的聲響，也怕紅色，所以過年期間人們都要屋子前面掛紅燈籠。
- 過年期間人們會在家裡掛著象徵好運的結繩吊飾等裝飾品。
- 大家在過年期間喜歡穿紅色衣服，因為紅色代表好運。
- 黑瓜子是過年常吃的零嘴。

Page 105

16 元宵節和端午節

中譯

Page 106 Reading Passage

元宵節

農曆新年的初十五是元宵節,這一天也被稱為第二個新年或「小過年」,代表了整個新年假期的尾聲。在元宵節期間,大家會製作精美的燈籠。過去只有有錢人才有能力製作這些燈籠,但是現在,人人都能做燈籠,這些燈籠也成為一種藝術。有些燈籠會做成動物、人物或物品的形狀,甚至有台北 101 大樓形狀的燈籠!這種傳統已經成功地現代化。

如今,台灣各地都會舉辦公開活動來慶祝元宵節,會運用現代科技營造精彩的燈光秀。

按照傳統,元宵節晚上要吃甜的元宵,元宵是糯米做的,有時包了甜餡,煮成甜湯來吃。猜謎語是另一個傳統活動。

端午節

另一個重要的節日是端午節,端午節在農曆的五月初五,國曆通常在六月。在古代的中國,夏季是個疾病頻傳的季節,這個節日就是為了驅逐會讓人生病的邪靈。隨著時間演變,後來又加上了屈原的故事。屈原是古代的大臣與詩人,因君主不肯採納他的諫言,便投江而死。他投江後,漁夫爭相救他,雖然時機太慢,救不了他的命,但漁夫仍然把粽子投入江中,以免魚群啃噬屈原的屍體。這就是端午節要划龍舟、吃粽子等傳統的由來。

划龍舟的隊伍來自各種不同的組織,有學生、商人,也有軍人。龍舟船身裝飾華麗,十分漂亮。這個節日不只在台灣很受歡迎,現在世界各地都有龍舟隊前來參賽,慶祝這個獨特的節日。

平溪天燈節
Page 109

新北市平溪的天燈節和台南的鹽水蜂炮,是元宵節的兩個重要慶祝活動。

平溪天燈節一年舉辦一次,大家會把自己的新年新希望寫在紙天燈上,讓天燈升空,年輕人尤其愛放天燈。

不過節日結束之後,紙天燈的殘骸落地往往污染環境,內含火焰的燈籠落地時甚至可能引起火災,因此今日已不再那麼推廣這項活動。

Page 108 Conversation

伊森	什麼是元宵節?
蘿拉	農曆年後的第一次滿月就是,那是新年節慶活動一個很好的結尾。
伊森	那天有什麼有趣的活動嗎?
蘿拉	你可以去體驗一下台北的燈會,從 1990 年開始,這個燈會就很有名,十分現代化,燈光秀好驚人。
伊森	聽來不錯。
蘿拉	另一個元宵節的特殊活動是台南的鹽水蜂炮節,不過那有點危險,蜂炮直接射入人群中,所以你得穿上厚厚的衣服,然後戴上安全帽。
伊森	喔,那聽來很危險,我看還是算了。
蘿拉	如果你的家人喜歡運動,或許應該在六月的時候來看端午節。
伊森	那是紀念什麼河神的節日嗎?
蘿拉	不是,是紀念古代的一位詩人屈原,他投江自盡。
伊森	他為什麼要這樣做?
蘿拉	他想給國君一些忠告,以拯救他的國家,但國君不聽他的諫言。
伊森	那為什麼叫龍舟節?有某種比賽嗎?
蘿拉	對啊,選手們會比賽划龍舟,這項傳統源自漁夫爭著搶救屈原,龍舟都裝飾得很漂亮,而且這個節日在全世界各地都很受歡迎。

鹽水蜂炮
Page 111

元宵節還有另一項瘋狂的放炮活動,是在台南舉辦的鹽水蜂炮節。主辦單位將炮竹和沖天炮射向群眾引爆,產生的聲光效果令人嘆為觀止。即便具有危險性,世界各地仍有人前來體驗這項刺激萬分的活動。參加者必須戴安全帽並且穿著防護衣。即便如此,民眾受傷的情形仍然一再發生,主辦單位仍在不斷改良炮竹的材料,以降低危險性。

17 鬼月與中秋節

Page 112 Reading Passage

鬼月

　　台灣人相信鬼魂每年會離開陰間一個月。為了確保這些鬼魂開開心心、別來找他們麻煩,台灣人在「鬼月」會遵守某些傳統。這個節日是在農曆的 7 月。家人在鬼月會祭拜祖先的鬼魂。他們也會在戶外擺設祭品,讓路過的「餓鬼」享用。台灣人也會焚燒特別印製的紙錢,好讓祖先在來世過得舒服。總而言之,鬼月被視為是一年中不吉利的時候。因為這樣,大家會避免在這個月裡結婚、搬家或開店。靠近水邊也是不可以的,因為遊魂可能會把你拖下去當替死鬼,好為他們換取投胎的機會。

中秋節

　　一年中最後一個重要節日是「月亮節」,也就是「中秋節」。這個節日是農曆的 8 月 15 日。在月圓這一夜,闔家齊聚吃「月餅」和文旦。這個節日是為了向月亮致敬,因此全家人會一起賞月。

　　中國和台灣流傳著各種關於月亮的傳說。西方人可能會談論月亮上的男人,台灣人則會提到一位名叫嫦娥的女子或是玉兔。長久以來,人們就流行在中秋節時以月餅致贈親朋好友。傳統的月餅是以蛋黃和麵粉做成,然而,現在的月餅則有多種口味,像是杏仁、巧克力和鳳梨口味。甚至還有包冰淇淋的呢!

Page 115
民間流傳著許多關於月亮的傳說,在中國神話中,有個名為嫦娥的女子與她丈夫后羿的故事。

嫦娥與后羿原是神仙,一日,玉皇大帝的十個兒子化為十個太陽,猛烈照射地球,人民苦不堪言。后羿擅長射箭,射下九日為民除害。玉皇大帝痛失九個兒子,一怒之下便將后羿與嫦娥貶入凡間。

后羿為尋求長生不老而向西王母求取靈藥,西王母也給了他長生不老之藥,唯獨這藥是兩人份,后羿和嫦娥必須一人服用一半。但是嫦娥卻大意吞服了全部的藥,身子變得輕飄飄的往上升,一直飄到月球上才停下來。她在月球上碰到一隻名為玉兔的兔子,玉兔住在月亮上搗藥,於是嫦娥就和玉兔互相作伴。

Page 114 Conversation

伊森	嗯,我不知道。我的家人也不是那麼熱愛運動。
蘿拉	如果他們想看看在全台都有,而且很中國的活動,他們可以在「鬼月」的時候來。
伊森	你在說什麼?
蘿拉	他們不避諱厄運這種東西吧?
伊森	不會,他們不太迷信。
蘿拉	他們膽子夠大吧?
伊森	他們不怕鬼、厄運、怪獸之類的東西。你為什麼這樣問?
蘿拉	中國人相信鬼門每年開一次,讓鬼魂出來透透氣。
伊森	所以,你所說的鬼魂、厄運,就是指這個啊。那大家鬼月都做什麼?
蘿拉	沒多少事可以做,鬼月是個不吉利的時候。
伊森	我猜猜看,大家不會想要結婚或買房子。
蘿拉	沒錯。大家不會做像結婚或開店這樣的大事。但是,他們會在準備食物放在戶外,這樣,鬼魂就不會來煩他們。
伊森	我家人可能不會愛聽這樣的鬼故事!
蘿拉	如果他們要避開這段時間,中秋節來也很有意思。
伊森	我聽說這是個闔家團圓的日子。
蘿拉	沒錯。家人團聚、吃月餅和文旦。大家通常會在戶外烤肉,一邊欣賞美麗的滿月。

Page 117
中秋節也是團圓節,全國在農曆 8 月 15 日都會放假一天,讓每個人都能回家與家人相聚一天。

台灣人喜歡一邊賞著月圓一邊烤肉。傳統上並沒有在中秋夜和家人或朋友烤肉的習俗,不過這項活動在今日卻非常受歡迎。

18 地方慶典

中譯

Page 118 Reading Passage

除了像春節和元宵節這樣的傳統節日外，台灣還有很多原住民和當代文化的慶典。在政府的推廣下，特殊產業如木雕等也開始受到歡迎。與產業相關的活動包括了三義木雕藝術節和新竹市國際玻璃藝術節。

台灣的當代文化活動很多元，台灣國際藝術節和春吶是這類活動的代表。台灣國際藝術節開始於 2009 年，邀來台灣及全球頂尖的表演者、製作人、演員和作曲家，演出舞蹈、音樂和戲劇。藝術節在台北的國家戲劇院和國家音樂廳進行，通常為期一個半個月。

春吶每年 4 月在墾丁舉行，最早是由兩位住在台灣的美國人於 1995 年首次舉辦，現在已是台灣最大型的音樂節。數百個表演團體和表演者聚集在南台灣，展現他們對音樂的熱情與才華，另有小販兜售手工藝品、衣服和小吃。這是台灣最令人興奮的活動之一。

如果你的行程會經過有原住民聚落的地區，如東海岸，運氣好的話可以看到原住民的慶典儀式。對原住民部落而言，豐年祭尤其重要，他們藉此感謝祖靈和部落的神祇賜予他們食物。阿美族、魯凱族和排灣族都會舉行這項傳統的慶典，而歌唱與舞蹈是慶典的核心。然而，豐年祭不只是感謝豐收而已，也是部落成員團聚的日子，有時還會舉行成年禮。

Page 120 Conversation

伊森　如果我要帶我爸媽和哥哥去參加文化活動，有什麼好的選擇？

蘿拉　有很多。你可以帶他們去參加日月潭花火音樂節，這在每年的 10 月舉行。

伊森　所以說，會有很多歌手和樂團在湖邊表演囉？

蘿拉　是啊，還不只這樣喔。晚上你可以欣賞煙火秀，還有交響樂團及歌仔戲的演出。

伊森　聽起來很好玩！

蘿拉　如果他們喜歡手工藝，你們可以去新北市鶯歌參加陶瓷嘉年華。

伊森　那是什麼活動？陶藝作品的展覽嗎？

蘿拉　會有很多商店和創作者販賣不同的陶藝產品，也會展出陶藝大師的傑作。而且，街道兩旁還有美食攤！

伊森　哇，聽起來真的很有意思！

蘿拉　你甚至可以自己做陶杯，帶回家當紀念。

19 台北：交通與博物館

Page 124 **Reading Passage**

　　廣義的來説，台北地區包括台北市和新北市（以前稱為台北縣）。台北是台灣的首都，有將近 700 萬人住在這裡。這是個日夜都充滿活動的城市，你永遠都可以在台北繁忙的街道上、夜市、公園和城市郊外的山區，找到事情做。在台北四處走走很方便，有計程車和公車可搭。台北的捷運系統也在快速發展，這套系統稱為大眾捷運或地鐵，在 1996 年啟用，仍在興建新路線和車站。台北捷運提供旅客多種觀光護照，有一日券、二日券、三日券和五日券。捷運上的廣播有四種語言，包括國語、台灣話、客家話和英語。此外，單車族可以帶著單車在特定的車站上下車。

　　台北有許多藝廊和博物館，當初蔣介石從中國撤退時，他和部屬帶走很多古代中國的藝術品，以便加以好好保存。雖然過程充滿危險，每件藝術品依然毫髮無傷地送到台灣。1940 年代晚期和 1950 年代初期，對台灣來説是艱困的時代，因此這些藝術品被安放了好幾年。不過，一等經濟開始起飛，政府就著手興建一所合適的博物館。國立故宮博物院在 1965 年開幕，此後就成了台北的主要景點。國立故宮博物院的館藏非常之多，因此每次只能展出其中一部分。有些藝術品長年展出，其他的在一小段時間後就被換下，並不時會舉行特展。翠玉白菜、肉形石和毛公鼎被稱為館方的「三寶」。

Page 126 **Conversation**

蘿拉	你覺得台北的生活如何？
伊森	這是個很有意思的地方，但每個人都很匆忙。台北有時候人好多。有時候，很難找到可以獨處的地方，但是換個角度想，你永遠不會覺得寂寞。
蘿拉	你喜歡博物館嗎？
伊森	我喜歡啊。我喜歡看以前的人怎麼生活。我也喜歡古畫、陶器、金屬品和其他種類的藝術品。
蘿拉	那你一定要去參觀國立故宮博物院，你絕對會愛上它！
伊森	它在哪裡？
蘿拉	在台北市北區的士林區。那裡展出 1940 年代為了保存從中國帶來的藝術品。
伊森	哇，聽起來要運送這些無價之寶，要冒很大的風險！
蘿拉	一點也沒錯。而且，在運到台灣之前，在中國境內就搬了好幾次。最後，每件作品都毫髮無傷地運到了這裡。
伊森	非常令人欽佩。館藏一定很豐富，館方不會一次展出全部的作品，對嗎？
蘿拉	不會，館藏實在太多了，館方只會展出一部分，其餘的則先收藏起來。展出作品會定期更換。
伊森	全都寫中文嗎？
蘿拉	不是，也有英文標示和導覽。
伊森	我還應該去看哪些博物館？
蘿拉	台北有不少。另一個值得去的地方是臺北市立美術館，展出台灣和國外藝術家的作品。
伊森	會展出當代藝術家的作品嗎？
蘿拉	嗯，那裡展的都是過去數百年來的藝術家。如果你想看比較新的作品，可以試試台北當代藝術館。

20 台北：熱門景點

Page 130
Reading Passage

台北有許多廟宇、博物館、老建築、有趣的商店和其他事物可看。這個城市結合了現代和傳統建築、中西方文化、綠意盎然的公園和摩天大樓、異國餐和本地夜市。

你第一個想看的景點可能就是中正紀念堂，它建於 1980 年，是為了紀念已故的中華民國總統，同時也是台北最迷人的公園之一。它以其傳統中國式圍牆和建築，座落在西式摩天大樓林立的市中心，讓人更加難忘。紀念園區裡有美麗的中國式花園景觀和水池，紀念堂裡則有一座故總統的大型雕像，由武裝軍人守衛著。裡面也有展覽廳，展出他的生平和擔任總統時的事蹟。在中正紀念堂兩旁的國家音樂廳和國家戲劇院，也推薦你去參觀。

台北另一個美麗的紀念園區是國父紀念館，這是為了紀念創建現代中國的孫中山先生所建，雖然其規模不如中正紀念堂，仍然很吸引人。你一走進園區，可能會立刻被紀念館雄偉的中式屋頂所吸引。館內有一座大型的孫中山先生雕像、紀念博物館和文化中心。你可以看到大家在這裡遛狗、慢跑、放風箏或只在園區裡散步。這裡的氣氛非常悠閒。

台北 101 大樓在 2004 年啟用，目前是全球第二高的建築物。大樓共有 101 層（508 公尺高），地下還有 5 層。大樓內的電梯不僅是全球速度最快的電梯，也採用某些全球最先進的科技建造。大樓裡有美味的餐廳、辦公區和一間購物中心。台北 101 的除夕煙火秀已是全球知名。

Page 132
Conversation

伊森　台北是這個國家的首都，一定有很多地方可看，對嗎？

蘿拉　沒錯。我想你一定已經去過中正紀念堂。

伊森　當然去過了。它就在台北市中心，而且園區非常美。我喜歡有士兵守衛雕像的紀念堂。等我爸媽來台灣時，那裡是我第一個要帶他們去的地方。

蘿拉　還有，別忘了帶他們去台北 101 大樓，那也是台北的一個重要地標。

伊森　從上面俯瞰台北一定很令人興奮。

蘿拉　是啊。台北 101 的觀景台在 89 樓，每天上午 9 時開放到晚上 10 時。你可以帶你爸媽去那裡看台北的夜景。

伊森　那裡有好吃的餐廳嗎？

蘿拉　101 大樓裡有些很棒的餐廳。

伊森　那太好了。有老建築物那類的景點可看嗎？我想他們可能也有興趣看看台北不同於現代化的一面。

蘿拉　我建議你去參觀林安泰古厝。那是一間保存下來的民宅，在 18 世紀末是個富商的宅第。原本在 1970 年代要把房子拆除，還好最後一刻被搶救下來。房子裡有漂亮的古董傢俱。

伊森　聽起來，台北有很多我爸媽可以去看的地方。

21 新竹與台中

cc by mingwangx

Page 138 Reading Passage

新竹

新竹是北台灣最古老的城市，也是台灣最重要的工業區之一。它有很多有趣的景點，而且從台北或台中都很容易到達。一些可看的景點包括新竹市立玻璃工藝博物館、十八尖山和城隍廟口夜市。新竹也是教育重鎮，國立交通大學（NCTU）就在這裡，交大被公認是台灣最好的理工大學之一。新竹的特色美食有米粉、貢丸湯和肉圓。

雖然新竹比台北小得多，但對台灣的經濟仍很重要，因為新竹有一座科學園區，數種高科技產業都集中在這裡。全台灣各地都有科學園區，包括台南和台中都有，高雄的也正在籌備當中。對遊客來說，這些科學園區帶來的好處顯而易見。越多科學園區代表有越多的外國員工，也就代表有越多美味的異國餐廳！

台中

台中是中台灣最大的城市，人口超過 200 萬，是僅次於台北和高雄的台灣第三大城市。台中市的文化豐富，有很多博物館和景點，也有多所知名的大專院校。雖然台中也是座大城市，但它的步調比起台北要緩和和悠閒得多。台中的周邊地區種植許多重要的農作物，例如香蕉、甘蔗和稻米。這些農作物會運往台中加工後，再送到其他地方。台中也有一些其他的重要工業，如機械、紡織和化學製品。

說到吃吃喝喝，來台中就對了。我們已經知道舉世聞名的泡沫紅茶就誕生於台中。然而「太陽餅」也是這裡的特產，太陽餅是一種包著麥芽內餡的甜糕餅。還有好多美食都起源於台中，如「雞腳凍」和「豐仁冰」。在台中的街上，你還可以找到「一心豆干」。台灣人來台中玩，常會買這些美食回家當伴手禮。

Page 140 Conversation

伊森	我聽說有個城市對台灣的科技很重要，它離台北近嗎？
蘿拉	有好幾個城市都以科學發展而聞名，但我想你指的是新竹，它在台北南方。
伊森	那裡有很多高科技人才嗎？
蘿拉	是的，新竹科學園區就在那裡，很像美國的矽谷。擁有科技背景的人多半都會去那裡找工作。
伊森	那裡也像其他城市有地方美食嗎？
蘿拉	當然有。如果你到城隍廟口夜市去，可以吃到好吃的米粉和貢丸湯。
伊森	我又開始流口水了！
蘿拉	在玩過新竹後，你也許想去台中。
伊森	台中在哪裡？
蘿拉	在新竹南方，是中台灣的最大城，也是台灣第三大城。
伊森	喔，我記得它是世界有名的泡沫紅茶的起源地。
蘿拉	沒錯。除此之外，還有一種出名的點心叫太陽餅。去台中玩的遊客通常會買這種餅回家分送家人和朋友。其他的美味點心如挫冰和豆干也很值得一試。
伊森	哇，我等不及要去了！

22 台中：熱門景點

cc by Jimmyarch81118

中譯

Page 144 Reading Passage

台中是個很適合欣賞傳統台灣文化的地方。如果你到民俗公園去，你可以體驗完整的傳統民俗活動，包括剪紙、竹編和傳統舞蹈。如果你是在節日時去，你會發現有更多活動在進行。民俗公園裡也有一座中國南方建築風格的房舍，和一間展出民俗藝術和古董的藝廊。如果你逛累了，可以到茶藝館休息，享受傳統的茶道。

如果你想暫時遠離城市的喧囂，那麼去高美濕地可能是不錯的主意。它是台灣僅存的幾個大型濕地之一，也是數種稀有鳥類如黑面琵鷺和唐白鷺的棲息地。如果你覺得賞鳥不夠刺激，別擔心，高美濕地裡還有很多事可以做。你可以去看當地的景點如風車或水壩，或沿木板人行步道及單車專用道探險。

對那些喜歡了解周遭世界的人來說，有國立自然科學博物館可去。這是台灣第一座科學博物館，以擁有 6 個場館而自豪，包括科學中心、生命科學廳和地球環境廳。館方也會舉辦特展，這樣遊客每次重遊都可以學到新東西。博物館內有 6 座不同的劇場，讓你可以觀賞 IMAX 或 3D 電影。

除了吃吃喝喝、接觸大自然之外，台中還有很多地方可去。東海大學的美麗校園很適合走走。此外，還有國立台灣美術館、豐樂雕塑公園和「茶街」精明一街，以及擁有藝術小店和主題咖啡館的東海藝術街。台中都會公園和逢甲夜市也不該錯過。台中有這麼多東西可以看，可能會讓人有點累但卻總是讓人興奮！

Page 146 Conversation

伊森 我記得你説過現在在台灣旅行很方便，那麼南下去台中要多久？

蘿拉 從台北搭火車或客運大約要 3 小時，但是，如果你搭高鐵只要大約 50 分鐘，起得夠早的話還可以一天來回。不過，説到台中，你知道那裡沒有捷運吧？你必須靠公車、計程車、單車或機車。

伊森 對我不是問題。

蘿拉 台中是個以教育和文化設施出名的城市，有很多可看、可做的活動。

伊森 有哪些？

蘿拉 有很多博物館，其中最有趣的一個是國立自然科學博物館，那裡有很多互動式的展覽。

伊森 嗯，學習是很好，但我比較想看影片。

蘿拉 國立自然科學博物館有自己的劇場喔！而且有 6 座。不同的劇場播放不同科學主題的影片。

伊森 除了博物館，還有什麼可看？

蘿拉 你可以去雕塑公園散散步，或去東海藝術街看它的咖啡館和小店。也可以去東海大學，它的校園非常地蒼翠美麗，比較像公園而不是學校！如果你去那裡，一定要去看路思義教堂，那是為了紀念 19 世紀一位名叫亨利·路思義的美國傳教士而建，教堂的外型非常獨特。

23 日月潭

Page 150 ## Reading Passage

在離台中不遠的地方，你會看到有名的日月潭。日月潭位於南投縣，是台灣最大的淡水湖。它是由兩個湖組合而成，一個形狀像太陽，另一個像月亮，因此名為日月潭。湖區及周邊地區非常美麗，而且全年氣候宜人。這裡是邵族人的故鄉，原住民會在這裡建立家園並不令人意外。現在，你可以在欣賞日月潭自然美景的同時，體驗原住民文化。

近年來，新建的飯店取代了舊有的旅館。人行步道、單車道和新的划船設施也相繼建造完畢。划船很受遊客喜愛，船隻可以在水社租借。遊客也可以探訪位在潭中央的拉魯島。如果你不喜歡一個人旅行，可以參加遊湖團體行程。大部分的行程都涵蓋了湖邊所有景點，有的還會加入賞鳥活動。你可以搭巴士，但有時會有點慢。其他的選擇包括租汽車或單車。

日月潭禁止游泳，只有在每年一次的日月潭國際萬人泳渡嘉年華時會開放。每年 9 月，來自全台各地的人會跳入湖中，努力游向對岸。當然，你得是游泳健將才能成功。

如果你想一窺從前台灣原住民的生活，那麼可以到九族文化村去。在這裡，你能了解原住民的傳統建築、民俗藝術、風俗習慣和部落舞蹈。這裡也提供遊客難得品嚐傳統原住民料理的機會。

日月潭四周還有其他有趣的景點，如孔雀園、原住民的德化社、慈恩塔和許多美麗的廟宇。

如果你是夏天來，還有機會看到邵族的滿月豐年祭，這項慶典會持續進行好幾天。

Page 152 ## Conversation

伊森 我真的好想去日月潭。每一本台灣旅遊手冊都提到這個美麗的湖泊。

蘿拉 是啊，只要你來台灣，一定要去日月潭，它是台灣最重要的景點之一。

伊森 為什麼叫做日月潭？

蘿拉 日月潭其實是由兩個湖泊組成的，一個形狀像太陽，另一個則是新月形。

伊森 真有意思！我猜，我在湖上應該可以划船之類的吧？

蘿拉 沒錯，沿著湖畔騎單車或散步也很棒。

伊森 是啊，我已經可以想像自己在湖邊騎著單車，一邊欣賞美麗的山林，也許還聽著鳥兒歌唱，度過美好的一天！但是，可以游泳嗎？

蘿拉 日月潭禁止游泳，除了年度泳渡嘉年華的時候。

伊森 你可以多說點關於這個嘉年華的事嗎？

蘿拉 每年，來自全台各地的上萬人都會聚集在那裡，游泳橫渡日月潭。

伊森 聽起來很刺激。

蘿拉 沒錯。如果你沒有那麼喜歡運動，你可以去探索原住民文化，那裡是邵族人的家鄉。

伊森 我可以在那裡過夜嗎？看起來，要欣賞風景，又想體驗當地文化，一天一定不夠。

蘿拉 當然可以，湖邊有許多很好的飯店。

台灣在 1999 年 9 月 21 日歷經一次芮氏規模 7.3 級的大地震，震央位於南投縣的集集。主震持續搖晃 102 秒，之後一個月內陸續發生 12,911 次的餘震，其中一次餘震規模強達芮氏 6.8 級。

Page 153 921 大地震重創全台灣，當時造成 2,415 人罹難，傷者達 11,305 人。許多建築物也在這次地震中倒塌。

全台飽受停電、交通通訊中斷之苦。來自世界各地的搜救隊伍協助尋找生還者，並且幫助災區重建。這是台灣自 1945 年以來最嚴重的一次震災。

24 台南：歷史

Page 156 Reading Passage

台南是一個歷史豐富的古老城市，位於南台灣，就在台中和高雄之間。台南人口超過 180 萬人，使它成為台灣第四大的城市。

在葡萄牙人發現台灣後，沒多久其他歐洲國家也得知了這個島嶼的存在，開始設法佔領。荷蘭人在現在的台南建立了一座堡壘（安平古堡）。後來一位名叫鄭成功（也稱為國姓爺）的明朝將領將荷蘭人逐出，並在此建立基地，以對抗那些想推翻明朝皇帝的勢力。不久，清朝打敗明朝，掌控了中國。大批中國移民湧入台南，這裡也就成了台灣最重要的城市。

因此，在台南可以看到老式的歐洲建築，十分難能可貴。安平古堡（原稱為熱蘭遮城）是由荷蘭人在 1624 年所建。雖然如今除了幾段磚牆外，看不到太多原先的堡壘遺跡，但日本人在原先堡壘所在之處，蓋了一些別具特色的建築。爬上高塔欣賞美麗的落日，光是如此就值得了。

安平還有一個重要的軍事設施稱為「億載金城」，原先是由清朝名臣沈葆禎在 1874 年所建，用以抵擋日軍可能的侵襲。因此，它的原始目的是為了海防。日本於 1895 年佔領台灣後，賣掉了億載金城裡大部分的砲台，以補償戰事所造成的損失。

鄭成功生前對台灣影響很大，為了紀念他的貢獻而建了延平郡王祠，這是島上唯一的官方國姓爺祠。旁邊是民族文物館，講述國姓爺的生平、安平古堡的歷史，傳統服裝、布袋戲等等。還好，所有的說明都有英文翻譯！

這座城巧妙融合了台灣、中國、歐洲和原住民歷史。這裡終年溫暖宜人，生活步調也較為緩慢，台南人更是出了名的親切、率直。對不會講中文的人來說，這是一個很好的旅遊點，因為很多標誌和資訊都有英文。

Page 158 Conversation

伊森	跟我說說台南的歷史吧。
蘿拉	就某方面來說，這裡是中華台灣的根源。
伊森	但是原住民是先來的吧？
蘿拉	對啊，可是就和美洲和澳洲一樣，一旦新人帶著更好的武器來，就準備要變天了。
伊森	你是指中國人嗎？
蘿拉	不，我是指歐洲人。
伊森	真的嗎？你是指什麼？
蘿拉	首先發現台灣的歐洲人是葡萄牙人，然後西班牙人也來了。接著，荷蘭人登台，並佔領了島上大部分的地方。
伊森	荷蘭人建造了台南最早的建築，對嗎？我敢說，大部分是軍事設施。
蘿拉	沒錯。如果你想佔領一個地方，就得先蓋自己的堡壘。所以，我們可以去台南看古老的荷蘭堡壘。日本人接管台灣之後，重建了其中一座。
伊森	台南以前不是台灣的首府嗎？
蘿拉	是啊，中國人和歐洲人都把台南設為首府。
伊森	中國人是什麼時候到台灣來的？
蘿拉	有些來得很早，不過，大部分都是在國姓爺把台灣變成反清基地以後來的。他在 1662 年把荷蘭人趕出台灣，並在台灣建了新政府。不過，他在戰勝之後沒多久就過世了。
伊森	中國的生活方式就是如此傳入台灣並落地生根囉。我猜台南有很多全台之最吧？
蘿拉	是的，它有台灣最古老的孔廟和武廟。那些美麗的歷史建築也為台南贏得廟宇之都的美名。除此，台南也有不少鄉村風情。

Page 162 Reading Passage

　　由於台南是台灣最早的的首府，因此它有許多歷史古蹟就不令人意外。台南的佛教和道教寺廟數量冠於全台。最重要的兩座廟宇分別供奉孔子和武聖。台南孔廟是全台最古老的孔廟，原先是孔子書院，因此大家才會稱它為「全台首學」。裡面有些石頭上刻有學生應守之戒律，例如學生不可飲酒。9 月 28 日這天，你來會看到許多祭孔的有趣儀式。

　　就像台南的孔廟一樣，武廟也是台灣最古老的。廟裡有一尊引人注目的關公雕像，刻畫他手持傳說中的「青龍偃月刀」的騎馬英姿。關公原是一名中國的將軍。政府官員和生意人，數百年來都會到這裡奉上供品，祈求關公賜福。多年來民眾捐給廟方的新裝飾和大量供品，使得武廟越建越華麗。傳說以前武廟的台階設得很高，讓女人無法進入。

　　台南有許多可看的景點，著名的有大南門、國立台灣文學館和赤崁樓，這是其中一部分。市區外的西濱公路沿線也以自然美景聞名，是個賞鳥的好去處！

　　台南有許多傳統美食。最受歡迎的美食之一是棺材板，它是將麵包挖空再填入咖哩雞等美味餡料的小吃。豬腳和蝦餅是另外兩種受歡迎的台南美食。去台南還應該嚐嚐一種叫做安平豆花的點心，和一種叫擔仔麵的特殊麵食。就像台灣其他城市一樣，這些特別的料理，你可以在餐廳、小吃攤、夜市，甚至巷弄間吃到。美食從來不會離你太遠！

Page 164 Conversation

蘿拉　你有沒有想過要去台南？那裡絕對值得一去，而且就在去高雄的路上。

伊森　到底有什麼好玩的？

蘿拉　它是台灣最古老、最有歷史的城市。

伊森　聽起來是我爸媽會喜歡的地方。真可惜，他們時間不夠。

蘿拉　那裡也有很多美食。光想到，我就肚子餓了。

伊森　我對發掘沒吃過的美食最有興趣！只要不是些什麼怪東西就好。

蘿拉　別擔心，不管是台灣人還是外國人都愛台南美食。

伊森　真的嗎？快説快説！

蘿拉　台南最有名的就是棺材板。

伊森　啊，你不是説台灣人不喜歡聽到死這類的事嗎？

蘿拉　是啊，很怪的名字對吧？

伊森　那為什麼要用「棺材」這個詞呢？

蘿拉　我也不是很確定。它有點像法式吐司，不過麵包是被挖空，塞了些海鮮或咖哩雞當內餡。

伊森　所以，餡料是屍體，麵包是棺材！聽起來發明棺材板的人有種黑色幽默。

蘿拉　沒錯喔。你應該會很高興知道其他的台南美食不但好吃，而且沒有這種奇怪的名稱。

伊森　像是？

蘿拉　豬腳啦、蝦餅和安平豆花。

伊森　聽起來我們會吃很好喔。

蘿拉　這就是台灣啊，有好多美食可吃。

26 高雄：概述

Page 168 **Reading Passage**

　　高雄位於本島的南端，人口超過 270 萬人，是台灣第二大的城市。這裡的居民比較多講台灣話，比較少說國語，這點和台北不太一樣。

　　高雄是全球最繁忙的貨櫃碼頭之一，台灣大部分的重工業都習慣設在靠近高雄港的地方。然而，高雄可不只有製造業而已。著名的愛河流經市區，由於新開了很多商店也新設步道，沿著河邊散步非常舒服。夜晚乘船遊河更能欣賞市區燈景。

　　高雄市政府一直致力於建造更多景點，讓高雄轉型為一個悠閒又浪漫的地方。2001 年，9 位藝術家獲邀合力完成「城市光廊」，在夜間營造光景，為此地增添一抹浪漫氣息。在另一個有名的景點「真愛碼頭」享受晚餐，也是很推薦的行程。高雄並沒有很多出名的在地美食，然而，坐在愛河邊或真愛碼頭的餐廳裡，你有機會品嚐到美味的異國料理。

　　對台灣北部的人來說，高雄是個值得一遊的好地方。雖然有些地區過於工業化，但郊區美景也不缺。如果你要到鄰近的墾丁或屏東來個一日之旅，高雄也是一個很好的住宿點。如果你想去更遠的地方，可以搭船或飛機到位於台灣與中國之間的澎湖群島。參觀這些島嶼，得以體驗傳統台灣漁村風情，宛如時光倒流一般。

Page 170 **Conversation**

伊森	高雄是什麼樣子？值得一遊嗎？
蘿拉	以前觀光和高雄沒辦法劃上等號。但是最近這幾年真的改善很多，高雄市政府已經讓當地搖身一變成為觀光景點了。
伊森	它在台中以南，對嗎？
蘿拉	對啊，從台北搭火車大約要 5 到 6 個小時。如果從台中去就比較方便。
伊森	那麼，這個城市有什麼可看？
蘿拉	愛河是觀光客會感興趣的主要景點之一。
伊森	從名字聽起來，我猜會到這裡的大部分都是夫妻和情侶。
蘿拉	哈，不只是夫妻和情侶啦。事實上，市政府興建了新的步道、餐廳和商店，所以，沿著河邊散步非常愉快。
伊森	愛河有遊河行程嗎？
蘿拉	有啊，很棒喔，我去年去過一次。
伊森	附近有什麼好玩的小島嗎？
蘿拉	附近是多近？如果你想的話，可以搭船到澎湖群島去。在那裡可以玩上幾天。
伊森	我們應該沒那麼多時間。有沒有比較近的地方，可以一日來回的？
蘿拉	那就去墾丁國家公園。
伊森	聽起來很棒！

Reading Passage
Page 174

自從高雄捷運在 2008 年通車後，大家的生活就更加方便了。在這之前，只能靠計程車或公車在市區觀光。

你看高雄馬路寬闊，可能會想要租車。可是很多外國人會發現在台灣開車並不容易。因此，除非你有在台灣開車的經驗，否則並不建議租車。

對很多人來說，高雄最重要的景點就是附近的佛光山。佛光山是著名的佛寺，不管來觀光還是來禪修，都可以在寺內過夜。寺方可以教導遊客很多台灣佛教的二三事。例如，這裡有開設人人可參加的禪修課程。寺外的美麗花園內有多尊佛像，最大的一尊高達 40 多公尺。佛光山曾在 1997 年停止對外開放，但在 2000 年重新開放遊客參觀。

去旗津玩也挺能放鬆的，而且很方便可到，搭船只要 5 分鐘，也可以經由海底隧道到達。旗津島上有很多好吃的海鮮餐廳，還有一座媽祖廟和燈塔。

高雄的客家文化中心裡保存了豐富的老照片，詳細記錄著客家人的傳統生活方式。高雄以前有很多老式的客家屋宇，都是謹守風水原則所建造。不幸的是，在過去幾十年裡，許多這類的房子都被拆除了。高雄市民已經團結一致，努力要保護在美濃和旗山碩果僅存的客家房屋。

Conversation
Page 176

伊森：市區觀光呢？像台中一樣只有公車可搭嗎？

蘿拉：不，還好高雄捷運在 2008 年通車了。

伊森：真令人鬆口氣！這樣我就不用租車了。

蘿拉：是啊，在台灣不是很建議外國人開車。

伊森：高雄的主要景點是什麼？

蘿拉：觀光客最愛的景點是佛光山。那是高雄附近的一所著名佛寺。

伊森：能在那裡過夜嗎？

蘿拉：可以，你可以住個幾天。當然，你必須遵守所有的規定，而且只能吃素。

伊森：還有其他值得去的地方嗎？

蘿拉：有很多博物館，有一座客家文化中心，市郊還有美麗的鄉間景致。

伊森：聽起來不錯。我們遲早會需要看點自然風景來調劑一下。你知道附近有什麼地方嗎？也許是可以一日來回的地方？

蘿拉：旗津島怎麼樣？從市區搭船只要 5 分鐘，或者你可以走海底隧道。

伊森：如果離高雄這麼近，真的有島的感覺嗎？

蘿拉：那裡的確有小島的氣氛喔。島上有燈塔、很多海鮮餐廳，還有一座媽祖廟。

伊森：誰是媽祖？就是你以前提過的民間海神嗎？

蘿拉：沒錯！你還記得！

28 高雄：熱門景點（2）

cc by Prattflora

Page 180 Reading Passage

如果你搭火車到左營車站，就會來到高雄最美麗的景點之一蓮池潭。這裡有一座很大的公園，裡面有許多美麗的建築物和廟宇。這些建築物都是基於中國的傳統信仰和故事而建造。沿著湖邊散步，你會看到春秋閣，這是紀念關公這位古代名將的。在春秋閣前面，有一尊騎龍的觀音雕像，觀音是中國的慈悲女神。據說觀音有一次以此姿態顯靈雲端，要求建造一座這樣的雕像。

沿路走下去，有兩座高大的中式建築，叫作龍虎塔，一座為虎、一座為龍。據說你從龍口進，虎口出，可得好運。塔內許多繪畫多是勸人行善，或警惕世人惡有惡報。這些畫都有中國傳統信仰的依據。

其他知名的景點有壽山動物園、西子灣風景區和位於城市北邊的半屏山。還有不要錯過雄偉的孔廟，這是台灣最大的孔廟，附近有一尊莊嚴的孔子雕像。

過去這些年來，高雄也設立了不少博物館，主要的有國立科學工藝博物館、高雄市立美術館和高雄市立歷史博物館。

Page 182 Conversation

伊森　市區附近還有哪些景點？

蘿拉　你一定會想去看蓮池潭。

伊森　名字好美，是個公園嗎？

蘿拉　當然是囉。精確說來是一座湖，附近圍著很大的公園，裡面有好幾座廟宇和有趣的建築。觀光客很愛來這裡。

伊森　我猜，這些廟宇是供奉你說過的海神是吧？

蘿拉　就我所知並不是。不過有一座全台最大的孔廟、兩座紀念武聖的塔樓，還有一尊美麗的大慈大悲觀世音菩薩的雕像。

伊森　你最喜歡蓮池潭什麼地方？

蘿拉　應該是龍虎塔吧，很多人從龍嘴進去，再從虎嘴出來，據說會帶來好運。

伊森　好運永遠不嫌少啊。那裡像台灣其他城市一樣，也有博物館或藝廊嗎？

蘿拉　當然有，也許你會對國立科學工藝博物館有興趣。

伊森　裡面有什麼展覽？

蘿拉　一整年都有很多展覽，例如有關於生物科技、水資源和食品工業的展覽，甚至還有恐龍特展哩！

伊森　哇，聽起來很有趣！我一定要去看看！

cc by Jessepylin

cc by Peellden

29 墾丁

Page 186 ## Reading Passage

　　墾丁國家公園是台灣最出名的夏季旅遊勝地。它位於台灣最南端的屏東縣，是島上的第一座國家公園，成立於 1984 年，面積有 333 平方公里，涵蓋陸地和海洋。

　　墾丁國家公園多為丘陵和台地。園裡的珊瑚礁和其他的特殊地形，是由地球的地殼運動和海水侵蝕所造成，裡面有許多特殊的景觀，例如，位於公園最南端的貓鼻頭就是典型受到侵蝕的珊瑚礁地形，由於形狀像一隻蹲伏的貓而得名。其他有名的景觀包括南灣、船帆石和鵝鑾鼻等。

　　由於是熱帶氣候，這裡有許多不同種類的動植物。此地是許多候鳥的冬季避寒處，如灰面鷲和伯勞鳥。海中則常見抹香鯨和許多種不同的海豚。

　　墾丁終年炎熱，對台灣人來說，這是個充滿沙灘與陽光的地方。夏天時，全台各地的年輕人，都會湧入墾丁享受各種刺激的水上活動。海邊和街上都是穿著休閒短褲的男孩，和穿著比基尼的女孩！你也許會看到拿著衝浪板的年輕人，他們不是正要去海邊衝浪，就是已經衝了好幾小時要休息了！墾丁絕對是一個青春與熱情洋溢、活力十足的地方！

　　大型活動經常選在墾丁舉辦，包括四月分辦的有名的春吶，以及風鈴季。公園裡也有許多觀光景點。

　　另外還有墾丁大街夜市，那裡有很多旅館、商店、小吃攤和酒吧。觀光客也可以在這條街上買到游泳和水上活動的設備。

Page 188 ## Conversation

伊森	你說過墾丁國家公園離高雄很近，那裡很受觀光客歡迎嗎？
蘿拉	當然。它絕對是個台灣人和外國遊客都熱愛的一個地方。
伊森	你可以介紹一下嗎？
蘿拉	沒問題。墾丁是由地球的地殼運動所造成，在被風及海水侵蝕多年後，形成了今天我們所看到的這許多景觀。
伊森	有些什麼景觀？
蘿拉	主要是小山丘、岩層和珊瑚礁！
伊森	好妙！那麼，它位於台灣南部，我想一定很熱！
蘿拉	的確很熱！由於是熱帶氣候，終年高溫。
伊森	那玩水一定最適合了！
蘿拉	沒錯，尤其是一個叫南灣的地方，每年夏天都湧入大量人潮來享受陽光！
伊森	哇，我可以想像海灘上擠滿帶著衝浪板或潛水裝備的年輕人，或者只是躺在沙灘上做日光浴！可是，我爸媽對水上活動沒興趣。
蘿拉	別擔心。公園裡有好多景點，如鵝鑾鼻燈塔，這是台灣最南端的燈塔。他們還可以去參觀形狀就像帆船的船帆石和貓鼻頭，這是形狀像一隻蹲伏的貓的石頭！
伊森	哇，我想他們會有興趣的！晚餐呢？有什麼好餐廳嗎？
蘿拉	你可以帶他們去有名的墾丁大街夜市，街上有許多小吃攤、異國餐廳和酒吧。

30 東海岸：概述

中譯

Page 192 *Reading Passage*

　　台灣的東部與其他地區被中央山脈隔開，因此，東部並沒有太多工業，大部分地區也都保持著原始未開發的狀態。東部沒有大城市，也沒有西半部那麼擁擠。以花蓮市來說，人口才 11 萬多人，即便整個花蓮縣也僅有 34 萬人。

　　鄉間風景、海岸線加上沒有工業區，使東部成為台灣風景最美、生活最悠閒的一個地方。這裡較為寬闊，生活也沒那麼忙亂。許多遊客都能盡情享受這裡的悠閒，參加潛水、騎單車和健行等戶外活動。夏季是東部的旅遊旺季，因為台灣人會和家人一起去度假。

　　東部是中國移民來到台灣後，最後遷入的地區。直到 1960 年代，新的公路開通，讓東部與台灣其他地區連結後，東部才完成現代化。東部的居民以他們的強韌和對生命的熱情而著稱。另一個東部的有趣事實是，由於被高大的山脈阻隔，在這裡太陽早早就下山了。

　　東部的兩座最大城市是花蓮和台東。雖然這兩地目前都還是台灣較為寧靜的城市，但政府正規劃將其打造成觀光勝地。

　　在台灣最長的隧道雪山隧道 2006 年開通後，台灣東西部間的交通已大為改善。從台北到宜蘭的交通時間，從兩小時大幅縮減到只要 40 分鐘。這有助於吸引更多遊客到東部玩。

Page 194 *Conversation*

伊森　我停留在台灣的期間，想去試試一、二種戶外活動，什麼地方適合呢？

蘿拉　你應該到東部去，那裡有很多戶外活動可參加。而且你在東部時，還可以享受那裡的開闊空間！

伊森　有哪些活動可以玩？

蘿拉　你玩過泛舟嗎？

伊森　哇，那可能太刺激了！就是那種你坐著橡皮筏、順著激流而下的活動嗎？

蘿拉　對啊，東部有很多河流。那裡是台灣最沒有開發的地區，因此非常地天然純淨。那是中國移民最後遷入的地區。

伊森　所以，那裡沒有大城市？

蘿拉　沒有，花蓮市有 11 萬人，台東市 10 萬 9 千人。

伊森　可以健行、游泳或潛水嗎？

蘿拉　可以，但你在出發前要作好計劃。台灣人也很愛去東部玩。

伊森　是因為較少工業化嗎？

蘿拉　那是原因之一。東部有很多自然景點可看。

伊森　我得現在就開始計劃！看來我有機會逃離大城市，呼吸些新鮮空氣了！

31

東海岸：花蓮與台東

Page 198
Reading Passage

花蓮

　　花蓮市的石雕很出名，每年都會舉行國際石雕藝術季，這項活動已是國際知名。傳統上，遊客來花蓮都會買大理石。不幸地是，開採大理石已對當地山區的環境產生負面的影響。因此，如果你去花蓮玩，也許改買玉製品會比較好。

　　那裡也有宜人的公園、廟宇、日式建築和海岸線。如果你到花蓮，一定要去以太魯閣峽谷命名的太魯閣國家公園。太魯閣在當地原住民部落語裡意指「壯觀而美麗的」。公園裡處處可見壯麗的峽谷和懸崖。這是台灣的國家公園之一，也是體驗島上未被破壞的天然美景的好機會。

　　花蓮也有些出名的美食與點心，如麻糬和扁食。

台東

　　台東是東部的另一個大城，人口約 10 萬 9 千人。遊客一定要去參觀國立台灣史前文化博物館和卑南文化公園。卑南文化公園是座考古遺址，是 1980 年要建造一座火車站時所意外發現。公園裡展現數千年前史前人類的生活。

　　如果你對當地藝術有興趣，那麼一定不能錯過台東鐵道藝術村。台東市政府將數個市內的老舊火車站站體，變身為展覽館供當地藝術家使用，成為融合現代藝術與當地歷史的舒適空間。

　　花蓮和台東有好多事物可看。當地的溫泉也很有名。台東縣的知本溫泉是台灣最有名的溫泉之一，屬於碳酸氫鈉泉，水溫可高達攝氏 85 度。

　　台灣東部既有文化體驗又有天然資源，你也可以從這裡前往離島的綠島或蘭嶼遊玩。來到台灣東部絕對不會無聊！只要記得放慢腳步，好好享受！

Page 200
Conversation

伊森	這些城市有博物館可以讓我多了解原住民文化嗎？
蘿拉	台東有國立台灣史前文化博物館和卑南文化公園。你可以學到很多台灣古代的歷史和文化。
伊森	台東還有其他景點嗎？
蘿拉	你可以去看看台東鐵道藝術村。
伊森	會有台灣鐵道文化的展覽嗎？
蘿拉	不盡然。它是把 80 年歷史的台東火車站變身為展覽館，展出當地藝術家的作品。
伊森	聽起來很有意思！東部有很多自然景點嗎？
蘿拉	當然啦！別錯過花蓮的太魯閣國家公園，它的美會讓你嘆為觀止。
伊森	「太魯閣」這個詞是什麼意思？聽起來不像國語。
蘿拉	它是當地原住民的語言，「太魯閣」意指「壯觀而美麗的」。
伊森	它像墾丁國家公園一樣，有山又有海嗎？
蘿拉	一點都不像。因為立霧溪貫穿公園，造成許多峽谷和懸崖。
伊森	我敢說東部保存了台灣的許多天然美景，那裡一定是一個讓遊客得以認識台灣的大自然的好地方。
蘿拉	沒錯。那是因為東部較少工業。也是台灣人很愛去度假的地方。所以，週末假期都擠滿了人！

32 東海岸：原住民文化

Reading Passage
Page 204

花蓮和台東的主要景點之一，就是當地保存到現在的原住民文化。可惜隨著觀光客數量日益增加，原住民文化的保存也面臨了危機。

東部有許多原住民部落：排灣族、阿美族、卑南族、布農族、魯凱族、撒奇雅族、噶瑪蘭族、太魯閣族和達悟族。這些古老的文化至今仍影響著人們的生活。他們的慶典都會大肆慶祝，尤其是每年七、八月舉行的阿美族豐年祭。每一個阿美族的村落都會慶祝豐年祭，並舉行男孩的成年禮。慶典本身就是一場包含歌唱、舞蹈、飲酒和美食的盛宴。

直到現在，布農族仍使用自己的語言。他們是唯一有曆法的部落，使用圖像記事。他們也舉行豐年祭，並在祭典吟唱「八部合音」，或稱「祈禱小米豐收歌」。布農族還有一種「打耳祭」，強調教導年輕男孩狩獵技巧，在每年四月舉行。

達悟族住在台東縣的蘭嶼島，他們的拼板舟、銀器和陶藝很出名。由於他們住在離台的小島上，因此要保存自己的文化較容易。然而，他們還是受到現代社會的影響。達悟族人傳統上住在深穴式地下建築，但政府在 1960 年代開始將他們遷入混凝土房屋。不幸地是，混凝土房屋不像傳統建築那樣適合當地的氣候。傳統建築可以在夏季隔絕熱氣而冬季則可隔絕寒冷，效果非常好。

東部有許多地方可以欣賞到原住民文化。花蓮有一座原住民木雕博物館。台東每年舉行南島文化節，試圖連結當地原住民文化與南島文化。台東還有一座國立台灣史前文化博物館，展出歐洲人和中國人來到台灣之前，原住民與台灣人的史前文化。

Conversation
Page 206

蘿拉	東部是許多原住民的家鄉。你運氣好的話說不定可以體驗到他們的慶典喔。
伊森	跟我多說些原住民的事。他們對台灣文化有很大的影響嗎？
蘿拉	在東部的確是的，原住民的慶典常常就在那裡的學校舉行。
伊森	我猜這些慶典包含成年禮。
蘿拉	是的。很有意思的是，東部有好多部落。布農族是唯一發展出以圖像標示一年中重要活動的部落。
伊森	真的嗎？你是說他們有自己的曆法？
蘿拉	沒錯，他們早在中國移民來到之前就有自己的曆法。他們也有個名稱特殊的慶典，叫作「打耳祭」。
伊森	這個祭典有什麼特殊的目的嗎？
蘿拉	用意在教導男孩如何成為好的獵人。
伊森	東部有什麼離島嗎？我想搭船旅行。
蘿拉	有，蘭嶼在台東縣，是達悟族的家鄉。
伊森	住在小島上的部落？那表示說他們的文化保存得比一些本島部落要好囉。
蘿拉	有很長一段時間的確是這樣，但要抵擋現代社會也是很難的。
伊森	你說的是沒錯。現在，全世界的情況都是如此。
蘿拉	是的。顯然，政府甚至要達悟族人住在地上的混凝土房屋裡。他們傳統上住在比較適合當地氣候的深穴式地下建築。
伊森	我敢說他們有很深的地下室！他們一定設法保留了這部分的文化。

解答 & 聽力原文

Unit 1

▶ Quiz p. 7

1 Taiwan is close to China and lying between the Philippines and Japan.

2 It measures 36,000 square kilometers. It is almost the same size as the Netherlands.

3 Yushan (Mount Jade).

4 Snakes, but visitors are not likely to see them.

5 Because they are good for their health.

▶ Practice p. 10

1 **Script**

1. It has a long tail about 40 centimeters in length and can be seen in many scenic spots.
2. They're mostly found in the mountains, and people like to soak in them.
3. There are several kinds, and some of them are poisonous!
4. It's close to Taipei, it's beautiful, and it's full of nature.

1. 牠有著約 40 公分的長尾巴，會出沒於許多景點。
2. 它多位於山區，人們喜歡泡著它。
3. 牠們有很多品種，其中有些有毒。
4. 它距離台北很近、很漂亮、充滿大自然氣息。

1 Taiwan Blue Magpie 2 Hot springs
3 Snakes 4 Yangmingshan National Park

2 1 a 2 d 3 c 4 b

3 2 Yushan is the highest mountain in Northeast Asia.
3 The Blue Taiwan Magpie is not afraid of people.
4 Visitors love to soak in Yangmingshan's hot springs.

Unit 2

▶ Quiz p. 13

1 A hot rainy climate.

2 Typhoons can bring about mudflows and floods.

3 The Plum Rain Season lasts from May to June.

▶ Practice p. 16

1 **Script**

1. Taiwan is half tropical and half subtropical because the Tropic of Cancer runs across the middle of the island.
2. Humidity is high in Taiwan, and the temperature in summer rarely drops below 30 degrees Celsius.
3. Take an umbrella with you at all times during the Plum Rain Season, or you'll certainly get wet.
4. During a typhoon, visitors should avoid visiting the outlying islands as it can be dangerous.

1. 由於北回歸線橫跨台灣的中部，台灣一半處於熱帶地區、一半處於亞熱帶地區。
2. 台灣的濕度高，夏季氣溫鮮少低於攝氏 30 度。
3. 在梅雨季節期間，要隨身攜帶雨傘，以免淋濕。
4. 颱風期間，外島較為危險，遊客應避免前往。

1 The Tropic of Cancer runs through Taiwan. 2 The summers in Taiwan are hot and humid. 3 It rains a lot during the Plum Rain Season. 4 Don't visit the outlying islands during a typhoon.

2 1 c 2 e 3 a 4 b 5 d

3 1 blossoms 2 offshore 3 mild
4 destructive 5 crowded

Unit 3

▶ **Quiz** `p. 19`

1 Twenty-three million.

2 On the flat western plains.

3 The indigenous people were the first people to live in Taiwan.

4 The Dutch took over Taiwan in 1623.

▶ **Practice** `p. 22`

1

Script

A: How many indigenous tribes are there in Taiwan?

B: There are 14, and the Amis tribe is the biggest.

A: Oh. Where do they live?

B: They mostly live in Hualien and Taitung on the east coast.

A: What's the population of indigenous people in Taiwan?

B: I'm not sure, but it's not much compared with the Hoklo.

A: Who are the Hoklo?

B: The Hoklo are descendants of the Chinese settlers who came to Taiwan a few centuries ago.

A: And how many of them are there?

B: They make up about 70% of the island's population.

A: 台灣有多少原住民族？

B: 有 14 個，最大的一族是阿美族。

A: 這樣啊。那他們都住在哪裡？

B: 他們大多住在東岸的花蓮和台東。

A: 台灣的原住民人口有多少呢？

B: 我也不確定，但是無法與閩南人的數量相比。

A: 閩南人指的是？

B: 閩南人指的是中國移民者的後代，這些中國移民在幾世紀前來到台灣。

A: 那他們的人數又有多少？

B: 他們佔了台灣人口的百分之七十喔。

1 – **2** ✓ **3** ✓ **4** –

2 **1** c **2** d **3** b

3 **2** The largest tribe in Taiwan is the Amis tribe.

3 There are over 640 people per square kilometer in Taiwan.

4 The Dutch ruled over Taiwan until Koxinga drove them out.

Unit 4

▶ **Quiz** `p. 25`

1 Several languages are spoken here because of the number of different people in Taiwan.

2 Mandarin Chinese.

3 No, they cannot.

4 Because Japan governed Taiwan for fifty years.

▶ **Practice** `p. 28`

1

Script

1. There are many different Chinese dialects, such as Hakka, Hokkien, and Mandarin.

2. A Hakka TV station was launched in 2003 in order to save the Hakka language.

3. Mandarin Chinese is a tonal language, which makes it difficult for foreigners to pronounce the words correctly.

4. Taiwanese, which is related to Mandarin, is spoken a lot more frequently in the south.

5. Because Taiwan was governed by Japan for fifty years, many of the older people can speak Japanese.

1. 中國有許多方言，例如：客家語、福建語和國語。

2. 為了拯救客家語言，在 2003 年時成立了一個客家電視台。

3. 國語屬於聲調語言，因此外國人很難發音正確。

4. 台灣話與國語有關係，南部人更會説。

5. 台灣曾受日本統治 50 年，因此許多老一輩的人會説日文。

1 dialects, Hakka **2** launched

3 tonal, pronounce **4** related, frequently

5 governed

2 **1** b, c, d, a **2** c, b, a, d **3** c, d, a, b

4 a, c, d, b

3 **1** number, Hakka, declining

2 speak, dialect, communicate

3 English, foreigners, around

4 Tones, tricky, characters

5 official, Mandarin, recognition

Unit 5

▶ **Quiz** `p. 31`

1 Buddhism and Taoism.

2 Matsu, the goddess of the sea.

3 The International Matsu Cultural Festival.

4 Farmers worship the land god because he truely understands the importance of a good harvest.

▶ **Practice** `p. 34`

<u>1</u>

Script

1. It's a mixture of several beliefs concerning gods, ghosts, ancestors, and luck.
2. It is an important philosophy based on the teachings of Confucius.
3. Farmers worship this god because they want a good harvest.
4. They often lead religious processions and are in charge of expelling evil spirits.
5. They are the two major religions of Taiwan, and Taiwanese usually believe in a mix of these two.

1. 它是由數個關於神、鬼、祖先和「運」的信仰所構成的。
2. 它是個以孔子教誨為基礎的重要哲學。
3. 農人會拜這位神明以祈求豐收。
4. 祂們經常是宗教活動隊伍的先導，專門驅趕邪靈。
5. 它們是台灣的兩大宗教，台灣人的信仰通常融合了這兩者。

1 Traditional folk religion
2 Confucianism **3** The land god
4 The Eight Infernal Generals
5 Buddhism and Taoism

<u>2</u> **1** a **2** d **3** b **4** c

<u>3</u> **1** People usually pray to Matsu for good luck and safety.
2 The Eight Infernal Generals are eight messengers from the underworld.
3 The International Matsu Cultural Festival takes place during the third month on the lunar calendar.

Unit 6

▶ **Quiz** `p. 39`

1 In a very colorful, eye-catching manner.

2 Taoist temples are usually managed by the local people.

3 They serve as community centers where local people can get together.

▶ **Practice** `p. 41`

<u>1</u>

Script

1. These antique carvings are so detailed. And look at these bronze dragons! They're amazing!
2. I really want to find my Mr. Right. What should I do?
3. I know it's been rebuilt several times, but when was Lungshan Temple first built?
4. What else happens in temples apart from praying?
5. What are those old people doing in the temple grounds? It looks like they're playing a game.

1. 這些古老的雕刻好精緻。你看這些銅鑄的龍！好傳神啊！
2. 我好想找到我的白馬王子喔，我該怎麼做呢？
3. 我知道龍山寺曾歷經多次重建，那麼它最早建於何時呢？
4. 廟裡除了拜拜還會做些什麼？
5. 那些老人家在廟宇的空地上做些什麼啊？他們好像在玩什麼遊戲。

<u>1</u> **1** d **2** e **3** a **4** c **5** b

<u>2</u> **1** b **2** c **3** d **4** a

<u>3</u> **1** Lungshan Temple has the only bronze dragon pillars in Taiwan.
2 Taiwanese temples are built according to special rules called feng shui.
3 The "bai bai" ritual can be used to venerate both ancestors and gods.

Unit 7

▶ Quiz p. 49

1 Confucianism.

2 Confucius.

3 Everyone has his or her own position in society. Each one should fulfill his or her own duty.

4 Traditional Chinese architecture is seen in a Confucian temple, with solemn entrances, grand red columns, ornate roofs, and colorful paintings and decorations.

5 Every year a memorial ceremony is held on the 28th of September to celebrate the birthday of Confucius.

▶ Practice p. 52

1

Script

A: So what kinds of things did Confucius teach?

B: He taught that everyone has their own position in society, and everyone must fulfill their duty.

A: What does that mean?

B: Well, for a family it means that parents must look after their children and that children must then take care of their parents when they get older.

A: Is that why so many Taiwanese families have elderly people living with them?

B: Yes, though it's changed a bit in recent years.

A: In what way?

B: Well it used to be that the parents would live with their eldest son. But now they sometimes live with one of their daughters because she sometimes has the better-paying job.

A: 那麼，孔子的教誨主要是些什麼？

B: 他主張每一個人在社會上都有自己的位置，人人都應守其本分。

A: 那是什麼意思？

B: 對家庭來說，父母親應該盡到照顧子女的責任，而子女在父母年邁時也應該侍奉父母。

A: 這麼多台灣的家庭都有老人同住，就是這個原因是嗎？

B: 沒錯，不過這個現象近年來也有了改變。

A: 怎麼說？

B: 以往呢，父母會和長子同住，可是現在有時候女兒的工作薪水比較好，所以他們也會和其中一個女兒同住。

1 ✓ 2 ✓ 3 – 4 – 5 ✓

2　1 peaceful　2 discrimination
3 ceremony　4 mentor　5 principles

3　1 in honor of　2 ornate　3 fulfill
4 influence

Unit 8

▶ Quiz p. 55

1 Traditional crafts like paintings or wood carvings.

2 The government and other groups.

3 It is usually performed outside temples.

4 Taiwanese puppetry.

▶ Practice p. 58

1

Script

1. A: Could you tell me something about Taiwanese performing arts?

   B: Well, Taiwanese performing arts include acrobatics, puppetry, and Taiwanese opera.

2. A: Is Taiwanese opera the same as Chinese opera?

   B: Not quite. Taiwanese opera has been influenced by indigenous music and Taiwanese folk songs. So it's a little different from Chinese opera.

3. A: What does the government do to promote traditional arts in Taiwan?

   B: It holds festivals and sets up cultural centers which support emerging art groups.

4. A: How are traditional art groups attracting younger people to come and study traditional skills?

   B: They're combining traditional art with modern technology and holding festivals specifically for kids.

解答 & 聽力原文

1. A: 你可以和我説説台灣的表演藝術嗎？
   B: 台灣的表演藝術包含了雜技表演、布袋戲，還有歌仔戲。
2. A: 台灣的歌仔戲和中國戲曲一樣嗎？
   B: 不太一樣，台灣的歌仔戲受到原住民音樂和台灣民間音樂的影響，所以和中國的戲曲已經不太一樣了。
3. A: 政府採取了哪些措施來推廣台灣的傳統藝術？
   B: 政府舉辦一些節慶、建立文化中心來支持新興的藝術團體。
4. A: 傳統藝術團體如何吸引年輕人前來學習傳統技藝？
   B: 他們結合了傳統藝術和現代科技，更特別為兒童舉辦許多節慶活動。

1 performing, puppetry　**2** indigenous, folk　**3** promote, festivals, emerging
4 traditional, technology

<u>2</u>　**1** a　**2** c　**3** d

<u>3</u>　**1** Taiwanese people are still interested in traditional crafts.
2 Carving, weaving and ceramics are examples of traditional crafts.
3 The government is trying to keep folk arts alive by holding lots of festivals.
4 Folk songs and indigenous music have influenced Taiwanese opera.
5 The performing arts use modern technologies to attract young people.

Unit 9

▶ Quiz `p. 61`

1 In the past, many buildings had distinctive Chinese-style roofs. Nowadays, most Taiwanese people live in Western-style apartment blocks.

2 Feng shui is an ancient Chinese belief that tells us how buildings should be positioned.

3 Sun Yat-sen Historical Events Memorial Hall, A Drop of Water Memorial Hall, and Huguo Chan Buddhist Temple of Linji School.

▶ Practice `p. 64`

<u>1</u>
　Script
　1. Taiwan's population has increased so much in the past few decades that it's impossible for everyone to live in traditional, Chinese-style houses.
　2. Dutch-style architecture from the 1600s can be seen in southern Taiwan and can be recognized by the Dutch's use of bricks.
　3. The Japanese-style building A Drop of Water Memorial Hall was moved to Danshui and reassembled there in 2009.
　4. To see a British-style building, go visit the former British Consulate at Takao in Kaohsiung, which was built almost a hundred and fifty years ago.

1. 過去幾十年台灣的人口大幅增加，已經不容許每個人都住在傳統的中國式住宅裡。
2. 在台灣南部可見 1600 年代所建的荷蘭式建築，最明顯的特徵就是荷蘭人使用紅磚。
3. 日式建築「一滴水紀念館」於 2009 年被移至淡水並重組建造完畢。
4. 若想看看英式建築，可以參觀高雄的打狗英國領事館，該館約為 150 年前所建。

1 decades, Chinese-style　**2** architecture, bricks　**3** reassembled　**4** Consulate

<u>2</u>　**1** c　**2** a　**3** b　**4** d

<u>3</u>　**1** construct　**2** apartment
　3 architecture　**4** principles
　5 old Chinese style

Unit 10

▶ Quiz p. 67

1 Taiwanese people sometimes get embarrassed when foreigners unknowingly do something wrong.

2 Yes, Taiwanese people often compliment their guests, but at the same time they are modest about themselves.

▶ Practice p. 70

1

Script

1. Taiwanese people are very polite to visitors and will often compliment their guests.

2. To solve their day-to-day or business problems, Taiwanese people rely on strong personal relationships.

3. Talking about death is considered very bad luck in Taiwan, so it's best to avoid the subject in conversation.

1. 台灣人對訪客十分有禮貌，經常會讚美他們的客人。

2. 台灣人仰賴密切的人際關係來解決日常生活或是生意上的問題。

3. 「談論死亡」在台灣被視為非常不吉祥的事，對話中最好能夠避免。

1 c **2** b **3** a

2 **1** d **2** e **3** a **4** c **5** b

3 **1** virtue **2** embarrass **3** assistance **4** Valley

Unit 11

▶ Quiz p. 73

1 In Chinese New Year.

2 Clocks and knives.

3 Clocks represent death, and knives represent the cutting of personal ties.

4 You should wrap it up nicely.

▶ Practice p. 76

1

Script

1. I'm going to visit my Taiwanese friend's family. Should I bring a gift?

2. This clock is very pretty. Shall I buy it? I want to give it as a gift to my Taiwanese friend.

3. I've been invited to a Taiwanese funeral. Should I give money as a gift?

4. Why do people give money in red envelopes?

5. Is there any special etiquette I should remember when giving a gift to someone in Taiwan?

1. 我要去拜訪一位台灣朋友的家，應該要帶禮物嗎？

2. 這個時鐘好漂亮，我可以買嗎？我想把它當作禮物送一位台灣朋友。

3. 我受邀參加一場台灣葬禮，我該包禮金嗎？

4. 為什麼大家要用紅包裝錢致贈他人呢？

5. 在台灣送禮給別人的時候，有什麼需要記住的禮節嗎？

1 b **2** e **3** c **4** d **5** a

2 **1** a **2** b **3** d **4** c

3 **1** <u>Money</u> is usually put in a <u>red</u> envelope when it's given as a gift.

2 Hospitals in Taiwan don't have a <u>fourth</u> floor because the words for <u>four</u> and death sound almost the same in <u>Mandarin</u>.

3 Umbrellas represent <u>separation</u> in Taiwanese culture.

4 When you give a gift you should offer it with <u>both hands</u>.

5 Remember to take off your <u>shoes</u> when you enter someone's <u>house</u>.

Unit 12

▶ **Quiz** p. 79

1 At breakfast.

2 Indian, Thai, Korean, French, and Mexican food.

▶ **Practice** p. 82

1

Script

1. Taiwan's food culture is incredibly rich. You can find almost every style of Chinese cuisine on the island as well as traditional indigenous food.

2. If you find yourself missing Western food, don't worry. There are plenty of Western restaurants in Taiwan.

3. Rice and noodles are the two basic foods in Taiwan. People eat them with almost every meal.

4. In the past, people would not eat beef in order to show respect for the work cows did in the field. Now, though, one of the most popular dishes in Taiwan is beef noodles.

1. 台灣擁有豐富的飲食文化，你可在各處找到幾乎各式的中國料理，還有傳統的原住民料理。

2. 如果你想吃西方料理，也別擔心，台灣有很多西式的餐廳。

3. 米飯和麵是台灣的兩大主食，大家幾乎餐餐都要有飯或麵。

4. 過去，牛是農耕動物，人們敬重牠們的辛勞而不吃牛肉。如今，台灣最受歡迎的一種食物就是牛肉麵。

1 Taiwan offers visitors the chance to eat a variety of different dishes.

2 There are many Western restaurants in Taiwan.

3 Almost every meal in Taiwan includes rice or noodles.

4 Taiwanese people eat beef more now than they did in the past.

2 **1** c   **2** a   **3** b   **4** d

3 **1** dishes, meat, banquet
2 cows, agricultural, eaten
3 fried, roadside, stalls
4 paramount, suffered, disasters

Unit 13

▶ **Quiz** p. 85

1 Stir-fried clams, three-cup chicken, grilled fish, grilled squid, stir-fried vegetables, and deep-fried tofu.

2 Sesame oil, rice wine, and soy sauce.

3 Oolong tea.

▶ **Practice** p. 88

1

Script

1. What kinds of snacks do Taiwanese people like to eat?

2. Mmm, this tea is so good. Was it grown here in Taiwan?

3. This three-cup chicken is really tasty. How do you make it?

4. Do Taiwanese people like milk in their tea, or do they drink it without?

5. What's the stuffing inside the dumpling made of?

1. 台灣人最愛吃哪些小吃？

2. 嗯，這茶好好喝，是在台灣種的嗎？

3. 這道三杯雞真好吃，你們是怎麼做的？

4. 台灣人喝茶喜歡加牛奶還是直接喝呢？

5. 這小籠包裡面的餡兒是什麼做的？

1 e   **2** a   **3** c   **4** b   **5** d

2 **1** influenced   **2** colleagues   **3** culture
4 pot   **5** dishes

3 **1** beerhouses   **2** renowned   **3** ethnic
4 burst

Unit 14

▶ **Quiz** p. 91

1 Stinky tofu, oyster omelets, shaved ice, bubble tea, and grilled sausages.

2 It is a form of fermented tofu that has a strong odor.

3 Bubble tea.

4 It was developed in Taichung, central Taiwan in the 1980s.

▶ **Practice** p. 94

1 **Script**

A: Wow! The night market is so busy this evening!

B: Yeah. Night markets get pretty crowded on weekends. What do you want to eat?

A: I'd really like to try stinky tofu. I've heard so much about it.

B: Are you sure you want to try it? Most foreigners are put off by the smell!

A: I know. But I can't leave Taiwan without trying it.

B: OK. But how about we get some pearl milk tea first?

A: Sounds good. I'm really thirsty.

B: And maybe later we can get some shaved ice too; it's so hot this evening!

A: 哇！這夜市今晚好多人啊！

B: 對啊，夜市一到週末都很多人。你想吃什麼？

A: 我很想吃吃看臭豆腐，老是聽人家提到。

B: 你真的想吃嗎？大部分的外國人一聞到那個味道就退避三舍。

A: 我知道啊。可是，來台灣總不能沒吃臭豆腐吧。

B: 好吧，不過我們先喝杯珍珠奶茶怎麼樣？

A: 好啊，我口也好渴了。

B: 等一下，我們還可以再吃點剉冰。今晚好熱啊！

1 ✓   **2** ✓   **3** –   **4** ✓   **5** –

2 **1** a   **2** d   **3** c   **4** b

3 **1** distinctive, Taichung, popular
2 Shaved, toppings, dessert

Unit 15

▶ **Quiz** p. 101

1 Chinese New Year.

2 No, it doesn't.

3 People don't like to sweep the floor during Chinese New Year.

4 Married couples go to the wife's house and spend time with her parents.

5 Because they don't want to sweep away good fortune along with the dirt.

▶ **Practice** p. 103

1 **Script**

1. It falls on the first day of the first month on the lunar calendar.

2. They are used to decorate houses during Chinese New Year.

3. They are usually closed during Chinese New Year.

4. They visit the wife's house on the second day of Chinese New Year.

1. 它是農曆的 1 月 1 日。
2. 農曆新年時會用它們來裝飾屋子。
3. 農曆新年時，它們通常不開業。
4. 農曆新年的初二，他們要回娘家。

1 Chinese New Year   **2** Couplets written on red paper   **3** Shops and restaurants
4 Married couples

2 **1** c   **2** a   **3** d   **4** b

3 **1** c   **2** d   **3** b   **4** a

Unit 16

▶ **Quiz** `p. 107`

1 On the 15th day of the New Year Season.
2 People make elaborate, beautiful lanterns.
3 He was a great poet as well as a great statesman during the Warring States Period in ancient China.
4 To stop the fish from eating Qu Yuan's body.
5 The Dragon Boat Festival.

▶ **Practice** `p. 110`

1

Script

1. For Lantern Festival, lanterns are made in all kinds of different shapes, like animals and people. Some are even made in the shape of Taipei 101.
2. Solving riddles is one of Lantern Festival's most popular activities.
3. At the Yanshui Beehive Fireworks Festival, fireworks are shot into the crowds of people. So if you go, make sure you wear a helmet and a thick coat.
4. Many of Taiwan's businesses, universities and organizations put together dragon boat teams to compete in the races, but teams also come from all over the world to compete, too.

1. 元宵節時，人們製作各種形狀的燈籠，像是動物或人物造型。有些還做成台北 101 的樣子。
2. 猜燈謎是元宵節普遍的活動之一。
3. 鹽水蜂炮節上，爆竹會被射向人群。你要去的話，一定要戴安全帽還有穿厚衣服。
4. 台灣很多企業、學校和機構都會組龍舟隊來參加比賽，也有來自世界各地的參賽隊伍。

1　1 b　2 c　3 d　4 a
2　1 a　2 a　3 d　4 b　5 c
3　1 rower　2 lanterns　3 helmet
　　4 minister　5 disease

Unit 17

▶ **Quiz** `p. 113`

1 It is seen as an unlucky time.
2 Moon cakes and pomelos.

▶ **Practice** `p. 116`

1

Script

1. Ghost Month is considered to be a very unlucky time of year, so people avoid doing important things like getting married or starting a new business.
2. People gather with their families on Moon Festival to eat moon cakes and look at the beautiful full moon.
3. Instead of seeing a man's face in the moon, the Taiwanese see the "Jade Rabbit."
4. Moon cakes are traditionally made with egg yolk and flour, but now they come in all kinds of different flavors, like strawberry, almond, and chocolate.
5. Some people say that going swimming during Ghost Month is a bad idea because you might get dragged underwater by a ghost.

1. 鬼月是一年之中相當不吉利的時刻，所以大家不會在這個時候從事結婚或開業這樣的重要活動。
2. 大家會在中秋節時與家人團聚，一起吃月餅和欣賞美麗月圓。
3. 台灣人不會在月亮上看到男人的臉孔，而是看到「玉兔」。
4. 傳統上，月餅就只有使用蛋黃和麵粉來製作，不過現在月餅有了各式各樣的口味，像是草莓、杏仁，還有巧克力口味。
5. 有些人認為鬼月時不能去游泳，因為可能會被鬼拖下水。

1 People try to avoid getting married during Ghost Month.
2 The Moon Festival is a time for families to get together.
3 The Taiwanese see the shape of a rabbit in the moon.
4 You can get strawberry-flavored moon cakes.
5 Going swimming during Ghost Month is considered dangerous by some.

2 **1** c, b, d, a **2** a, d, b, c **3** c, a, d, b
 4 a, c, b, d

3 **1** observe, ensure, wander
 2 superstitious, forbid, water
 3 honor, reunion, pomelos
 4 frightened, monsters, underworld
 5 full, shapes, Chang-e

Unit 18

▶ **Quiz** `p. 119`

1 The east coast.

2 It invites top performers, producers, actors, and composers from Taiwan and around the world to present dance, music, and drama performances. The festival takes place at the National Theater and National Concert Hall in Taipei.

3 It is the largest music festival in Taiwan.

▶ **Practice** `p. 122`

1
 Script
 1. A: I'm going to travel down the east coast. Do you think I'll be able to go to an indigenous festival?
 B: I'm sure you will. It's August, so the Amis will be celebrating their Harvest Festival.
 2. A: We're going to Yingge today. I want to take you to the Ceramics Festival.
 B: Great! I can't wait to see all the beautiful pots on display! Maybe I can buy one as a souvenir.

 3. A: Have you heard about Spring Scream? It's this amazing music festival held in Kenting every April.
 B: I know. Apparently hundreds of bands play there, and people party all weekend on the beach.

 1. A: 我要去東岸旅遊，你覺得我可以去參加原住民的慶典嗎？
 B: 一定可以啊，現在是八月，正好是阿美族的豐年祭。
 2. A: 我們今天要去鶯歌，我想帶你去看陶瓷嘉年華。
 B: 太棒了！我等不及要看展出的那些美麗茶壺呢！說不定我還可以買一個當紀念品。
 3. A: 你有沒有聽過春吶？這個節慶每年四月在墾丁舉辦，是很瘋狂的音樂節唷。
 B: 我知道啊。大概會有好幾百組樂團在那裡演出吧，而且大家會在沙灘上派對一整個星期呢。

 1 east coast, celebrating, Harvest
 2 Ceramics, display, souvenir
 3 Spring, Kenting, bands

2 **1** held **2** spirits **3** masterpieces

3 **1** Spring Scream was started by two Americans living in Taiwan.
 2 You can often see indigenous ceremonies on the east coast.
 3 The Sun Moon Lake Music Festival takes place every year in October.

Unit 19

▶ **Quiz** `p. 125`

1 Nearly 7 million.

2 The National Palace Museum.

3 To store the ancient Chinese works of art which were brought to Taiwan from mainland China to keep them safe.

4 It has a massive collection that includes Jadeite Cabbage, Meat-Shaped Stone, and Mao-Kung Ting.

▶ **Practice** `p. 128`

1　**Script**

A: I want to go to the National Palace Museum. How can I get there?

B: The best way is to take the MRT to Shilin and then take a bus from there.

A: The MRT? What's that?

B: It's short for Mass Rapid Transport. It's what people call the subway here.

A: Oh, I see. Is it expensive?

B: No, it's pretty cheap. You can even buy a travel pass to save money.

A: Cool. So when I get to the museum, what should I look out for?

B: Well, the Jadeite Cabbage is a must see. It's one of the museum's most famous treasures.

A: 我想去故宮博物院,請問要怎麼去?

B: 最好是先搭捷運到士林,再轉公車過去。

A: 捷運?什麼捷運?

B: 是「大眾捷運系統」的簡稱呀,這裡的人這麼稱呼地鐵的。

A: 喔,原來如此。會很貴嗎?

B: 不會,很便宜喔。想省錢的話,還可以買觀光護照。

A: 酷耶。那我去故宮的時候,有什麼特別需要看的嗎?

B: 這個啊,一定要去看翠玉白菜,那是故宮最知名的館藏之一。

　1 –　**2** ✓　**3** ✓　**4** –

2　**1** e　**2** a　**3** c　**4** d　**5** b

3　**1** artifacts　**2** Announcements　**3** routes
　　4 priceless　**5** abundant

Unit 20

▶ **Quiz** `p. 131`

1 The Chiang Kai-shek Memorial Hall, the Dr. Sun Yet-sen Memorial Hall, and Taipei 101.

2 It was built in 1980 to commemorate the former president of the Republic of China.

3 People usually walk their dogs, jog, fly kites, or simply take a walk there.

▶ **Practice** `p. 134`

1　**Script**

A: Wow. There are a lot of skyscrapers in Taipei. Is there any traditional architecture at all?

B: There's plenty. And here's the best example right in front of us—the Chiang Kai-shek Memorial Hall.

A: Amazing! My guidebook says it was built in 1980, but the architecture makes it look so ancient.

B: Yeah. It was built in the traditional Chinese style. There are some beautiful gardens here too. It's a real contrast to the city surrounding it.

A: Are there any other buildings like this in Taipei?

B: Well there's the Dr. Sun Yat-sen Memorial Hall, which is smaller than this one, but it has a very grand golden Chinese roof that is really worth seeing if you like Chinese architecture.

A: 哇!台北真的有好多高樓大廈,到底有沒有一些傳統建築啊?

B: 很多啊,我們眼前就是一個最好的例子——中正紀念堂。

A: 太美了!我的旅遊手冊上面說,它建於 1980 年,不過建築風格看起來更古老。

B: 對啊,它是採用傳統的中國風,還有幾座美麗的花園,跟它周遭的城市形成強烈的對比。

A: 台北還有其他像這樣的建築嗎?

B: 還有國父紀念館,比這個小一點,可是卻有著非常宏偉的金黃色中式屋頂,你如果喜歡中式建築的話,真的很值得一看。

　1 ✓　**2** –　**3** ✓　**4** ✓　**5** –

<u>2</u> **1** d **2** b **3** c

<u>3</u> **1** The Taipei 101 Observatory is open every day from 9 a.m. to 10 p. m.
2 The Lin Antai Historical House used to belong to a prosperous family.
3 The statue of Chiang Kai-shek is guarded by armed soldiers.

Unit 21

▶ **Quiz** **p. 139**

1 rice noodles (*mifen*), meat ball soup, and stuffed meatballs.

2 National Chiao Tung University is one of the best technical schools, and it is located in Hsinchu.

3 Taichung.

4 Some of its food and drinks.

5 Sun cakes.

▶ **Practice** **p. 142**

<u>1</u>
Script
1. It has a science park which contains several high-tech industries and is important to Taiwan's economy.
2. They are a culinary invention from Taichung which Taiwanese tourists buy to take home and give as gifts.
3. It's south of Hsinchu and is the third largest city in Taiwan.
4. They are grown in the area surrounding Taichung and are taken to the city for processing before being sent to other places.
5. It's one of Hsinchu's main tourist attractions, along with the Municipal Glass Art Museum and Shibajian Mountain.

1. 這裡有一座涵蓋多種高科技工業的科學園區，對台灣經濟有舉足輕重的影響。
2. 它們是來自台中研發的食品，台灣的觀光客喜歡買這樣東西回家當伴手禮。
3. 它位於新竹以南，是台灣第三大的城市。
4. 它們被種植在台中周圍地區，被送往城市加工之後轉運到其他地方。
5. 它和市立玻璃工藝博物館、十八尖山同為新竹主要的觀光景點。

1 Hsinchu **2** Sun cakes **3** Taichung
4 Bananas, sugarcane, and rice
5 Chenghuang Temple Night Market

<u>2</u> **1** b **2** a

<u>3</u> **1** c **2** a **3** d **4** b

Unit 22

▶ **Quiz** **p. 145**

1 There are many traditional activities, such as paper cutting, bamboo weaving, and traditional dancing.

2 Gaomei Wetlands, the National Museum of Natural Science, Tunghai University, Fengle Sculpture Park, and the Fengjia Night Market.

3 Six.

▶ **Practice** **p. 148**

<u>1</u>
Script
1. The teahouses in Taichung's Folk Park allow visitors to experience a traditional tea ceremony.
2. The Gaomei Wetlands are home to several rare bird species and attract many keen bird watchers.
3. There are also many biking trails in the Gaomei Wetlands for cyclists to explore.
4. Many visitors like to take a relaxing walk around the beautiful campus of Tunghai University.
5. There's so much to do in Taichung that you might find a visit exhausting as well as exciting.

1. 台中民俗公園的茶藝館提供遊客體驗傳統茶道的機會。
2. 高美濕地是幾種罕見鳥類的棲息地，吸引許多熱衷賞鳥的人士來此。
3. 高美濕地也有許多鐵馬道可供自行車友遊覽。
4. 許多遊客喜歡到美麗的東海大學校園裡輕鬆地散步。
5. 在台中，你絕對不會閒著，來此一遊可能又累又刺激呢。

1 c **2** a **3** b **4** d **5** e

<u>2</u> **1** a **2** c **3** e **4** b **5** d

<u>3</u> **1** bamboo **2** boardwalk **3** Sculpture
4 stroll **5** windmills

Unit 23

▶ **Quiz** p. 151

1 It is located in Nantou County. It's not too far from Taichung.

2 It is the combination of two lakes, one of which is shaped like the sun and the other shaped like a crescent moon.

3 The weather is very pleasant all year round.

4 Walking, cycling, boating, and bird-watching.

5 Once a year in September.

▶ **Practice** p. 154

1
Script

1. Visitors can learn about indigenous folk art, customs, and tribal dancing at the Formosan Aboriginal Cultural Village.

2. Cycling around the lake is a very popular activity for tourists because it allows them to take in the beautiful mountain scenery.

3. Tours visit all the major sights on the lake and may even include a little bird-watching.

4. Sun Moon Lake is so named because it is composed of two lakes, one in the shape of the sun and another in the shape of a crescent moon.

1. 遊客可以在九族文化村裡瞭解到原住民的民俗藝術、習俗和部落舞蹈。

2. 遊客普遍喜歡沿著湖邊騎自行車，這種方式最能將美麗山林盡收眼底。

3. 旅遊行程都有涵蓋湖邊的主要景點，有的甚至還加上一點賞鳥的活動。

4. 日月潭是由兩個湖所組成，一個形狀像太陽，一個形狀新月，因而得名。

1 customs, dancing　**2** Cycling, scenery
3 sights, include　**4** composed, crescent

2　**1** a, c, b, d　**2** d, c, b, a

3　**1** annual　**2** freshwater　**3** solo

Unit 24

▶ **Quiz** p. 157

1 Because many Chinese immigrants began to come to Taiwan.

2 Over 1.8 million.

3 The Dutch built Anping Fort in 1624.

4 He took over Taiwan in order to support the Ming dynasty against the Manchu-ruled Qing dynasty.

▶ **Practice** p. 160

1
Script

1. They were the first Europeans to discover Taiwan.

2. It's next to the Koxinga Shrine and tells the history of Fort Anping, Koxinga and traditional puppetry and clothing.

3. They took over Tainan in the 17th century, but were driven off the island by Koxinga.

4. It was the original Dutch name for Fort Anping.

5. They came to Tainan after the Qing dynasty defeated the Ming and took over China.

1. 他們是最早發現台灣的歐洲人。

2. 它位於延平郡王祠的旁邊，內部展示包含安平古堡的歷史、國姓爺鄭成功的生平，以及傳統布袋戲和服裝。

3. 他們在十七世紀時佔領台南，但又被國姓爺鄭成功逐出台灣。

4. 它是安平古堡原來的荷蘭文名稱。

5. 清朝推翻明朝、佔領全中國之後，他們便來到了台南。

1 The Portuguese　**2** The Taiwan Cultural Museum　**3** The Dutch　**4** Fort Zeelandia
5 Chinese immigrants

2　**1** b　**2** a　**3** b　**4** b

3　**1** Koxinga used Taiwan as a base to attack the Qing dynasty.

2 Koxinga established a government on Taiwan but died soon afterward.

3 The oldest Confucius temple in Taiwan is in Tainan.

Unit 25

▶ Quiz p. 163

1 It was the first one built in Taiwan.

2 Guan Gong.

3 Because people have donated new décorations and lavish gifts to the temple over many years.

4 Coffin sandwiches and danzai mian.

▶ Practice p. 166

<u>1</u> **Script**

1. This is a strange-looking snack. It looks like a hollowed-out piece of toast with filling inside it.

2. Why do so many businessmen go to pray at the Martial Temple?

3. Why is the Tainan Confucius Temple called the "first school in Taiwan"? It's not a school, is it? It's a temple surely.

1. 這是一種長得很奇怪的小吃，很像是中間挖空的土司，填了內餡進去。

2. 為什麼那麼多生意人要去武廟裡面拜呢？

3. 為什麼台南孔廟被稱為「全台首學」？它並不是一所學校，對吧？他是一間廟呀。

1 a **2** c **3** b

<u>2</u> **1** d **2** a **3** c **4** b

<u>3</u> **1** blade **2** alleyways **3** donate

Unit 26

▶ Quiz p. 169

1 Over 2.7 million.

2 It is very beautiful and pleasant to walk along the water's edge. You can take a boat cruise there.

3 The Penghu Islands.

▶ Practice p. 172

<u>1</u> **Script**

1. Before being turned into a tourist destination, Kaohsiung was mainly an industrial city focused on manufacturing goods.

2. The bridges and banks of the Love River are all lit up in the evening, and the best way to appreciate this lovely night view is to take a boat cruise along the river.

3. The Penghu Islands are a living history lesson for those who want to know what life used to be like in traditional Taiwanese fishing villages.

4. Located on the coast, Kaohsiung is a true port city, and it has one of the world's busiest container ports.

1. 高雄在轉型成為一個觀光區之前主要是一座工業城，以製造貨物為主。

2. 愛河上的橋樑和河岸到了夜晚燈火通明，欣賞如此美好夜景最好的方式就是乘船遊河。

3. 對於想瞭解傳統台灣漁村過去的生活方式的人來說，澎湖群島可以說是一本活歷史教材。

4. 高雄位居海岸，是個名符其實的港都，也是全球最為繁忙的貨櫃港口之一。

1 c **2** b **3** d **4** a

<u>2</u> **1** shortage **2** day trips
3 city government **4** admire **5** fairly

<u>3</u> **1** The boardwalks along the edges of the Love <u>River</u> are a great place for taking romantic <u>walks</u>.

2 From Kaohsiung you can take a <u>boat</u> to the Penghu Islands, which lie <u>between</u> Taiwan and China.

3 In the past, Kaohsiung was not considered a good destination for tourists, but over the last few <u>years</u> it has improved a lot.

4 In 2001, nine <u>artists</u> were invited to work on lighted decorations for the Urban <u>Spotlight</u> Arcade.

Unit 27

▶ **Quiz** p. 175

1 The MRT.

2 Fokuangshan, Qijin Island, and Hakka Cultural Center.

3 It's in Kaohsiung, and it is a famous Buddhist monastery.

4 Many Hakka-style houses have been torn down over the past few decades. Citizens of Kaohsiung have tried to save the remaining ones in Meinong and Qishan.

▶ **Practice** p. 178

<u>1</u>　**Script**

A: We're going to Qijin Island today, right? How are we getting there?

B: We're taking the underwater tunnel. I get really seasick, so I'd prefer not to take the boat.

A: OK, sounds good. What's there to see on the island?

B: There's a temple of Matsu—the goddess of the sea—a lighthouse, and lots of seafood restaurants.

A: I love seafood! I can't wait to try some. I'm sure it'll be really fresh.

B: Definitely. It'll be a nice change from the vegetarian food we've been eating at the monastery.

A: Yeah. Oh, that reminds me. We have to be back at the monastery by 3 o'clock.

B: What? Why?

A: Because we have that meditation class, remember?

B: Of course. I almost forgot.

A: 我們今天要去旗津島對不對？我們要怎麼去？

B: 我們要走海底隧道，因為我很容易暈船，所以不想坐船去。

A: 好啊，這樣不錯。島上有什麼可看的？

B: 有一間媽祖（海神）廟，還有一座燈塔和好多海鮮餐廳。

A: 我愛吃海鮮！我等不及要吃吃看了啦，一定超新鮮的。

B: 那是當然的啦。我們才在佛寺裡面吃了素食，換換口味也不錯。

A: 對啊。喔，這倒提醒了我，我們得在三點以前回到寺裡耶。

B: 什麼？為什麼？

A: 我們報了禪修班呀，記得嗎？

B: 對呴，我差點忘了。

1 – **2** – **3** ✓ **4** ✓

<u>2</u>　**1** b **2** e **3** a **4** d **5** c

<u>3</u>　**1** vegetarian **2** tunnel **3** spiritual **4** citizens **5** lighthouse

Unit 28

▶ Quiz p. 181

1 Lotus Lake.
2 Go into the dragon's mouth and out the tiger's mouth.
3 The National Science and Technology Museum, the Kaohsiung Museum of Fine Arts, and the Kaohsiung Museum of History.

▶ Practice p. 184

1
Script
1. In front of the Spring and Autumn Pavilions is a statue of Guanyin, the goddess of mercy, riding a dragon.
2. Paintings inside the Dragon and Tiger Pagodas show people the punishments they will suffer if they do bad deeds.
3. Kaohsiung's National Science and Technology Museum has exhibitions on biotechnology, water resources, and the food industry.
4. Lotus Lake, near Zuoying Train Station, is surrounded by a large park and is very popular with tourists.
5. Kaohsiung's magnificent Confucius temple is the biggest of its kind on the island.

1. 春秋閣前方有一尊乘龍的觀音像，觀音是慈悲之神。
2. 龍虎塔內的繪畫警惕世人，作惡將有惡報。
3. 高雄的國立科學工藝博物館有關於生物科技、水資源和食品工業的展覽。
4. 鄰近左營車站的蓮池潭位在一座大型公園之中，是觀光客非常喜愛的地方。
5. 高雄孔廟十分宏偉，是全台灣規模最大的孔廟。

1 statue, dragon 2 punishments, deeds
3 exhibitions, resources 4 surrounded, tourists 5 Confucius, biggest

2 1 a 2 b 3 a 4 b 5 b

3 1 c 2 e 3 a 4 b 5 d

Unit 29

▶ Quiz p. 187

1 It is located in Pingtung County, in the southernmost part of Taiwan.
2 They were formed by movements of the earth's crust and erosion caused by the sea.
3 Yes, because of its tropical climate.
4 Maobitou, Nanwan, Chuanfan Rock, and Cape Eluanbi.

▶ Practice p. 190

1
Script
1. Kenting National Park has a total area of 333 square kilometers. It was established in 1984 and covers both land and sea.
2. Maobitou, or Cat Nose Rock in English, was so named because it's shaped like a crouching cat.
3. Many birds migrate to Kenting during winter because of its year-round tropical climate.

1. 墾丁國家公園總面積 333 平方公里，成立於 1984 年，涵蓋了陸地與海面區域。
2. 貓鼻頭，英文字面上是 Cat Nose Rock，是因其形狀像一隻蹲伏的貓而得名。
3. 由於墾丁終年維持熱帶氣候，許多鳥類到了冬季便遷徙到這裡過冬。

1 Kenting National Park has been established for more than 25 years.
2 Maobitou is shaped like an animal.
3 Kenting stays warm throughout the year.

2 1 b 2 b

3 1 movements, wind, landforms
2 months, surfboards, heading
3 buzzard, migratory, weather

Unit 30

▶ Quiz `p. 193`

1 110,000 people in Hualien City and 340,000 people in Hualien County.

2 They are well known for their toughness and passion for life.

3 The sun goes down early because it is cut off by the massive mountain range in the west.

▶ Practice `p. 195`

1
   Script
   A: OK, so I've been down the west coast; now I want to try the east coast.
   B: That's a great idea. The east coast of Taiwan is very different from the west coast.
   A: In what way?
   B: Well, for one, it's far less crowded. There are only two big cities—Hualien and Taitung.
   A: Oh, right. Does that mean there's not much to see and do?
   B: Quite the opposite. There's plenty to see and do. You can go hiking, rafting, cycling . . ., pretty much any outdoor activity you can think of.
   A: Excellent. I love cycling. But is the east coast
     difficult to get to and get around? It sounds like it's quite remote.
   B: Well, before 1960 it was, but not now. There are plenty of new roads connecting east and west, and there's the new Xuehshan Tunnel, which has made getting to the east coast by car a lot faster than before.

   A: 好，我已經玩過西岸了，現在我想去去東岸。
   B: 很好啊，台灣的東岸和西岸大相逕庭呢。
   A: 是哪些方面？
   B: 嗯，一來那裡的人少多了，那裡只有花蓮和台東兩個大城市。
   A: 喔，這樣啊，那代表說那裡沒有什麼可看可玩的嗎？
   B: 恰恰相反，那裡好看好玩的可多了。你可以去健行啦、泛舟啦、騎自行車啦，幾乎想得到的戶外活動都可以去做。

   A: 太棒了，我愛騎自行車。不過東岸那邊會不會不好到達，或者交通不便呢？聽起來好像挺偏遠的。
   B: 這個嘛，在 1960 年以前是這樣沒錯，現在可不同了。新建了許多連接東西岸的道路，還有全新竣工的雪山隧道，使得開車到東岸比以往要快得多了。

1 – **2** ✓ **3** ✓ **4** – **5** ✓
2 **1** c, d, a, b **2** b, c, d, a
3 **1** breathe **2** toughness **3** rafting
    4 pristine

Unit 31

▶ Quiz `p. 199`

1 Taroko National Park.

2 Mochi and wonton.

3 National Museum of Prehistory, Peinan Cultural Park, the Taitung Railway Art Village, and Zhiben Hot Springs.

4 Sodium bicarbonate.

▶ Practice `p. 202`

1
   Script
   1. Unlike Kenting National Park with its low, rolling hills, the landscape of Taroko National Park is full of deep gorges and high cliffs.
   2. The archeological site at Peinan Cultural Park can let you see how people lived thousands of years ago.
   3. Hualien holds a yearly stone-carving festival where artists from around the world can show off their stone-carving skills.

   1. 太魯閣國家公園不像墾丁國家公園以低矮、起伏的山丘為主，它反而充滿了深谷和高聳的峭壁。
   2. 卑南文化公園的考古遺跡，可讓人一窺人類在數千年前的生活。
   3. 花蓮每年舉辦一次石雕節，邀請來自世界各地的藝術家展現他們的石雕技術。

1 a **2** c **3** b
2 **1** d **2** b **3** c **4** a
3 **1** b, f **2** a **3** e, c **4** d

Unit 32

▶ **Quiz** `p. 205`

1 The indigenous culture.
2 the Paiwan, Amis, Puyuma, Bunun, Rukai, Sakizaya, Kavalan, Truku, and Tao.
3 The Bunun speak their own language and have a calendar system using icons.
4 The Tao are well known for their carved boats, silver items, and pottery. They traditionally live in underground houses.

▶ **Practice** `p. 208`

1

Script
1. A: Why is the Amis Cultural Festival so important to the young people in the Amis tribe?
   B: It's important to them because the festival is a cultural rite of passage where the boys of the tribe become men.
2. A: I know that the Tao live on Orchid Island, which is quite far from Taiwan. But what else are they well known for?
   B: They're best known for making beautiful carved boats, as well as pottery and items made from silver.
3. A: How difficult is it for Taiwan's indigenous people to keep their culture and traditions alive?
   B: It can be difficult, especially with increased tourism. But there are also plenty of festivals and museums which try to help keep indigenous culture alive.
4. A: Why did the Tao people use to build their houses underground?
   B: Because those houses were much better at keeping the heat out in summer and the cold out in winter.

1. A: 阿美族的文化慶典對部落裡的年輕人來說，為何那麼重要？
   B: 這慶典是代表族裡男孩成為男人的成年禮，所以對他們來說很重要。
2. A: 我知道達悟族居住在離台灣有點遠的蘭嶼上，那麼他們還有哪些著名之事呢？
   B: 他們最出名的就是會建造美麗的拼板舟，他們的陶器和銀器也都很出名。

3. A: 台灣的原住民在保存文化和傳統上面，到底遭遇多大困境？
   B: 確實是有難度，尤其觀光業又開始發展。不過，也是舉辦了很多節慶，並且建立多間博物館來協助保存原住民文化。
4. A: 為什麼達悟族以前要把房子蓋在地下？
   B: 因為那種房子比較能在夏季避暑、冬季驅寒。

1 young, cultural, passage **2** Orchid, carved, silver **3** alive, tourism, museums
4 underground, keeping

2 **1** a **2** b **3** c

3 **1** The Bunun's ear-shooting ceremony teaches young boys how to be good hunters.
2 The Bunun tribe developed a calendar for marking important events during the year.
3 You can learn about indigenous history by visiting the National Museum of Prehistory.
4 The ancient cultures of Taiwan's indigenous people still influence life to this day.

用英文介紹臺灣
實用觀光導遊英語

發 行 人　周均亮
編　　著　Paul O'Hagan/Peg Tinsley/Owain Mckimm
審　　訂　Cheryl Robbins/Zachary Fillingham

翻　　譯　蔡裴驊／郭菀玲／丁宥榆
編　　輯　丁宥榆
主　　編　黃鈺云
製程管理　蔡智堯
出 版 者　寂天文化事業股份有限公司
電　　話　886-(0)2-2365-9739
傳　　真　886-(0)2-2365-9835
網　　址　www.icosmos.com.tw
讀者服務　onlineservice@icosmos.com.tw
出版日期　2012 年 8 月初版一刷 160101

郵撥帳號 1998-6200 寂天文化事業股份有限公司
• 劃撥金額 900 元（含）以上者，郵資免費。
• 劃撥金額 900 元以下者，請外加郵資 60 元。
〔如有破損，請寄回更換，謝謝。〕

國家圖書館出版品預行編目 (CIP) 資料

用英文介紹臺灣：實用觀光導遊英
語 / Paul O'Hagan, Peg Tinsley, Owain
Mckimm 作；蔡裴驊, 郭菀玲, 丁宥榆
譯 . -- 三版 . -- [臺北市]：寂天文化,
2012.08　面；　公分

ISBN 978-986-318-034-0 (16K 平裝)

1. 英語 2. 讀本 3. 臺灣

805.18　　　　101016143